T0046872

Lacandon
DREAMS

Also by the author

The Quality of Mercy

Lacandon DREAMS

A MILAGRO MYSTERY

KATAYOUN MEDHAT

Leapfrog Press
Fredonia, New York

Lacandon Dreams © 2019 by Katayoun Medhat

This is a work of fiction. Names, characters, businesses, places, events and incidents are either the products of the author's imagination or used in a fictitious manner. Any resemblance to actual persons, living or dead, or actual events is purely coincidental.

All rights reserved under International and
Pan-American Copyright Conventions

No part of this book may be reproduced, stored in a data base or other retrieval system, or transmitted in any form, by any means, including mechanical, electronic, photocopy, recording or otherwise, without the prior written permission of the publisher.

Published in 2019 in the United States by
Leapfrog Press LLC
PO Box 505
Fredonia, NY 14063
www.leapfrogpress.com

Printed in the United States of America

Distributed in the United States by
Consortium Book Sales and Distribution
St. Paul, Minnesota 55114
www.cbsd.com

First Edition

Library of Congress Cataloging-in-Publication Data

Names: Medhat, Katayoun, author.
Title: Lacandon dreams / by Katayoun Medhat.
Description: First edition. | Fredonia, NY : Leapfrog Press, 2019. | Series:
A Milagro mystery
Identifiers: LCCN 2019021077 | ISBN 9781948585040 (softcover : acid-free paper)
Subjects: | GSAFD: Mystery fiction.
Classification: LCC PR9110.9.M43 L33 2019 | DDC 823/.92--dc23
LC record available at https://lccn.loc.gov/2019021077

. . . when I waked I cried to dream again.
— Shakespeare, *The Tempest*

CONTENTS

CHAPTER ONE

It was as if a malign force had been unleashed to operate to the limits of its destructive capacities: piles of stone and rubble, terrain crisscrossed by gaping trenches, bushes torn up, tree trunks hacked to splinters, their severed roots upturned and extending skywards as though pleading for mercy.

The old oak alone had been spared, its gnarled branches spreading over the wreckage. The solitary tree had the effect of somehow making the spoilage more pronounced—a fragile memorial to what once had been.

The young woman was crying. Tears were running down her face, leaving grimy trails on her cheekbones, the grooves of her mouth, pooling below her chin, dripping on her T-shirt, dotting it with grey splotches.

She was an Amazon of a woman, a good six foot one in socks, which made her crying particularly disconcerting. She had the open face of an idealist or had had—because as they were looking out on the bleeding root-work, ruin and blight that had been Goosewash Wilderness, K fancied he could see hope, trust and faith vanishing from her features one by one.

It wasn't something he was keen on witnessing.

"Thank you for alerting us," he began.

She hiccupped, wiped her nose on a sinewy forearm and raked dirt-crusted fingers through her leonine mane.

"What are you going to do?"

K's eyes followed the Amazon's outstretched arm.

"Please! What are you. . . ?"

K could think of no answer. He shrugged.

"You don't care?" sobbed the woman. "You see this. . ." she made a sweeping motion that missed K's jaw by a quarter inch, "and you shrug?"

K thought it unwise to explain to the Amazon that it had been a helpless, not a careless shrug. It was easier to have confidence in a heartless than a powerless cop. He could give her that at least.

They stood like the last survivors of the final apocalypse amidst truncated trees and seeping bark on gravel that glistened like a burn scar in the ravaged landscape.

"When did this happen?" K asked.

"You tell me," began the Amazon, then shook her head and hung her shoulders. "I don't know," she whispered. "Last week I was here for the wildlife audit. Everything was okay then. I mean, not okay, how could it be with all of this going on?"

"Wildlife audit? You are with the federal Wildlife Service?"

"The Wildlife Service? No. No! I'm not. I wouldn't help them! They are against wildlife. Everything they do is bad for nature."

"Are you associated with an NGO, a grassroots project?" K asked.

"Do you have to be? Is it not enough to care?"

"No, it isn't," said K firmly. "Are you affiliated to any group or are you doing this on your own?"

"Somebody's got to do something."

"I take it you are alone in this?"

"Yes," the young woman said, and her tears began to flow again.

•   •   •   •

For once K was grateful to get back to the station. His drive from Quorum Valley to Milagro had been haunted by the specter of the Amazon as he had left her, standing amidst chaos and ruin, inconsolable. There had been nothing he could say to comfort her; nothing he could promise to give her hope; nothing he could do to assuage his own rage.

Milagro PD's break-room was filled with the lively hum of cops kicking back. Small wonder that the town's crime rates remained the only concern withstanding recession. K rooted around for a clean mug, finally located one in the far corner of a shelf, and poured himself a coffee.

"They caught the Delgado Walmart shooter," said Smithson.

Around lunchtime a man had opened fire on customers waiting in line at the Delgado Walmart self-service checkout, fatally wounding two customers and one employee.

"Alive?" asked K.

"Alive and calm like nothing happened. He ditched his gun in the dairy aisle, went over to the electronics section and did some browsing. They only got him because he was the only one that looked happy when everybody else was freaking. He was hanging out by the TVs waiting for the news broadcast and checking updates on his phone to see if he was trending yet."

"If Walmart had the damn sense to let their associates pack, that whole mess wouldn't have happened," said Dilger.

"A no brainer," said K, "more guns is always the answer."

Gutierrez made a warning "tsk" sound and patted the chair next to him. "You don't look so happy."

"I'm not," said K. "Just got back from a call-out to Quorum."

"Quorum Valley? That's way out," said Gutierrez, "I've never been out there."

"Too late now," said K.

"Too late?" asked Gutierrez.

"Quorum's as good as gone now," K said, and it was now that the irrevocable destruction of Quorum Valley's wilderness fully hit him.

"They bought the land and they didn't waste any time. They went straight to Goosewash Wilderness and tore it up, just in case the environmentalists try to find some protected species there. They weren't going to let anything get in the way of their fracking. So they beat the eco-folks to it. That poor girl who called us out—she had been doing a wildlife audit—there was nothing I could do for her. Nothing."

"It's really getting to you, huh?" said Gutierrez. "Who's 'they'?"

"XOX Energy Corporation. The guys with the pipeline. They pretty much own every stretch of land between here and Galveston."

"XOX?" Gutierrez frowned.

"Surely you know XOX, our new overlords? They won't leave us anything worth living for. But our economy will be rocketing."

Gutierrez shook his head. "Sure I know about XOX. They just put in a bore hole at the end of my road. But there's something else. I think we had some dealings with them, you and me?"

K couldn't recall ever having had any dealings with XOX and more the pity. XOX had been welcomed with open arms by a Milagro municipality hungry for a recap of the town's oilfield boomtown days and determined to let nothing whatsoever get in the way of its categorical pursuit of commercial prowess.

"I don't recall," said K. "Do let me know if you remember. I'll be glad for anything we can get on that scum."

•   •   •   •

"You looking for something?" asked Becky.

K was standing in Milagro PD's reception, studying the framed regional map hanging on the wall.

"No," said K.

"Just taking some time out, huh?"

"I guess," said K.

"Sure," said Becky.

It was a given that before K had become the weakest link of Milagro PD, Becky would have torn a strip off him, subjected him to her particular brand of merciless teasing, would not have missed the opportunity to make clear exactly what she thought of cops taking "time out" during working hours.

He had become the weakest link of the Milagro squad because he couldn't deal with his responsibilities like a true cop; or because he couldn't deal with the consequences of having dealt with his responsibilities like a true cop; or because he dealt with the consequences of having dealt with his responsibilities like a true cop like any person—any ethical person—who had a life on their conscience should: he had cracked.

K went back to looking at the map. A scant one hundred miles from Milagro town, Quorum Valley was light-years away from the contemporary small town hub that was Milagro.

Quorum Valley was scattered ranches; the cemetery on top of the hill that marked the midpoint of the valley; the steepled community hall, the old-time grocery store and the one-room elementary school. Quorum Valley was so remote that it was a miracle anyone had ever found it, let alone settled in it. The people who settled in Quorum Valley must have been brave and hardy, perhaps foolhardy.

"Do you happen to know anything about XOX? The Texan Energy Corporation?" K asked.

"XOX?" said Becky. "Sure I do. What happened to that guy?"

"What guy?"

"The DWI dude you caught. Don't you remember? The guy that worked for XOX. You called him 'motherfracker.' That was kind of cute."

"I thought you don't hold with cussing," K said.

"Motherfracker's not a real word," said Becky. "Anyways, you ought to remember him. He broke some kind of record. You and Gutierrez booked him and you couldn't believe he was still driving when he should've been in a coma? It was a while back. Around the time when all that stuff happened. . . ." Becky's voice trailed off.

"What's his name?" K asked.

Becky shook her head "He's their CEO. Want me to dig out the log book?"

"No," snapped K. He hadn't known that being treated kindly could be so wearying.

In Becky's eye he spied a glint of her old pre-compassionate combative self. Maybe there was hope for him yet.

"Don't bother," he said. "Even I know how to Google."

Indeed it took him no more than three minutes including starting up the devil's machine.

Lucky Easton, XOX Energy Corporation Southwest's CEO, complete with mug shot, Mission Statement and an assortment of inane quotes promising a golden dawn of abundant natural resource squandering, drawn straight from a 1950s mind-set where the dire consequences of rapacious energy consumption were an as yet undiscovered continent.

K thought of the weeping Amazon who all on her own was trying to stem the tide of destruction, like the little boy plugging the hole in the dyke with his finger.

•   •   •   •

"Becky helped me recall the dealings we had with XOX. Lucky Easton was the guy with the epic 0.43 BAC. We were going to nominate him for the regional DWI heat. Remember?"

"0.43? That guy? Oh boy!" Gutierrez looked up from his computer. "I got his wife to pick him up and he was so out of it, he called her by the wrong name. So that guy works for XOX?"

"He's their CEO."

"Great role model," said Gutierrez.

"Driving on 0.43's small fry compared to what XOX are doing to Quorum. Any chance we can get them on environmental vandalism?" K said.

"I don't think so," Gutierrez said. "Milagro needs the jobs. XOX are practically free to do anything they put their mind to."

"It's not right," said K. "Somebody should pay for all the havoc they're creating. I have a mind to look in on Mr. Lucky. Make him feel not so lucky."

"Mind if I come with you?" asked Gutierrez.

"The more the merrier," said K gratefully.

CHAPTER TWO

No expense had been spared on XOX Energy Corporation's Milagro headquarters. The general impression was of the kind of ostentatious bad taste that was being role-modeled by the highest in the land. Gilded wall-cladding featured prominently, as did capriciously displayed neo-classicist ornamentation.

"Welcome to XOX ENERGY CORPORATION! How may I help you today?" The receptionist was a pertly décolletéed blonde of tender years.

It was the type of scripted formula usually doled out over the phone but rarely ever face-to-face. Most people did not have the gall to speak to anyone's face like this. But she was still young and maybe she thought she was doing a good job.

"We are here to see Lucky Easton," said K.

"Mr. Easton?" asked the receptionist.

"The very one," said K.

"Mr. Easton is in a meeting," said the receptionist.

"Until when?" asked K.

"It is a priority meeting," the receptionist stated. She had some way to go to being a good liar.

"How long is the meeting scheduled for?"

There was panic in the receptionist's eyes. "Mr. Easton must not be disturbed," she pleaded.

Gutierrez approached the desk and lifted the leather-bound and gold-embossed diary with nimble fingers. He studied the schedule and looked at his watch. "I reckon there's enough time for us to visit with Mr. Easton before his meeting starts," he said. "It's through here, isn't it? Don't trouble yourself Ma'am. We do remember the way."

They turned their backs on the receptionist's feeble protestations.

Gutierrez led the way.

The boy Gutierrez had grown into a man. Not so long ago he had been shy, introverted and self-effacing. K found in himself a mixture of awe and envy.

They walked along a hallway that was hung with ornately framed photographs of XOX's crimes against the environment, and stopped before an oak-paneled door with a polished brass plaque on which Lucky Easton's name was surrounded by a halo of etched sunrays.

Gutierrez knocked briskly and opened the door.

K caught sight of an indistinct flurry of separating shapes.

Lucky Easton, straightening his shirt, strode to a behemoth mahogany desk and seated himself on a high-backed chair with elaborately carved armrests.

"Thank you, Miss Alvarez. That will be all."

Miss Alvarez nodded, head held high. Her face was haughty, her long hair dark brown with the shimmer of honey, her body in a clinging jersey dress sensuously curvaceous. She opened the door and was gone with the lightness of a breeze. A trace of scent lingered in the air.

"Can I help you guys?" Lucky Easton asked, gritting his teeth.

At a glance Easton was in his late forties, one of those guys who perpetually looked as if they were about to slide off the cusp of the prime of life into the bloated dissipation of middle age. His jaw bore a hint of jowls, his eyes had a bloodshot tinge, and his forehead was grooved with furrows that spoke of ill temper. Easton bore sideburns and a coarse and coppery moustache trimmed to the lesser brigand style. "Can I help you?" he repeated tersely.

"How about explaining your activities in Quorum Valley," K said.

"Our activities in Quorum Valley?" Easton's eyes roamed to Gutierrez and back to K. His lips stretched to a self-satisfied sneer, buoying the coppery brigand's mustache.

"All's going just swell." Easton's sneer broadened. He leant back on his chair and spread his arms wide. "What can I tell you: All's going great. We're progressing fast. Even faster than we thought we would."

"I imagine you are," K agreed. "Considering that you don't seem to bother applying for permits for your activities."

"You trying to accuse me of something?"

"Not trying," said K. "I *am* accusing you of trespassing and destroying wildlife habitat."

"You can prove that?" Easton's smile was gleeful now and not at all abashed. "How about you come back when you got something on me?"

"How come you're so sure we haven't got something on you right now?"

"Yeah, I'm sure. You betcha I'm sure," Easton gloated. "You got nothing on me, boys. Nothing. Zilch. Nada."

The man's audacity could only be explained by the existence of friends in high places.

So certain was Mr. Lucky that his buddies had his back that he barely bothered with appearances. Easton's smug contempt was starting to seriously mess with K's self-control.

"Anyways, Sir," Gutierrez intercepted genially. "We are mainly here to help you, Sir."

"Help me?" Easton's sneer lost some of its expanse. "You are here to help me?"

"How are you doing, Sir?" Gutierrez asked.

"How am I doing?" Easton repeated, his sneer now almost completely gone.

"How are you doing, Sir?" Gutierrez repeated in a tone somewhere between concerned good Samaritan and patronizing social worker.

"You are asking me how I am doing?"

"We try our best, Sir, to help citizens," said Gutierrez.

Easton's hands fastened around the carved griffins or phoenixes or turkey vultures or whatever they were supposed to be, on his armrests. His moustache bristled.

"Can't recall asking for your help," Easton snarled.

"That is part of the illness, Sir," said Gutierrez.

"What?"

"Your alcoholism, Sir," said Gutierrez.

"My alcoholism? I am not an alcoholic!"

"Denial," said Gutierrez, "is part of your illness too. There is nothing wrong with you, Sir. It is an illness. Don't blame yourself. Just take one day at a time."

"Is he for real?" Easton appealed to K.

"How is the program going?" K inquired.

"The program?" Easton asked.

"The rehabilitation program, Sir," K said evenly.

"What rehabilitation program? I'm in no rehab program!"

"You are not?"

"No!" boomed Easton.

"Are you quite sure you are not?"

"Sure I'm sure!" Easton was crimson with rage.

Gutierrez looked at K and K looked at Gutierrez. They shook their heads weightily.

"This is unfortunate, Sir."

"Damn you, what is going on?!" Easton yelled.

K produced the logbook, leafed through it and began reciting, in a droning monotone, comments grouped under the rubrics: Date of Apprehension; BAC; DWI Citation; Conditions of Discharge; Mandatory Treatment Details.

"Are you for real?" Easton's voice had a hysterical kink to it. Gone the smug veneer.

K said flatly, "Certainly, Sir. The condition for your discharge and for retaining your driver's license is the mandatory attending of a program specializing in the treatment of alcohol and substance dependency."

Gutierrez took over. "Your license, please."

"You gotta be joking," said Easton.

"Your license!" roared Gutierrez.

K flinched. Never before had he heard Gutierrez so much as raise his voice. Anger in Gutierrez was somehow much more disconcerting than in most other folks he could think of.

Easton must have felt it too. He handed over his Texas-issued driver's license, and meekly accepted the receipt issued by Gutierrez.

They left him deflated and momentarily subdued, emptily contemplating his reflection on the polished mahogany desk.

• • • •

"I had fun," said Gutierrez as K accelerated out of the XOX parking lot. "What about you?"

K considered. "It was okay," he said. "But I would have had even more fun if we could have made him smash something or really lose it. Or if we had lost it and ripped all those gold-framed photos of drill towers and uranium yellow cake off the walls and stamped on them and crushed the glass into powder and maybe banged him over the head with that oil painting in his office, you know so that his head would've stuck through the canvas. . . ."

"You were about to go for him, weren't you?" said Gutierrez. "Let's just hope Mr. Easton doesn't get any loco ideas once he realizes we took his license and want him to go to rehab before he gets it back."

It was a bit late to start worrying about having sailed rather close to the wind. What they had just done in there was unlikely to be compatible with law or order or professional code of conduct.

Walking in and confiscating someone's driver's license was rather Wild West. But that's where they were—the Wild West.

"At least taking away his license really got to him where nothing else would. Who do you think is covering Easton's back with XOX's rampaging?"

Gutierrez shrugged. "The good ol' boys. They're all covering each other's backs."

"So we got to stand by and watch them doing whatever they choose to do?"

"Pretty much," said Gutierrez. "What did you make of the girl—that Miss Alvarez?"

What K knew of Mr. Lucky Easton was that he was a guy they had caught driving on 0.43 BAC and who had carried in his wallet a photo of his daughters and a twin pack of raspberry flavored condoms.

"I'm sure he is banging her," K said.

There was an odd sound from Gutierrez. K stole a sideways glance. Gutierrez was frowning and staring intently at the road.

"Sorry," said K. "I didn't mean to be crude."

"You really think they are having an affair?" asked Gutierrez.

"I don't know about an affair, but I'm pretty sure they are . . . having sexual relations."

"Sexual relations are not an affair?"

"No," said K.

"I don't understand," said Gutierrez unhappily.

Gutierrez was happily married with two young, much adored children and an equally adored bichon frise and, it seemed, led a very sheltered life.

"What don't you understand?"

"Why would a young woman like that have—uhm—relations with a nasty guy like Easton?"

Because he's got status and money, thought K. He didn't think Ms. Alvarez was into Easton for reasons of love or lust. He knew better than to say what he was thinking.

"There's many women that get involved with guys that are not worthy of them."

"I still don't get it," Gutierrez insisted.

K was starting to feel somewhat impatient with Gutierrez' willful naivety.

"Surely this can't be the first time that you've seen relations that are built on opportunism and mutual exploitation?"

Gutierrez obstinately shook his head.

"There's something about these two that is getting to you."

Gutierrez frowned. The silence grew oppressive. Just as K was about to break up the uncomfortable void with an inane comment about—let's say this month's precipitation to date—Gutierrez cleared his throat.

"I think—" he began ponderously, "I kind of feel responsible for her."

"Do you know her?" asked K.

"I don't think so. I know some Alvarez, but I don't know if she is related to them. It's just . . . she's Mexican too. With things as they are now our people are getting kind of a hard time, you know? Like we are all criminals, pushers and rapists. We got to look out for each other."

K thought that this was maybe the one good thing to be said about these interesting times they lived in, that they inspired solidarity among the beleaguered. Well, one could choose to believe that—if one chose to be optimistic.

"Easton is Ms. Alvarez' boss," said K. "With those hierarchical deals you never know if they are consensual or coerced, you know? It's hard to say no to your boss. And it's harder to get out of a thing like that once it's got going. She might lose her job."

"That's why women should behave so that guys like that don't get any ideas." Gutierrez said.

They lived in interesting times.

CHAPTER THREE

"You did what?" Sheriff Weismaker did not look impressed.

"He hadn't complied with the conditions, Sir," Gutierrez mumbled.

"Let me get this straight: you took away his driver's license?"

"Yes, Sir," said Gutierrez unhappily.

"Coffee?" asked Weismaker.

"Yes, Sir." "No, Sir," Gutierrez and K said simultaneously.

"You sure you don't want coffee?" Weismaker glared at K.

"Three sugars, Sheriff," K mumbled.

Weismaker meted out coffee, sugar, creamer, and distributed steaming mugs from which emanated the incomparably awful aroma of his special brew—his test of loyalty in a mug.

K, conscious of Gutierrez waiting for him to take the first sip, felt like being delegated to royal food taster. He took a sip, struggled for a neutral expression and swallowed. No matter how prepared you thought you were, the first sip of the sheriff's coffee always managed to devastate.

Gutierrez sipped, swallowed and choked.

"I'm listening," said the sheriff.

"Easton had plenty of time to comply with the mandated treatment and didn't," said K over Gutierrez' spluttering. "He was so sure he didn't have to comply, that he completely forgot about the mandated treatment. He was caught with 0.43 BAC and yet someone thought it was okay to hand him back his license and let him go."

"What are you saying?" inquired Weismaker.

K thought it over and decided there was no way of putting it nicely. "That man must have some friends where it counts."

"Who would they be?" asked the Sheriff.

"Your guess is as good as mine. This can't be the first time you have come across the good old boys working their magic?"

"Easy, Son," said Weismaker.

K shrugged. "Anyway. He got off. And I guess he'll get away with it. Until the time when it happens again and someone gets hurt, or killed. Depending of course just who it is that gets hurt or killed. Whether they are dispensable or not."

He was conscious of the sheriff looking at him and was careful to avoid his eyes.

"And y'all think he should be punished," said Weismaker.

"No," said Gutierrez.

"Yes," said K.

The sheriff raised his brows. "There's some disagreement?"

"No, Sir," said Gutierrez.

"Yes," said K. Then he realized that he had forgotten what it was that they were supposed to be having a disagreement about—or not.

Everything crawled along so slowly these days and there never seemed to be any conclusions to anything. In his newfound fool's paradise that had been created for him through the team's collective indulgence of his trauma-acquired sensitivity, he found that he could be honest about his confusion.

"What are we disagreeing about?" he asked.

"Nothing," said Gutierrez. "Everything's just fine."

"Thank you, Nurse," said K, and for a moment thought he had gone too far.

At least there was no exchange of meaningful glances between Weismaker and Gutierrez—not as far as K could see. Maybe they were just very subtle.

"I agree that we need to educate irresponsible drivers," said the sheriff. "This year's been one of the worst for road fatalities."

K remembered what the disputed disagreement had been about. "The DWI is not Easton's only wrongdoing, Sir," said K.

"It isn't?" asked Weismaker.

"Not by a long way, Sir. The corporation he works for is single-handedly destroying Quorum Valley. And nobody's calling them out on it."

The sheriff listened while K described the desolation he had found; the wildlife auditing girl weeping amidst the uprooted trees and torn up soil.

"XOX acquired the hydraulic fracturing rights for Quorum," said the sheriff. "So I guess they are in their rights to do whatever they need to do to get at the shale."

"It looks like they are straying mightily out of the designated area. There's this protected area northwest of the Merced River. It's got all kinds of plants and wildlife that struggle everywhere else but that thrive there because of the micro-climate. It's a pretty special place. You heard of it?"

The sheriff nodded. "Goosewash Wilderness?"

"Goosewash is wilderness no more," K said. "XOX have done for it."

"There was no one else protesting? Standing up for Quorum Valley?" asked the sheriff.

"No one," said K, "just this one very distraught young woman. Quorum's just like Milagro. They want the jobs and the money. XOX did everything pretty much in plain sight. They must have caught on to this environmentalist and her wildlife audit and knew they had to act fast. They didn't want any rare species to get in the way of their drilling."

The sheriff looked at his watch.

Gutierrez shot up from his chair and inched towards the door. The sheriff nodded. Gutierrez exited. K rose and made to follow.

"Stay," said the sheriff. "More coffee?"

"I'm okay. Thanks."

"You're okay?" asked the sheriff. "How's the counseling going?"

"I stopped going," K said.

He tried to sound matter of fact and assertive. How he did sound was defensive.

The sheriff regarded him broodingly. K realized he wasn't going to get out of the office so easily.

"It wasn't working for me," he explained. "It was either go into things so far that there was a chance that I couldn't get back, or deal with stuff the way most folks do."

"What way is that?" asked the Sheriff

"Forgetting. Letting stuff go. It does work, you know."

Not according to the counselor, who had called it repression, denial, manic defense.

"Fair enough," said Weismaker. "Though I guess you know you still got a ways to go."

"Probably," admitted K.

"Just mind you don't take it out on others, agreed?"

"I'll try my best, Sir," K said and beat it.

·   ·   ·   ·

The squad had gathered in reception, uniforms starched, holsters greased, guns polished and faces set.

"Y'all look like you mean business," said K.

Young nodded, coughed and spat.

"Maybe you should stay at home until you're cured?" suggested K.

"Some of us gotta do real work." Young jeered.

"Is it Black Friday already?" asked K.

"We are going out to schools to train the teachers," Smithson explained.

"Train the teachers? In what?"

"You been living under a rock? You ain't heard of the School Marshal Plan?" asked Young.

"The School Marshal Plan gives educators armed capabilities

and responsibilities," Smithson recited weightily. "We're training teachers to keep their schools safe."

"Is that the thing about 'hardening schools' and tooling up teachers?" asked K. "How do teachers like your Marshal Plan?"

"They like it just swell," snarled Dilger.

"How else are they going to keep their students safe from the bad guys?" reasoned Smithson. "The only way to stop a bad guy with a gun is—"

"—to stop the sale of guns?" K asked.

So the NRA lobby had won and Milagro was going full tilt for turning its educators into armed militia. Already most schools had installed entry systems, metal detecting gates and bullet-proof doors that evoked penal institutions rather than places for learning. Some schools had employed armed guards to patrol the perimeters of campuses. Now teachers were being made to acquire live fire qualifications and every scheme that K had taken for a dystopian pipe dream was being made reality.

• • • •

The sheriff stood at the glass door, watching his men leave. K joined him. The cortege of patrol cars fanned out right and left, toward Milagro elementary, middle, junior-high and high schools.

"This Marshal Plan thing—do you think it's a good idea, Sheriff?" asked K.

"We aren't here to have ideas," said Weismaker. "We are here to protect citizens."

"Wouldn't it be better to protect citizens from living in a martial society?"

"Too late, Son," said the Sheriff and turned to leave.

"Sir, about Quorum Valley—"

"You don't give up, do you?" said the sheriff. "What about it?"

"Goosewash Wilderness," said K. "Shouldn't we do something about what happened there?"

"Why?" asked the sheriff.

"As you just said, Sir, we are here to protect citizens. Shouldn't we protect citizens from unscrupulous corporations too? It's not just shooters that destroy lives."

"Great motto for a bumper sticker," said the sheriff. He contemplated K's stricken face. "Well . . . most everyone is out there working with the schools. So I guess it's just you."

"Are you saying I can look into this, Sheriff?"

"Go ahead, Son," said the sheriff.

"Thank you, Sir," said K. Knock yourself out, Officer Franz Kafka, patron-saint of lost causes.

•　　•　　•　　•

So now K found himself taking the turn to Latep and chugging along the ill-maintained road leading through Petalia Plain, sunbaked, parched and bleak.

Petalia Plain had been named by the small group of Mormons who, on reaching Quorum Valley, had unaccountably and capriciously kept going until they found themselves on this arid plain they named Petalia. You had to hand it to those Mormons, they didn't let reality get in the way of a good name.

K assumed Petalia referenced the petals of flowers that only lived in peoples' imaginations and the old timers' oral traditions. Naming somewhere for something it lacked seemed less like nostalgia than like rubbing salt in a wound.

Petalia Plain's main hub was to be called—what else—Petal. When the expertly hewn and lovingly carved letters had been assembled, ready to be mounted on a sign at the hamlet's boundaries, some busybody had brought the devastating news that some way to the west a town named Petal already existed.

The Mormon founders contemplated the letters P-E-T-A-L before them and decided they weren't going to let good work and wood go to waste. After some regrouping and consideration, they decided that Latep was as good a name, if not better, than Petal. And they could be reasonably certain that theirs would be the only Latep.

Which taught you something on how to survive in the middle of nowhere and nothing, on not much more than the power of your dreams and the brawn of your compromises.

· · · ·

On his way to Quorum K had often passed Latep Library, though he had never before stopped there.

It was a wonder that a flea-pit place like Latep had a library at all. Not only did Latep have a library, but they had housed it in an impressive civic building that was light and spacious with a high ceiling, which also served as community center and crèche.

Inside, the eye was drawn to a wall covered in crayon drawings depicting the usual infant offerings of house plus sun plus cloud plus mummy-daddy-dog; K spied one with just a dog and one that just showed a solitary tree on a hill, produced probably by infants with attachment disorders. There were tables where students could study and social groups meet; there were armchairs for readers; in short, it was a thoughtfully appointed library—albeit with somewhat scant evidence of books.

The librarian was a benign-looking lady in her far sixties with tightly curled hair of a peculiarly intense copper color that made K wonder if she'd mistaken oxidized drain cleaner for hair dye at the drugstore.

Her smile was as wide as if she was welcoming him into her own home.

"Welcome to Latep Library," she said.

She did not say anything else. She beamed at K for what seemed like a stretch of time bordering on awkward, then went back to knitting a grey woolen sock.

"Just looking around," he addressed the coppery head bent over grey wool.

He strolled around the room. Here and there were low shelves bearing hardback books. As far as K could determine, the library's stock consisted mainly of romance novels, supplemented by a few military and hunting tomes. A couple of tables displayed newly published books. These seemed to be hardback mysteries without exception.

At the far end of the library K came upon a table that held books with ecological themes. Books that did not doubt that global warming existed, that climate change was man-made and that natural resources were finite. There were half a dozen books or so on the uranium industry and the grave dangers of hydraulic fracturing. Given the plans for Quorum Valley and environs, the looming project of a uranium mill and XOX's fracking frenzy, the literature was timely and relevant, though surprising nonetheless, considering the degree of enthusiasm and avarice with which the valley had welcomed energy corporations to the area.

"Ma'am?" said K. He had to repeat himself twice before the librarian was roused from her knitting.

"Who orders the books here?"

"You like our books?" beamed the lady. "We got more hunting and fishing books over there. And right next to it is our leisure collection. We got a lot on gun sports, there's a new one just come in on ATV trails and. . . ."

K nodded vigorously. "Impressive. I was just looking at your environmental books—"

"Oh," knitting lady said.

"A comprehensive collection. Very impressive."

"I suppose so."

"You haven't read them yet?"

"Nope," said the lady curtly. "Doubt I will, too."

"There's many that look interesting though," insisted K, "and relevant."

"Relevant?" echoed the lady.

"Well," said K "there's a lot going on here, isn't there? XOX—
"

"Where are you from?" the woman asked.

"Milagro," said K.

"You got an accent," diagnosed the lady. "Where is your accent from?"

"Wales," said K.

The woman put down her knitting. "Neat! I didn't know they could talk."

"They talk quite a lot as it happens," said K, piqued.

"I heard about the dolphins," said the lady. "They're supposed to be real good communicators."

"The dolphins?"

He should have stayed at home. Here he was, in Latep Public Library, having a full-blown psychotic breakdown, albeit without the dramatic bells and whistles that he had supposed accompanied psychotic breakdowns. This here was a rather domestic scenario, one where knitting elderly ladies sporting ill-advised hair colors spoke about talking to dolphins—maybe he should have taken her blinding copper hair as a warning.

The woman rested her knitting on her lap. "I do recall that they have these songs. I think we even have a book on them," she gestured toward a shelf.

K obligingly trotted over. The books seemed to be all about wildlife.

"The big blue one," called the lady.

K drew the book out of the shelf. *Whale Songs*. Who was it that was mad here? Did she really believe he had learnt to speak English from whales? He decided he didn't have the nerves to try and find out.

"Call me the Prince of Whales," he said, and put the book back into the shelf.

The lady frowned slightly.

"Who orders your environment books?" he asked.

"Those books? We got a new librarian. Mind she's only temporary, until LaRee Hinkley is back. She's away in Vernal looking after her daddy. He's been unwell for a while now."

"Hope he gets well soon," said K. "So who is your temporary librarian?"

"Miss Solanas." The woman gathered up her knitting and stuffed it into a bulging purse. "She's due any minute now." She looked at the wall clock. "She better be on time. I got to leave right away."

K wandered over to the notice board. Most notes seemed to be about selling agricultural equipment, ATVs, feed, hay; one was a photo of a litter of red heeler puppies straining over the rim of a basket with a phone number scribbled underneath. There were two petitions, one "Stop XOX Corporation," the other "Down Winders against Quorum Uranium Mill." There were three signatures on each—the same names on both petitions.

"Some folks are plain ungrateful," stated the woman. She had joined him at the notice board. "They got no sense. We should be grateful we got XOX coming here. They could go anywhere, you know?"

"Not quite anywhere," said K mildly. "It would depend on the occurrence of natural resources, I imagine."

There was no curbing her enthusiasm. "A big, important corporation like that choosing us! They're going to do great things here! And they pay real well for land, you know?"

"I bet," said K.

The woman stepped closer. "We don't need these folks—" she pointed at the petitions, "—spoiling everything for us."

The entrance door opened.

"Here's Miss Solanas. You ask her about those books. Have a great day!"

She left, clutching her bulging bag.

Solanas shrugged out of a faded denim jacket and draped it over the back of the chair. She wore a moss green T-shirt, jeans and dirt-crusted hiking shoes. She moved with the sinuous grace of an athlete and had the resolute and steely air of one who got things done.

"You got some questions?" she asked. She began sorting books on a trolley.

"The eco books over there," said K. "You got a very comprehensive collection."

"You didn't expect to find these kinds of books here?" Solanas observed astutely.

"No," admitted K.

"Where do you stand?" Solanas was certainly forthright.

K shrugged. "I am surprised," he said, "at the alacrity with which XOX has been welcomed by people here. And the uranium mill project too. There's not a lot of resistance, is there?" He nodded toward the notice board.

"They are being offered a lot of money for their land."

She wheeled the trolley along shelves and began to fit books into gaps fast and with economy of movement.

K watched her sliding books into slots. He could see the play of muscles under her honey-colored skin. Her ruthless efficiency was impressive.

"You'll find nobody hereabouts who believes in climate change," she said.

"That's why they have no problem with XOX?" said K.

"You got it." said Solanas. "They expect nothing but good things from XOX. Jobs, money, investment."

"You are the temporary librarian?"

Solanas nodded.

"You seem to know a lot about what goes on here," K said.

Solanas shrugged. "What about you?"

The rapidity of the question made K guess that Solanas wasn't the confiding kind.

"Just passing through," he said.

"Passing through, huh?" Solanas raised her eyebrows.

Because Solanas looked at him as if she was expecting to hear more, K said nothing. He held her eyes, trying to look neutral. This was difficult because he found that Solanas interested him. And there was something in her eyes that made him think that the interest was mutual.

But he was damaged goods, a broken man, who at this point had just about reached the stage when he was able to oblige women he felt indifferent to, which probably showed him up as a closet misogynist or a self-loather or maybe both, probably both, because the two traits seemed to go hand in hand.

"Good meeting you," he said, and turned toward the door.

K got into his truck and took a left on the potholed disaster they euphemistically called Petalia Highway.

CHAPTER FOUR

Great Spearstone Valley's expanse was bathed in a veiled light that spoke of distant dust storms. On an impulse K turned on to the dirt road heading west.

After a mile or so he began to regret that impulse. On a scale of bad and worse this road definitely was worse, with holes the size of craters, washboard ridges of an industrial scale and razor-sharp gravel everywhere. By now he was far enough in, he was damned if he did and damned if he didn't go on. So on he went.

After a while the whiplash-inducing bouncing had the unexpected effect of a mood enhancer, K was beginning to feel quite bouncy within himself.

Even better, the moving dots he had registered from afar were a herd of the elusive wild horses of Great Spearstone Valley, who usually could be relied upon not to be seen when you counted on seeing them.

Here they were, in sizeable number, fanned out and tucking away at the thorny shrubs that were all the sustenance that Great Spearstone Valley had to offer.

It was pretty impressive how these creatures managed to thrive in such a forbidding environment— and look good on it, too.

Maybe they snuck down to Quorum when no one was looking and dined on alfalfa and roses.

K got out of the truck, attempting to coax the horses by making clicking noises with his tongue. The wild horses ignored him and continued to concentrate on stripping fibrous leaves from lavishly thorned bushes.

"Howdee!" K said to the horses. A couple of them raised their heads, contemplated him indifferently and went back to pursuing their arduous meal. K stood by and lost himself in the primal soundscape of horses chewing. He decided that these horses had never tasted Quorum vale's bounty. That's why they were here, content with their tough lot at Great Spearstone, innocent of sweeter pleasures and an easier life. Not knowing what you were missing was the key to contentment, no doubt.

"Cheerio!" K called out to the enviable horses as he got back into the truck. This time not one looked up.

•　•　•　•

The road to Quorum Valley led west through farmland, open range, alfalfa fields and orchards. Ranch homes here were sprawling one-story buildings that often had started out as one-room shacks that had been solidified and built onto over time. The houses were set far back from the road. To shield against the scorching summer sun, early settlers had surrounded their homes with oaks, walnut trees and weeping willows that had grown to majestic dimensions, casting generous shadows.

K drove past the place he used to dream of spending his twilight years. It was a small, compact dwelling with a lopsided aspect about it. The house was girdled by a porch that ran along most of the circumference of the building, so that you merely had to shift your chair along with the course of the sun. The house also had a couple of haphazardly tacked-on, rickety balconies and an attic with a window and a shingled roof, all of which made it look somewhat alpine and therefore eminently unsuitable to the local climate. The attic would be unusable in summer, unless you had an urge to fry your brains in the true sense of the word rather than with the prescription opioids that were getting to be so popular with country folk around here.

In these climatic extremes even the porch would only be useful for a short time at the tail-end of the seasons, late spring and Indian summer. For most of the year it would either be too hot or too cold to hang out in outdoor spaces.

Still, K had set his heart on the house. There had been a time when he had paid frequent visits to see if had been abandoned in the meantime or if it had been put up for sale. Now he saw that it had indeed changed owners, as evidenced from improved grounds and prettified environment. The house had gotten a new lick of paint, missing roof shingles had been replaced, the porch had been sanded and varnished; and there was an abundance of flowers planted in glazed terracotta pots that it would take ages to water.

But K didn't want the house anymore anyway.

Because when you looked west across the valley, where once there had been red rock cliff sheltering a verdant band of trees marking the course of the Merced River, now there were drill towers stretching all the way to the old North Road, which XOX had doubled in width to serve its purposes.

Before XOX, the road had been all but invisible; you practically had to be on it before you saw it—it had been a narrow serpentine of a mountain road that demanded to be taken in the lowest gear. Now all was road and no mountainside.

That desolate view of the ravaged land was far too mild a punishment for the greedy fools of Quorum Valley.

•　　•　　•　　•

It must have been sheer masochism that had made K choose to get on the XOX case and that was now guiding him back to what had been Goosewash Wilderness.

In the few days since his last visit, the mighty energy corporation had gotten busy some more. Evidence of willfully defiant vandalism was everywhere. XOX must have hired a squadron of goons, instructing them to go ahead and do their worst.

K picked a path through heaps of bark, twigs, broken branches, rubble, making his way along the deep grooves torn into the soil by diggers, to where there had been the tree line. He wondered what had moved XOX and their goons to leave the Gambel oak standing. The oak had managed to grow to a full sixty feet in height through sheer freakish determination and now towered above the wasteland like a mourning Methuselah.

The old tree had inspired all kinds of local lore regarding its properties, which was split—like the collective mind of Quorum Valley—into benign and malign projection.

On the benign side the oak was said to progress courting to successful and harmonious conclusion; its bark cured infertility, tea brewed from its leaves shrank certain types of tumors, and urinating on its roots was sure to bring wealth.

Those favoring the malign lore, as usual, had the more compelling stories. Therein witches featured largely, spreading drought and infertility and pestilence; holding Sabbaths and orgies and lasciviously leading innocent country yokels into temptation and from there straight to damnation.

The tree's bark, leaves and acorns could be used to cast spells, maim, kill and paralyze. To the oak's roots they had transferred without any editing the Old World lore of the mandrake. Whenever anyone tugged at the tree's roots it would emit an unearthly sound that inevitably drove mad and eventually killed transgressors. Naturally the oak itself had grown out of the blood—semen was not mentioned—of a slain man.

K, per inclination, favored the malign lore. Also the gargantuan tree really did look grotesque, out of place, ominous.

Obligingly, K's fertile imagination produced something like a mandrake sound, a sighing brought forth by leaves rustling in the wind, and a rather disconcerting groaning—probably the creaking of morbid branches and the straining of roots against the soil.

The nearer he got the more human the damn tree sounded. It really did sound like groaning. He was tempted to turn back, but knew that this would make him feel even more of a loser than he already did. So he walked on. And all the while the tree's groaning grew louder and more eerie, more desperate—as if the poor lonesome tree was suffering a terrible agony.

K determined that he would walk up to the tree, circle it once—clockwise just to be safe—to assert himself vis-à-vis his head, which was more and more going its own way without consulting at all with common sense.

K whistled his old standby, "Always look at the bright side of life. . . ." which, mingling with the tree's moaning, made for an obscenely inappropriate mix.

Whistling determinedly K began to circle the tree. There was no nobility about the old oak; it was a mess: gnarled, weathered trunk; a thicket of low-hanging branches; chaotically intertwined limbs competing for light, surrounded by heaps of age-old vegetative matter in various stages of decay.

The light fighting its way through the foliage was playing tricks with his vision, casting all kinds of shapes.

What was the origin of the mandrake myth? The root that grew from an executed man's final ejaculation? K wondered if the thing about dead men ejaculating was true. Darwin would have needed no other proof as to the primal imperative of propagating the species.

Maybe the oak was old enough to have hosted executions. What had been the preferred method of execution in the old West? Shooting? Or hanging?

Over there was a branch that pretty much looked like a hanging person.

What a terrible species people were, taking the wondrous miracle of natural creation that was a tree, and using it to kill a human being. What infernal imagination would look at a tree and behold in it a tool for murder?

That branch over there really did look like a hanging human. You practically needed no imagination to picture how it would have been when they hoisted up the body, the person condemned to die struggling, pleading, writhing in fear.

How did they get a body up the tree? Who did the placing of the noose around the neck, the tightening and the pushing—did they ever get a night's sleep thereafter? After watching the kicking, the struggling, the spasming, the moaning. . . .

He could hear the moaning now and it was unbearable.

It was that branch, that very branch that was moaning and it was a human, he even recognized the human that the branch was, or had been, or soon would have been, if he didn't get her down from that branch she had hung herself from and he did not know how to get up there, or even whether to get up there and cut the rope from above or whether to try to get her down from below, but he knew one thing: that time was of the essence and he did not have long, she did not have long, because already she was blue in the face and her lips were a ghostly color and her tongue was black and protruding and her eyes were bulging and the noises she made were not groaning now, nor moaning, they were a terrible gurgling and the sound of lungs bursting for lack of air.

"Don't worry," he said to the dangling woman while frantically constructing a podium of logs and twigs and leaves and whatever else he could find. "All is fine. We'll have you down in no time and all will be fine. Do you hear me? All will be fine. I promise you. All will be well. All's fine."

He stepped on the tree-trunk she must have used to reach the strong branch around which she had fastened the rope, wrapped his left arm around her supporting her weight and lifting her, used his pocket knife to hack at the rope. How long they had depended on how tight the rope around her neck was. And how long he could manage to support her weight.

"Don't worry," he said. "I got you. I got you."

The woman moaned. The rope broke. K let the knife drop and held onto the woman with both arms. His arms wrapped around her, he went into a crouching position and lowered her body on to the bed of twigs and leaves. He collected his knife off the ground and severed the rope around her neck in one swift cut.

K cradled the girl's head with one hand, gently tilted it backward, pinched her nose with forefinger and thumb, fastened his lips on hers and began to breathe into her. All he had was the will to make her breathe. Breathe and survive. He breathed into her, shared his air with her, all that was of him and her was the air between them, moving from his lungs into hers.

She convulsed and spluttered and fought for air in great, wracking gulps.

The rope's friction had left burn marks on her neck.

He located his cell and prayed for reception. Much of Quorum Valley was a communication dead zone, a fact that under normal circumstances bothered him not at all, but today it did. Oh brother, today it did. The signal was weak. there was just one bar. "Please God," K prayed to the god he did not believe in—or in any case only when it suited him—"please God, let this call go through." And dialed 911.

God heard his prayer and the call went through. What was more, the emergency response was the very model of calm and contained efficiency: ascertaining location, ordering the ambulance and guiding K through a series of checks which indicated that the woman was alive.

The Amazon was mewling now, pitifully. Her eyes were closed. She was breathing, albeit with an odd whistling sound. K brushed her hair out of her face and rested his palm on her damp forehead. The Amazon whimpered. K took her hand in his, carefully, as not to hurt her, and covered her hand with his other hand, as if shielding a wounded bird.

"Help is coming. They'll be here soon," he said, to calm himself as much as the Amazon, who probably at this moment felt less worried than he did. Because she had after all relinquished all responsibility and left him with it.

Because he had been at the right place at the right time, or at the wrong place at the wrong time. There were different ways of looking at situations like this.

K wondered where the ambulance would be dispatched from. And how long it would take. They were smack in the middle of no-where. He was trying to think where the nearest hospital or health center was. There was none close by, that much he knew. And these roads did not lend themselves to speeding. He tried not to think about what would happen if the Amazon had sustained life-threat-ening injuries. Or what would have happened had he gotten there just a couple of minutes later. He alternated stroking the woman's forehead and holding her hand.

It seemed callous and uncaring just to be sitting there, doing nothing. Besides, his touch seemed to calm her. She looked quite serene now. At ease even. If you ignored the blossoming bruises around her neck.

"You didn't have to do that," K said to the girl. "You really didn't. You shouldn't have."

He wasn't sure if he was just imagining it or if she really was frowning. "You're okay," he said quickly. "All's good. Everything is going to be well. I promise."

• • • •

Paramedics had taken her vitals, strapped the young woman on a stretcher and loaded the stretcher into the ambulance. The ambu-lance been dispatched from Gopher but would take the woman, who was critical, to San Matteo General Hospital.

"How critical?" K asked hoarsely and the paramedic shrugged and did not answer.

"We will need to speak to you," one of the paramedics said. His tone sounded authoritarian bordering on menacing.

In the ambulance the other paramedic was applying an oxygen mask to the motionless woman's face.

"Is she going to be okay?" K asked.

"Can't tell yet," the paramedic said. "How can we get hold of you?"

K showed his shield. The paramedic grew somewhat friendlier.

"Suicide protocol is similar to homicide protocol," he confided. K didn't know what he meant. Except that it sounded as if the paramedic found suicide a less titillating version of homicide, though still a tad more interesting than a broken leg.

The paramedic opined they would need a crisis assessment. A psychiatric social worker might be called in.

K hoped the Amazon had insurance without too many deductibles. People had lost their life's possessions for less.

"Where's her vehicle?" asked the paramedic.

"Her vehicle?" asked K. He hadn't seen one.

"She must've gotten here somehow," said the paramedic.

"I don't know," said K. He was pretty sure there had been no vehicle along the stretch of the North Road that he had taken.

"Maybe she parked higher up?" K asked. "Do you want me to have a look?"

"Sure," said the paramedic. "We better get her to the hospital."

He watched the ambulance slowly driving downhill and then south on North Road.

And then he was alone, with the oak leaves rustling in the breeze and either the breeze was getting stronger, because the rustling was getting louder, a rustling cacophony—or he just imagined it was.

Neither possibility was particularly reassuring.

CHAPTER FIVE

Juanita Córdoba was one of the few people who treated K more or less like before. Córdoba treated him with the same sober neutrality that used to frustrate him then, and that he felt grateful for now. Then he had still been capable of whiling away staid meetings by entertaining erotic fantasies wherein Córdoba featured prominently.

"How come you're not at the school for the teachers' target practice?" K joked lamely.

Córdoba regarded him somberly. "Becky said you got called to an emergency?"

What hope was there for efficient work if facts got muddled at the first stage? Like the sucker he was he had once again found his way to a place he needn't have been, which had gifted him a baboon-sized monkey on his back.

"It was an emergency, but I didn't get called to it." K limped through his tale.

Córdoba quietly listened to his convoluted narration.

"You aren't going to start blaming yourself for this one too, are you?"

"No. Yes. Shouldn't I?" K answered, covering denial, actuality and doubt in rapid succession.

"No, you shouldn't," said Córdoba firmly. "If you hadn't found her she'd be dead."

"I found her too late," K mumbled.

"Stop it!" Córdoba said sharply. "You need to learn to let things go."

K was about to parry "do you?" when he remembered that not too long ago one of Córdoba's domestic abuse clients had been murdered in a particularly sadistic way by a violent partner. Maybe Córdoba did practice what she preached. So he told her about driving around Quorum Valley trying to locate the young woman's car.

Córdoba frowned. "There was no car?"

K shared his theory that the woman might have parked the car in the valley where it was less conspicuous, and walked up to her destination.

"You found her bag?" Córdoba asked.

"Her bag?" K echoed.

"You reckon she walked all that way carrying a rope?"

K shrugged. He hadn't really considered how the woman had transported the rope. In truth he hadn't considered anything much. He'd just hoped she would be okay. "Well. . . ," he said, "she could have just slung it on her shoulder, in a coil—"

"It would be pretty hard to carry a heavy coil of rope all that way," Córdoba said.

K tried to imagine the Amazon walking along the North Road with a coiled rope slung over her shoulder and began to share Córdoba's doubts.

To be so blatant that you walked to your appointed location of suicide in plain daylight carrying a rope you had to be bold and brazen, and during their first encounter K had formed the impression that the Amazon was neither and that her physical statue belied her vulnerability.

"I think you are right," K said. "I don't think she would have walked up there intending to kill herself with the rope in plain sight for everybody to see."

Córdoba nodded.

"If she really wanted to die she would have tried to make

sure that nobody could guess what she was planning," K mused. " But if she didn't really want to die and it was, as they say, a cry for help—then it would have made more sense to park her car near to where she. . . ." He tried hard to suppress his memory of the moaning, discolored woman with her bulging eyes and lolling tongue.

"No car. No bag," said Córdoba. "There's something weird here."

K cleared his throat. "I suppose you wouldn't care to come along to the hospital to see how she's doing?"

"Sure," said Córdoba. "Let's go."

• • • •

"Here." Córdoba handed K a Styrofoam cup. "I put sugar in it." She took a sip. "It's hot."

"Can't be worse than the sheriff's," said K.

Córdoba nodded. That was the one downside about Córdoba. It was not altogether apparent whether she had a sense of humor. On evidence K had to admit to himself that she probably didn't.

"What do I owe you?" K asked.

"Don't worry," said Córdoba.

"Thank you. Next one's on me." He thought it likely that they'd have enough time for him to repay his debt today. They sat and sipped their coffees. The lobby was quiet. It was starting to feel as if they had been sitting there for ages.

"Did you bring your dinner?" asked Córdoba, pointing at the paper bag K was holding.

"Grapes," K said. "I brought her some grapes."

"Grapes?" said Córdoba skeptically.

"In England that's what you take on hospital visits," K explained, though he wasn't sure if that was true. Maybe it was just something he thought they did. He doubted that Córdoba was going to trouble herself verifying his assertion. "I hope she is okay," he said.

Córdoba nodded.

This was kind of hard going. And somehow it didn't seem appropriate to feast his eyes on Córdoba's delectable bust here in San Matteo General Hospital while waiting to hear how the as yet nameless suicidal Amazon was faring.

K got up and strolled to a low table that was decked out with magazines. The selection suggested a recycling station for staff discards. Ecologically sound it perhaps was, though in terms of PR it did little to inspire confidence. It was to be hoped that the cheapness of reading matter did not reflect the quality of treatment.

K picked up a Time magazine that was so old as to be relevant again. "Would you like one?" he called over to Córdoba.

"What do they have?"

"Cookery and old news and . . . Hobby Dolls."

"Hobby dolls?"

K grabbed the magazine and took it over to Córdoba.

Córdoba began leafing through the dog-eared magazine. Her frown deepened.

"I don't understand," she said.

"Understand what?"

Córdoba handed him the magazine. "Who is supposed to read this?"

It seemed to be a catalogue mostly for doll-related matters: clothing, wigs, dolls' houses, dolls' house furniture, doll-related advice, suggestions, anecdotes, stories, prizes. . . .

"People who like dolls," K said.

"Kids?" asked Córdoba.

"Adults."

Córdoba shook her head. "Creepy."

"That's a bit harsh—I'd call it childish."

Córdoba looked at the magazine with distaste. To K, it seemed a fairly strong reaction to something so innocuous. He pictured a hardworking low-paid nurse or maybe a nursing aide, on his or her feet all day; all day having to deal with desperation and death with a sprinkling of patients' unreasonable demands for light relief, getting home at the end of a shift and kicking back with a Hobby Dolls zine, whose world consisted entirely of dinky, wholesome, trouble free and easy care replicas.

"Not childish," K reconsidered, "escapist."

"Huh?" said Córdoba.

"Here," K said and handed over his Time. "It's barely five years out of date."

He got up and approached the nurses' station.

"Can I help you?" asked the nurse.

The tone of the nurse's question belied the sentiment it was supposed to convey.

"That would be great," said K. "There was a young woman admitted a couple of hours ago?"

The nurse looked at him blankly. Perhaps she was thinking of dolls' houses.

"What is the name of the patient?" the nurse asked.

"We have no name," said K. He had told them all that already, but never mind. Whatever it took.

"I don't understand," the nurse said.

"Did the paramedics not tell you?" K asked in desperation.

"I just started the shift," said the nurse.

Did they not have handover, for God's sake? K was reaching the end of his tether. Not only did the nurse not know what she was supposed to know, she also seemed indignant that she was asked to know what she should know. K was starting to revise his indulgent assessment of nurses' legitimate interest in hobby dolls.

Córdoba joined him at the nurses' station. "The patient brought in from Quorum Valley—we need to see her," she said crisply.

"Let me call through," said the nurse.

They stood in uncomfortable silence for what felt like ages. Eventually a tiny woman in scrubs appeared.

"Are you relatives?" the tiny nurse asked.

"Police," Córdoba said and flashed her ID. "What is the patient's name?" she asked.

The nurse shook her head. She looked frightened. "I don't know. I didn't know I was supposed to know. . . ."

"Don't worry," said K. It was a day of repetitions. "You didn't do anything wrong. How is she?"

"I don't know," said the nurse, wide-eyed with panic.

K started to appreciate that San Matteo General's indifferent reputation was well-deserved.

"We need to see her," Córdoba said.

"I need to ask my supervisor," said the tiny nurse and bolted.

Córdoba frowned. "I heard they like doing that."

"Doing what?" asked K.

"They make trainee nurse aides run the shift."

"She's a trainee? She isn't a nurse?"

"Trainee nurse aide. Did you not see her ID?" asked Córdoba.

"No," said K. "I just assumed she was a nurse."

"Trainee nurse aide," said Córdoba. "That's not even a nurse aide. Nurse aides get paid bad enough. Trainee nurse aides get paid barely anything at all. That's how San Matteo General keeps in profit."

"Where does all the money go?" A while back an uninsured visiting friend had incurred a bill of $540 for a stubbed toe.

"To the management," Córdoba said.

K wondered where the trainee nurse aide's supervisor was hiding out. She was certainly taking her sweet time.

When she finally arrived, she was a he and K could bank another proof of his latent sexism. And add another one because he found that he did not trust men working in the caring professions— and what was even worse, that he regarded them with something amounting to contempt.

The exploited trainee nurse aide's supervisor was a shambling dude of unkempt appearance with too much facial hair and an aura of vagueness about him. His eyes seemed to have trouble focusing. K guessed that he had been torn away from some game where he had to pursue trolls through labyrinths and execute malevolent minotaurs with the aid of a Magick Sword.

"What level are you at?" K asked.

"Seventy-seven!" the dude said enthusiastically.

"Good on you!" K said.

He felt Córdoba's eyes on him. Pity that Córdoba wasn't a gossip, otherwise she could have helped K claw back some kudos down at the station.

The supervisor apparently found nothing remarkable in K's powers of deduction. Maybe he thought that everyone in the world was cosmically united in his game of trolls and minotaurs and magick swords.

"I guess you could go in and see her," the dude said. "Do you know her name?"

"Did you not find out who she is?" asked Córdoba sharply.

The dude shrugged: "Millie?" he said imperiously. "Did you get the patient's name?"

Tiny Millie shook her head. The whites of her eyes showed and she looked like a shying pony.

"No??" the dude said in a menacing tone.

Troll-hunting mega asshole.

"That would be your job, I guess," said Córdoba, icily.

For a split second it looked as if the dude was going to protest, but the expression on Córdoba's face shut him up.

Something had happened to Millie. She looked taller and held her head high.

"I guess you can go in now and see her," she said.

"Is she well enough to talk to?" Córdoba asked Millie.

"I can't say," said Millie. "They can tell you more on the day shift after they examine her."

What about conditions where time was of the essence? What if the Amazon's condition was such a one? But K felt his brain shutting down—it was too much to contemplate ifs and whats. To survive, to save himself from going crazy, he needed to believe that this was a responsible institution where staff was doing the right thing. Though at this very moment, their hirsute gaming buddy was inching his way back toward his lair.

Evidently there were more important things to do than save patients.

CHAPTER SIX

They said you were connected eternally to the person whose life you had saved. It was a notion that filled K with trepidation.

He had no wish at all to see the Amazon again, eternal bond or not.

Actually he felt so ill at ease that he wondered if he was in fact not wishing her dead rather than having to meet her again.

Well—maybe not dead, just gone. He'd be happy to know that she was living happily ever after. He just had no need to see her ever again, that was all.

The girl was hooked to a drip and connected to a monitor. Her neck was thickly bandaged, her face mottled and her eye sockets black and bruised. She looked awful.

Millie walked up to the bed and gently touched her arm. The Amazon did not startle or stir. She did not open her eyes.

"Is she sleeping?" Córdoba asked tensely.

Millie lifted her shoulders. It wasn't a callous shrug, it was the helplessness of one burdened with a responsibility that was far too great but that she was obliged to continue carrying. "The day shift will know more," she whispered.

K looked at the utterly still and faraway Amazon and recognized something of the aura around her. Here was another one who did not want to live. She had finished with everything and had made her peace with leaving this life.

Perhaps she had not yet realized that her suicide had not been successful and that she was still alive. Maybe she thought that this was what the afterlife was like: A random assortment of strangers hovering over you backed by the rhythm of a beeping machine.

K cleared his throat "We'll let her rest for now. We'll come back later."

He left the room, carrying the bag of grapes, without waiting for the others. He crossed reception, walked through the exit door, leant against the wall and breathed deeply, holding each breath while counting to five like the counselor had taught him.

Eventually Córdoba appeared. She stood next to him and said nothing.

"Sorry," K said.

Córdoba stood in silence.

"Do you think she is alright?" K asked.

Córdoba hesitated.

"No," she said.

"No?" asked K.

"I'm not a medic," said Córdoba.

"I know," said K.

"I was thinking . . . maybe . . . she has something, you know, something they didn't pick up . . . she was starved of oxygen, you know. . . ?

"You're saying she sustained some brain damage?"

"I don't know. I just got this feeling she isn't there. It's hard to say. Maybe she's just sleeping—" Córdoba bit her lip.

"Maybe it is still the shock? The trauma?" K suggested. "Maybe she just needs time to regenerate?"

"Sure," said Córdoba unconvincingly. "I guess we should talk to the consultant who treated her."

Which made Córdoba trump K in the naivety stakes.

• • • •

As K could have told Córdoba, no consultant had treated the Amazon.

This being San Matteo General and the patient being nameless,

ID-less and relative-less, all factors that increased the chance that she was insurance-less too, care had been taken to keep treatment as basic as ethically defensible.

Actually K couldn't remember how the weasel of a bureaucrat whom Córdoba had confronted had euphemized this particular instance of medical negligence.

It had taken a while to sink in that no doctor, never mind a consultant, had gone near the nameless Amazon.

The case had been wholly left to paramedics and auxiliary staff.

Córdoba was imposing in her anger, eyes blazing, breasts heaving, skin flushed to a bronze glow. The bureaucrat remained unimpressed and unapologetic.

All that had been done, or not done, had been done in accordance with hospital protocol.

Did hospital protocol include overlooking possible brain damage in a patient? Córdoba wanted to know.

Eventually, by a variety of subtle hints and not so subtle threats, they extracted the concession that a doctor would be deployed to assess the patient.

"Probably an intern," mumbled K.

The harried individual that eventually appeared did not have a reassuring air. For one, he had a stethoscope flung around his neck, which made K think that this was indeed an impostor—maybe the janitor who'd been paid a couple of bucks extra to get rid of nuisance cops.

The impostor was at least a passable actor. He was doing a great job portraying stress and impatience, employing a whole arsenal of nonverbal communication conveying that:

a) this was a bullshit task wasting precious time,

b) he had been bullied (into wasting time on this bullshit task), and

c) they were attempting to undermine the constitutional right of the poor to suffer and die for lack of adequate medical care.

At the nameless Amazon's door the impatient medic ordered them to wait outside, much like commanding dogs to "stay!" and "sit!" He vanished into the room and shut the door in their faces.

"How do we know he really examines her?" K asked Córdoba, making sure it was loud enough for the medic to hear.

"He shouldn't be in there alone," Córdoba said. "He needs to be chaperoned. You stay here."

K cracked his knuckles, paced a while, perused the pictures on the corridor that showed a somewhat baffling variety of subject matter, as if whoever managed these things had decided that there needed to be something for everybody and every taste, so that at any given time any one target group would be pleased by 5 percent of the hospital's artistic offerings and aesthetically offended by 95 percent.

He had looked at all the artwork on display and had covered a considerable distance pacing and still there was no medic and no Córdoba.

Maybe he should have chaperoned her? Some women went for white coats. Particularly when white coats were accessorized by dangling stethoscopes.

The longer they were taking in there, the more anxious he felt.

When he could just about bear it no longer the door opened and the tense-featured medic emerged. He strode past K without acknowledgement and hurried along the corridor. K stuck his head through the door.

Córdoba put a finger on her lips and shook her head. She left the room and closed the door behind her, slowly, softly, and motioned for him to walk along.

"Coffee?" she asked.

"My turn," K said.

He sat down next to Córdoba and stirred his coffee.

"If you go on like that you'll make a hole in the cup," Córdoba said.

K stopped obediently.

They sat in silence. Córdoba sipped her coffee. "This needs some more sugar," she said and got up. "You want more sugar?"

"I'm fine," said K.

Córdoba took a long time ripping open a sachet of sugar, pouring it into the coffee, stirring, tasting the coffee, taking another sachet of sugar, ripping it open. . . .

"So. . . ?" K asked eventually.

Córdoba ripped open another sachet. "He said he needs to get the consultant."

K said, "That's not good?"

"No," Córdoba said. "I don't think so."

He thought of the girl, hanging from the old oak tree, the groaning. Oh, her groaning. It had been terrible. An end of the world kind of sound. And maybe that was what it had been. The end of her world, her conscious world.

So he hadn't gotten her down off that tree in time. Maybe he had done something wrong, had committed some fatal error that had cut off her oxygen, that had injured her brain.

He stared at his bag of grapes, got up and walked over to the nursing station and put the bag on the counter. Maybe tiny Millie had some use for fruit.

CHAPTER SEVEN

"Robbie Begay," said K.

He had felt a sudden need for his old buddy's astute, no bull-shit counsel to help him put things into perspective.

"Officer Robbie Begay. Please."

Not that the abominable Sheryleah, receptionist at Redwater Navajo Tribal PD, beneficiary of clan-based nepotism, was either deserving of or receptive to good manners, but in K hope sprung intermittently.

"He's not here."

"When will he be back?" asked K.

"Dunno," said Sheryleah.

"Don't you have his schedule?" asked K.

"Huh?" said Sheryleah.

"Would you look at the schedule and tell me when Officer Begay is due back?" K enunciated carefully.

Sheryleah, he could hear all the way up from Redwater, was chomping her way through a wad of gum, which made it hard to understand just what she was saying.

"Pardon?" asked K.

Sheryleah repeated herself. This time she sounded as if she was talking through gritted teeth.

It was fair to say K and Sheryleah hadn't ever hit it off, but Sheryleah answering "shit" was pretty strong stuff, even when K factored in their historically ropey relations.

"There's no call for that," K said primly.

"Huh?" said Sheryleah.

"Maybe we should start over and try to be civil?" suggested K.

"Huh??"

K's patience, scarce at the best of times, snapped. "Just tell me when Robbie Begay's going to be back. Now."

There was a plopping sound. K wondered if Sheryleah had spat out the gum in preparation of giving him the what for.

"Shot!" yelled Sheryleah.

"What?" asked K.

"He was shot!"

"Robbie Begay? Was shot??" K asked, stunned.

"Yeh."

"How is he? Where. . . ."

"Hospital," said Sheryleah and slammed down the receiver.

•　　•　　•　　•

K caned it down Highway 288.

Atmospheric pollution had its aesthetic upside. Air-borne dust particles had given Needle Rock a pink halo.

K kept his foot on the accelerator, raced through speed restricted zones, overtook an 18 wheeler within a few spare yards of oncoming traffic, grimaced into oncoming drivers' shocked faces, flew over potholes, swerved around the bloody remains of a run-over dog and made it to Redwater Indian Health Service hospital in twenty-two minutes, including a five-minute grape-buying stop-over, which had to be a record. Taking grapes to hospitals was getting to be some kind of a ritual or superstition, though not exactly an effective one so far.

He shunted the car into a priority parking space and raced into the hospital.

Standing in the large, domed, homage-to-the-hogan main hall, it occurred to K that he did not know where Robbie Begay was being treated.

Begay might not even be in this hospital. If things were bad they would have taken him to Albuquerque.

Please God, K thought, let him be here. Let Robbie be okay.

If K had been God, he really would have weighed up whether to respond to Franz Kafka the Lesser's pleas or to teach him a lesson. Maybe God felt that s/he had to try extra hard when addressed by agnostics?

"You lost?"

K turned round and saw a young man in paramedic uniform.

"I'm trying to find a friend. But I don't know which department he's been admitted to."

The paramedic raised his eyebrows. "Don't ask them." He cocked his head toward the adobe-clad, petroglyph-facsimile-edged reception counter.

"No?" asked K.

"They won't tell you," said the young man, "Confidentiality— they take it real serious. Your mom could be dying in there and they wouldn't tell you where to find her. Just go through to the nurses' station at Inpatients and say your friend's name like you mean it." He pointed his pursed lips toward the sign spelling "Inpatients."

Seeing the old-time Navajo way of using pursed lips rather than fingers for pointing cheered K up.

K hurried along the corridor, strode into Inpatients, marched to the nurses' station and barked assertively, "Robbie Begay."

The nurse glowered. Damn right she was. As usual he'd overdone his brief. Barging in and barking commands like some Übermensch-type.

The phone rang. The nurse said "Six" and picked up the receiver.

K bolted down the corridor before the nurse could change her mind.

Most doors stood open and in almost all the rooms the sick beds were surrounded by groups of relatives of multiple generations. Grandpa, grandma, mom, siblings. In every sickroom there was a tower of stacked-up chairs, a sufficient number of chairs for the average Anglo family's Thanksgiving.

In an entirely theoretical way K admired Diné close family relationships that had survived historical adversity and the dominant society's relentless foray into forced assimilation.

In an entirely subjective way K could imagine very few things worse than having a gaggle of relatives ogling him while he was languishing in a hospital bed. It made him wonder what his xenophile tendencies were rooted in.

The door to room six was ajar. K paused a moment and braced himself for what he was to encounter. His pulse had started to race and his mouth was dry.

Oh God, he thought—today he was rather testing the Almighty's indulgence of agnostics—let Robbie be okay.

The door opened in his face and a nurse stepped out. She was young, with a cherubic face and a dimpled smile.

"How is he?"

"He's being naughty," the nurse said and giggled.

K knocked and entered.

At least there was no assembly of relatives crowding the room. Begay was sitting in bed. The bandage around his chest and shoulder gleamed white against his brown skin. He was grinning broadly.

Jammy sod, K thought. He's hoping to get lucky with the nurse.

Judging from the nurse's smile K thought that Robbie might be in with a chance. Perhaps it was his duty to warn her, innocent young girl.

"Oh Lord, have I not suffered enough?" groaned Begay, when he set eyes on K.

"Sheryleah sent me to make sure you are fine," K said.

"Ha," said Begay. "Trust you to make me feel better."

"What happened?" asked K, drawing up a chair.

"What's that?" Begay asked greedily, pointing at the paper bag K was carrying.

"Grapes," said K and handed Begay the bag.

"Organic grapes," he said into Begay's frown. Begay did not look any more impressed.

"Grapes?" yelped Begay in an outraged tone.

"Grapes!" asserted K. "I'm not feeling the gratitude."

"Why do you bring me grapes?" Begay asked, as if K was guilty of an unspeakable act.

K thought it wiser not to confess that these grapes were a kind of sacrificial offering, a symbolic gift for an immutable god, a kind god who had heard K's pleas and who had kept Robbie well and annoying. Although God could have done better on the Amazon.

"They are the number-one offering to the ailing and infirm. Have been since time immemorial."

"This one of your 'the dictionary I swallowed is repeating on me' days?" Begay asked irritably. "Don't mess with me, Dude, coz the first thing they done when I lie there bleeding and in pain, PAIN! is send in the dietician, one of those whispering Anglos, and she put me on carrot sticks and celery and whatsit, the white stuff that ain't cheese nor cream and tastes of sour nothingness?"

"My life?" suggested K

Begay snorted. "There's nothing we can do about that, my friend. But you can do something about sweetening up mine. I'm talking crullers and Bavarian torpedoes. Better get going, coz City Market sells out of crullers pretty early."

•　　•　　•　　•

"Are you fixing for the nurse to give you a sponge bath?" K was watching Begay stuffing down Bavarian torpedoes as if there was no tomorrow.

His bandages were flecked with chocolate icing and his chest was splotched with custard and cream. Maybe there were people who found that kind of thing erotic.

"What you staring at?" asked Begay, jamming three inches of torpedo into his cakehole.

K shook his head. "So what happened?" he asked.

Begay shrugged. "Remember the meth lab?"

K nodded.

"Remember I told you nobody was going to bother because the boss' relatives got themselves a sideline in meth labs?"

"Your boss is mixed up with meth?"

"Could be," Begay mused. "It's about the only secure investment you got nowadays. . . ."

"Are you thinking about investing?" asked K.

Begay shook his head. "The business partners you got to deal with are kind of high maintenance for me. Anyways, so nothing happens for months and I am starting to chew over all that stuff you were whining on about: taking responsibility, making the world better, yada. Then one time in this meeting the boss and his butt-kissing posse get me so pissed, I want to show them. So reckon I better go after those hombres, because if I don't nobody else will. I drive out there and they're getting ready to haul out the stuff and—" Begay pointed at the bandage.

"I'm glad you are okay," K said sincerely. "You're not looking too bad."

"You're not looking so hot," Begay said.

"Thank you," K said.

"I mean it," Begay said seriously.

"Hey," protested K. "I'm supposed to be visiting you!"

"How are you?" Begay asked.

K looked away. From where he was sitting he could see Needle Rock.

"Million dollar view!" he said.

"Franz!" said Begay sharply.

K flinched. Begay rarely ever called him by his first name. "Don't look at me like that," he said.

"Like what?"

"Like you care," K said and pulled his face into a shape that he hoped resembled a grin.

Begay closed the donut box and put it on the table. K stared at his knees.

Begay cleared his throat. "Look," he said, "for a while out there I thought I was gonna die. They'd got me here," he pointed at his shoulder, "and there was a lot of blood. There was no one around. And I'm just lying there. . . . You know . . . stuff happens when you got time to think about . . . dying."

"I'm so happy you made it. When I heard. . . ."

Begay shook his head impatiently "Yeah, I made it, bro. But I ain't so sure about you. I'm not asking you. I'm telling you: It's about time you snap out of whatever it is you got going there. You need to forgive yourself and forget, okay? And start living again."

"Could you—if you were responsible for something like that?"

"Sure," said Begay. "Get up and go, that's me. Besides, it's just your way of thinking that makes you think you are guilty. All you did wrong was doing your job right."

"You reckon?" said K sarcastically.

"Yes, I do. And your grinding is getting me pissed."

K thought it wiser not to share his new burden of self-blame that had joined the old burden of guilt.

"You just tell me if your guilt and beating up on yourself is changing anything." said Begay irritably. "Does it help you do your work better? Does it help you to help people like you were always chewing my ass about? Like we are some type of social workers? Does all that guilt help you do anything useful?" Begay was starting to look pretty angry. "Let me tell you what it does: it makes other people feel bad. That's all it does. You feeling bad: does it roll the clock back? Does it make anything un-happen?"

"Un-happen," K echoed.

"Don't start doing that word-thing. Or you'll really get me pissed!" Begay jabbed a finger at K. "Ouch." He put his hand on his shoulder. Blood seeped through the bandage.

"You're bleeding!"

The white gauze bandage was turning crimson with oozing blood.

"You're bleeding!" K yelped. He sprinted out of the room and to the nurses' station.

"He's bleeding!" he said.

"Who?" asked the nurse.

"Room Six!" said K. "Robbie Begay."

The nurse nodded and continued to scribble in a file.

"Excuse me!" said K.

"Yes?" said the nurse and looked up.

"My friend: Robbie Begay. Room six. He is bleeding!"

"Did you do something to him?" asked the nurse.

"Me?" asked K. "No! His wound started bleeding."

The nurse nodded and went back to scribbling in her file.

"Aren't you going to do anything?" croaked K.

"We'll rebandage him later. At ward round."

"How much later?"

The nurse looked up. "You trying to tell me how to do my job?" she asked sharply.

There was a choice between denial and challenge.

"Yes," K said.

"You are?" said the nurse.

"Yep," said K.

"Well, tough, Mister," said the nurse. "Coz I had thirty years of dealing with folks trying to tell me how to do my job—and guess what?"

"What?" asked K.

The nurse burst out laughing. Her laugh was infectious.

"Go back and sit with your friend. He needs some handling," said the nurse.

K trotted off obediently.

"You look better already," said Begay.

"There's nothing better than getting yelled at," said K.

"Want a cruller?" asked Begay.

CHAPTER EIGHT

"There's someone wants to file a Missing Person's." Becky had that pinched look around her nostrils that K had learned to mind.

"No problem," K said peaceably. "I'm on it."

Becky tilted her head toward the station's waiting area.

Milagro PD's waiting area had seen more than the average amount of wear and tear, an impressive amount of tear in fact, inflicted by irate citizens who were intent to max out on the Law's ill will they had so far accrued. No use being hanged for a mere sheep, when there were herds of sizeable rams to be had.

K walked over to the cluster of seats set out in rows. He felt rusty, as if he hadn't done anything in an official capacity for a long time. He had forgotten how to portray kudos and authority.

The woman sitting on a front row chair shot up. There was an aura of agitation and seething anger about her. At least K assumed it was anger.

"The interrogation room is free," Becky called out. Becky who always corrected him when he used the old, pre-enlightened-era term: "It is the Interviewing Suite."

K took it as a not-so-veiled instruction as to how Becky wished this particular visitor treated.

He led the way to the Interviewing Suite/interrogation room. The room's air was stale and smelled of fear and loathing, or maybe just Young's BO.

K pulled out a seat at the table for the visitor. He opened the window, grabbed the Missing Persons forms and returned to the table.

She was a young woman with long glistening dark hair, olive skin, wearing a scoop-necked fitted T-shirt that displayed the rounded tops of her breasts. A delicate cross dangling from a thin gold chain nestled in her cleavage. If the cross was supposed to connote piety, it had quite the opposite effect on K. But then K wasn't Christian.

"You'd like to report someone missing?" asked K.

He noticed belatedly that asking if one would like to report someone missing was perhaps using a rather unfortunate turn of phrase—unless it was someone of whose considerable estate or life insurance payout one expected to be the main beneficiary.

K couldn't quite decide what the young woman's expression suggested: anger had been his first guess, though trepidation, panic and fear were also possibilities.

She was very good-looking, could have even been called beautiful were it not for a certain unyielding quality in her expression. Also K felt as if he had seen her sometime, someplace that he couldn't quite recall. His memory for faces was crap. Not a good thing in a policeman.

"Who is missing?" K asked.

"My sister," said the young woman.

"When did she go missing?" asked K.

"She didn't come home from school."

"What day was that?" asked K.

"Today," the young woman said. There was a hint of outrage in her voice.

"Did you try her cell phone?"

"She doesn't have a cell."

"What time is school out?" he asked

"2:30," said the young woman.

K looked at the wall clock. It was 4.50 pm.

"How old is your sister?" asked K.

"She is fifteen years old," said the young woman.

K was starting to feel some warmth for the tardy kid with the pushy sister. Had he been related to a control freak like that, he wouldn't have carried a cell either. Whatever it took to give a body some peace and space.

"She is fifteen years old and she is two hours and twenty minutes late from school," said K carefully, "and you would like to report her missing?"

"Yes," said the young woman.

K nodded. He grabbed the diary that somebody had left lying on the table, opened it and leafed through it. It took just a couple of turns of pages for him to wish he hadn't. A lot of doodling of the kind that would make the average whorehouse-keeper blush. There seemed to be a surfeit of bestiality on view. Bizarre-looking critters humping and being humped; unfeasibly shaped genitalia, speech bubbles filled with obscene verbiage. Someone here had a questionable attitude.

K looked up. The young woman was eyeing him suspiciously. So he went on nonchalantly turning pages, hoping that there would be an end to the sketched out horror, hoping that he would find a couple of blank pages on which to add his own doodles.

He needed to be seen to be doing something. He needed some space to clear his head and to consider strategic options.

This lady would not be gotten rid of with any of the well-trodden "calm down dear" formulas that were the first aid kit of police work. This dame wouldn't tolerate any distraction maneuvers and any fobbing off, of that he was certain.

She was a pretty intimidating personality. Under her fitted T-shirt her breasts rose; her lips were parted, allowing a glimpse of glinting sharp incisors.

K found this both vaguely frightening and pretty erotic. He was starting to feel more tolerant of the diary's pornographic doodles. Sometimes a man needed to create an outlet for himself.

"Usually someone would have to be missing for 24 hours before a Missing Person's report is filed," he explained.

The woman glared.

"12 hours in case of a minor," K appeased.

"You want me to come back at 2:30 am?" she asked incredulously.

K couldn't very well ask her to return at 2:30 am to file a Missing Person's with Young, who would be on shift then—and who knew what control Young had over his libido in the wee small hours.

Damn, she looked familiar. He'd seen her someplace, he was sure.

"When does your sister usually get home?"

"It depends—ten to three when she takes the bicycle; three thirty when she walks; between two forty-five and three fifteen when the neighbor gives her a ride."

"Which was it today?"

"Today she walked—she was supposed to walk. . . ."

So in effect the girl was just one hour and twenty minutes late, which meant that her sister must have started to freak a scant hour after the girl had been due home.

"I already drove down Oak Street two times to see if I can find her. . . ." The young woman's voice had a frantic pitch.

"Did your sister have any plans that she needed to be punctual for?" K asked.

"No!"

"Tell me something about your sister's habits," K said gently.

"Her habits? She gets up, goes to school, comes back home, studies, helps mamá and abuelita with the cooking, studies some more, watches TV—and then they go to bed."

K waited.

The young woman shrugged. "What do you want me to say?" she asked.

"Does your sister have any hobbies? Does she play sports? How does she spend her leisure time?"

"She stays at home. She likes to study. She is a real good student."

"She is fifteen," K reminded her.

"So?"

"You were fifteen once," said K.

If the little sister was anything like her big sister K had a damn good idea where she was and what she was doing right at this moment.

"Does your sister have a boyfriend?" asked K.

"No!" said the girl, as if he had issued an unspeakable accusation.

"She is fifteen," he said again.

"My sister is a good girl," the girl said. There was no mistaking the despair in her voice now.

"You are very protective of her," said K.

The girl looked up. Her eyes were huge and shone with a film of tears.

"I can see that you are very worried," said K softly. "Do tell me what makes you so sure that your little sister wouldn't be late. Help me understand how different your sister is from an average fifteen-year-old."

From the young woman came a growl.

K saying the wrong thing had stopped her crying.

"My sister is a good girl," she hissed.

K stifled a sigh. He could see no way to getting Older Sister to break down for him exactly what made her so sure that her younger sister was different from practically every other hormonal teenager, who could be relied on to NOT return home on time and not spend their leisure time with mamá and abuelita watching TV. Every night.

K started shuffling the Missing Persons forms. He saw that he had the wrong forms. It was the Missing Child form he needed. He smiled apologetically into the woman's mask-like face, got up and went to the wall-mounted sorter unit that held the forms. Was supposed to hold the forms. Where were the damn forms? He rooted around in various folders and drawers without result; turned around to issue another apology.

69

The girl was sitting as if carved of stone, staring sightlessly into the distance. There was about her a look of utter despair.

This was way more than the usual relative's worry. Still he did not understand it. The kid had been late barely two hours. It was daylight outside and would be for a good while yet. The little sister wasn't so little anymore either. At least K assumed that she wasn't, unless she had dwarfism or some other medical condition that stunted her growth. And she wasn't a kid, she was a teenager of an age that many cultures perceived as imminently marriageable.

At last K located the Missing Child forms on the filing cabinet; they'd been sitting there right in front of his nose—which was how things always went.

"Name?" asked K.

"My sister's?"

"Next of kin," K read out. "As you are here that would be you. Unless you would prefer to give the names of your parents?"

"No," said the young woman impatiently. "Put my name: Alvarez,"

"First name?" asked K.

"Maribel," said the girl.

Now was the time to congratulate himself on all the necessary skills and personal accomplishments he brought to police work: photographic memory, perfect recall and razor sharp analytic skills.

The fragrant Ms. Alvarez, Maribel Alvarez, whose possible relations with the abominable Lucky Easton of the environmental nemesis XOX had so disturbed Gutierrez.

The little sister was called Luisa. Her birthday was close to K's own. They were both born in the month of dreamers and idealists. It took a good while to complete the form and still K felt he'd gotten no closer at all to understanding what was going on.

"Ms. Alvarez," K said gently, "thank you for this information. Have you had any more thoughts on why your sister has gone missing?"

Maribel Alvarez eyes burnt a hole into his skull.

K pretended not to notice. "Any thoughts?" he repeated.

"What are you going to do?" Alvarez demanded.

"To look for Luisa and to find her it would help us to have as many facts and aspects on her life and habits as we can."

"She goes to school, she studies, she. . . ." Alvarez started her litany.

Something snapped in K.

"Let's get real here," he said.

Maribel Alvarez looked at him, stunned at first, then her surprise turned into hatred. Her nostrils flared and her teeth were showing again.

"I am not here to insult your sister's honor and you are not here to defend it," K said. "You are here because your sister is missing."

He wisely did not say "because you think your sister is missing," though that would have been closer to what he believed. As soon as he heard himself saying 'your sister's honor' he started to comprehend something. Luisa was supposed to be the good girl and Maribel was the bad girl. It was a case of the Older Sister projecting all of herself that was good into her little sister.

Splitting, as K only knew too well, was endemic in families. But this seemed to be rather extreme, bordering on the delusional.

Dealing with whatever neurotic setup the Alvarez family had going was far outside of the bounds of police work and pretty much belonged in the territory of a professional therapist. There was no way K was going to suggest that, though.

In the silence the clock ticked loudly. Outside the windows traffic was rumbling by. K could see a pulse fluttering on Maribel's neck. He almost fancied he could hear her heart racing.

"Ms. Alvarez, I don't know if you remember: We met before—"

Maribel frowned. Clearly she had no recollection of their short meeting in Lucky Easton's plush office.

"Lucky Easton's office," said K. "We met in Mr. Easton's office at the XOX Energy Corporation."

K made no attempt to disguise the implication.

He held her eyes, steadily and, as he hoped, neutrally, though it was hard to maintain neutrality when thinking of just who it was that Maribel Alvarez was granting her favors to.

The girl looked at him and something odd was going on in her face. It was something that he recognized—and then he understood: Alvarez was going through the same thing that he had just gone through: the dilemma of fight or flight.

"Find Luisa," she hissed.

"You tell me," said K, "why you think that Luisa is so different from you."

"Luisa is not like me!"

The young woman's cry was one of pure agony. It tore at K's heart.

"Maribel," K said softly. "I can see that you love your sister very much. But surely Luisa does not need to be a saint for you to love her?"

Maribel Alvarez froze, as if he had thrown a bucket of ice water at her. She stared at him, white face, black eyes, pulse fluttering under her skin like a trapped butterfly.

K knew that there was no way anybody at Milagro PD would agree to activate a Missing Child's case when the child had only been missing for two hours, especially when the child was a teenager. The way Milagro PD's budget and resources stood the Alvarez family would be lucky if after a week or so anything would be done at all, other than missing posters being tacked on random stores' notice boards.

"Give it a few more hours," K said. "Give your sister a chance to come back home."

Maribel Alvarez shook her head.

"There's a good chance Luisa will return today. Most teenagers missing turn up alright. Don't worry just yet. Maybe your sister is already back at home?"

Maribel Alvarez looked at him. There was no hope in her eyes at all.

•　•　•　•

Gutierrez arrived punctual to the minute, carefully carrying a red-lidded Tupperware box probably filled with choice morsels lovingly prepared by his doting wife.

Young was ten minutes late and did not apologize. He planted himself on a chair. The chair creaked in a way that made K prepare for it collapsing into a slapstick-like heap of matchstick-sized wooden splinters.

Throughout the handover Young subjected various body parts to vigorous scratching. He just stopped short of his rude bits, but even so the noise of nails on polyester was pretty grating. As usual Young lasted halfway through handover, when he hoisted himself up from the chair and beat it. Maybe it was Happy Hour on Triple G Cup Redhot Mamas.

This was K's moment to tell Gutierrez about the Missing Child case whose relative might come in for a follow-up.

"How old is the missing kid? Fifteen?" asked Gutierrez. "And she was only missing for like—two hours?"

K was reassured that Gutierrez reacted much as he had. He had been worried that he had not given the disappearance enough consideration.

"The older sister was probably overreacting," K said.

"That's nice though," said Gutierrez, "It's always good to know there are still families out there that care, right?"

"Yes," said K. "By the way, we do know the older sister. We met her before."

"Yeah?" said Gutierrez without curiosity.

"Yes," said K, "do you remember Ms. Alvarez?"

"Miss Alvarez?" asked Gutierrez.

"We met her only for a moment," said K, "The woman in Lucky Easton's office? We disturbed them, remember?"

Gutierrez' brow furrowed. He nodded slowly.

K watched a blush spread from Gutierrez' throat to his face.

"Very good-looking," said K.

He knew he was being an asshole. He did not quite know why he was being an asshole.

Maybe he wanted to punish Gutierrez with his Tupperware box that his loving wife had filled with culinary offerings, for coveting another woman whom he was conceivably blaming for being coveted.

Being old-school, Gutierrez worked hard on sublimating his untoward desires—through cultivating a prissily self-righteous, moralistic attitude for instance.

"Maribel Alvarez is having a hard time," K said to Gutierrez, "and she is very worried about her sister. Be kind to her. She is judging herself harshly enough as it is."

Gutierrez shrugged, possibly feeling that no amount of contrition could make up for Maribel Alvarez' loose morals and allure.

"Be kind to her," K repeated and left.

CHAPTER NINE

"Boy, this is driving me nuts. I almost wish I was back at work. Do you believe that?"

Begay was calling from home. He had been discharged and apparently was missing the nurses' special attention.

"Shocking," said K. "Why don't you go back?"

"They are making me take all that sick leave. They are forcing me, man."

"Forcing you? How about being grateful for a change?"

"Grateful? What for?"

"For the sick leave. There are places that make people on Chemo show up for work. They make them provide their own sick bucket too."

"Don't be weird. Anyways, one thing I have learnt is that those guys never do anything because it is good for us, the little people. There's got to be something in it for them. Maybe they're running scared that I'll plant a compo claim on them, because of neglecting duty of care or whatever you call it when the big boys refuse to provide backup for one brave cop taking on those badass meth dudes out there in the boondocks."

"Maybe you should sell the film script," K suggested.

"That's not what I'm really thinking," said Begay, undeterred. "What I really think is that they want to keep me out of the way, 'cause the chief got something going with those meth-cookers. That's how he can afford to move off the Rez to that house in Appleton he's building for himself. On Gold Hill Drive, right up there with all the other scumbags."

"So what are you doing with yourself? Besides working out your compo claim?" asked K.

"Just hanging," There was a pause. "I told you it's driving me nuts. I'm not joking. I thought it would be fun hanging out with a carton of crullers and watching those cop shows with all these hot women, and their aim is always straight, and when they run they don't get out of breath, and all their hair is in place, and their shirts tucked in all neat—how do they do that, you suppose? I thought it'd be fun watching other people run around and get shot. But all it is doing is getting me pissed."

"Where's Gloria? They tell me there's nothing as restorative as the love of a good woman—"

"We had a situation. . . ." said Begay glumly.

"Sorry to hear that," said K. Though devotedly commitment phobic, he had a tendency to invest in the happiness of others' relationships. Gloria was a good woman; and a tolerant one too. Nevertheless, Robbie managed to drive her away with predictable regularity.

"She'll come back," K said confidently.

"This time I'm not so sure," Begay muttered.

"Why? What did you do?"

Begay's silence left K ample time to develop his own hypotheses. Well, it was none of his business. Besides, it was somewhat cheering in a schadenfreudig kind of way to see life-coach Robbie hoisted by his own petard.

He started picturing Begay with his box of crullers watching low-production-value police procedurals in a darkened room.

"Hey," said K. "Why don't you come up and stay with me? I could really use some cheering up."

"Ha," said Begay mirthlessly.

K realized that Robbie Begay thought he had been joking. And he realized that he had not.

"And this one. Hold on, there's another one." Robbie Begay was in his truck, handing down paper bags. They were bulging and heavy and K wondered if Robbie was traveling with all his earthly possessions in the time-honored fashion of his Navajo nomadic forbears.

Robbie shifted his limbs with the caution of one who had learnt the hard way about the consequences of rash movement. K was pretty sure the doctors had forbidden him to drive.

"No more lifting and jumping about today, hear?" K said. "I'm not in the mood for another trip to the hospital."

Begay however was not to be deterred from unpacking the bulging paper bags and presenting K with their contents, one by one.

"Eggplant!' he said proudly. "Looks like something that ET left behind, huh?" and laid the dark purple shiny vegetable on K's kitchen counter.

"I love eggplant," said K.

"Never tried it," said Begay. "Is it that color all the way through?"

He didn't wait for an answer but produced squash; zucchini; a trio of bell peppers, green, red and yellow, that he seemed particularly taken with, and:

"A cucumber. An ENGLISH cucumber. Just in case you got some home sickness."

K mimed delight though in truth he preferred native tough-skinned country cucumbers and the aromatic poblano peppers they sold at a third of the price.

At the same time he felt strangely moved by Robbie's beaming, expectant face that spoke of the pure joy of altruism, of Begay's happiness in surprising his oddball vegetarian bílagáana friend with a medley of weird vegetables.

"Baa ahe nisin, shik'is," K said, and tried to keep his voice from catching.

K brewed a pot of coffee before retrieving the box of crullers he had stowed on top of the kitchen cupboard out of Wittgenstein's way.

"Crullers!" said Begay. "Baa ahe nisin, shik'is."

It was one of those moments, fleeting as mist and sweet as honey, when they both knew that the world was a friendly place after all.

• • • •

Begay was into his third cruller when Wittgenstein made an appearance. He jumped on the couch and eyed the cruller. Begay plucked off a piece of pastry and held it out. Wittgenstein sniffed and carefully took the crumb from his's fingers.

"I didn't know Wittgenstein has a sweet tooth," K said.

"What?"

K repeated: "I didn't know Wittgenstein has a sweet tooth."

"Who?" said Begay.

"Wittgenstein."

"What's that supposed to mean?"

"Wittgenstein was an ill-tempered philosopher who wrote about the impossibility of saying what you mean and who once hit another philosopher with a poker," said K. He didn't really know if he was being accurate, because, truth be told, he'd never quite gotten what exactly Wittgenstein was saying—and even if the iron poker thing was true. In truth K had given the cat that name because whenever he said "Wittgenstein" he evoked Grandpapa's melodic Viennese vowels.

But K was damned if he told anyone that, ever.

"How come you got yourself a cat?" asked Begay.

"I didn't get myself a cat. He got himself a sucker. One day he was there. And the next. And then it got cold and he wouldn't take no for an answer. . . . I guess we got used to each other," he added, lest he had offended Wittgenstein.

"I'm surprised he didn't run away when you gave him that name," Begay said, and scratched the cat's ear: "Eh, puddytat?"

Somewhat to K's disappointment, Wittgenstein made no attempt to tear Begay's arm off.

• • • •

"So," said Begay licking sugar off his fingers, "Fill me in, bro. Tell me about yo' White Man's burden in Anasazi land."

"We've been busy . . . you know how it is."

"I'm starting to forget how it is," said Begay. "You got yourself some interesting cases?"

K told Begay about the Amazon. And when he was done with the Amazon, he told Begay about missing little sister Luisa. To his surprise he found sharing lightened the dread, the guilt and the confusion somewhat.

Begay listened and remained silent after K had finished his account.

Begay's pensive mien was starting to freak K out. Begay's silence felt ominous.

"And?" K prompted. What he really wished for now was a jolly "can do" attitude that rode ruddy roughshod over his high-strung sensibilities.

Begay looked as if he was considering his options very carefully.

"Those aren't happy cases," he said eventually.

"No?" said K.

"Leastways not the way you are telling them," said Begay.

"How am I telling them?" K asked.

Begay got his damned-if-I-do, damned-if-I-don't: better-really-think-how-I'm-gonna-say-this expression going.

"Just say it, will you?" K said irritably.

Begay said softly, "Could be you are telling stuff like it is. Could be it's more about stuff left from last time. The way you are telling it, there's not a lot of hope here."

Things for some reason always sounded worse when said out loud. Particularly when said out loud by someone else.

"I don't know if it is the way I'm seeing it or it's the way things are," said K. "But you tell me where to find reason to be hopeful about a young woman who may be brain damaged because she tried to kill herself because a big corporation is destroying the environment and there's nobody to stop them? And nobody's interested in her anyway, because it's way more important to teach teachers how to shoot people. Tell me a better way to look at that and I gladly will."

"Maybe not," said Begay. "Maybe things are like that. But you can't tell me that you—" he paused. "How long is it you worked as a cop?"

"Ten years," said K, "Yikes! Ten years!"

"Time sure flies," said Begay. "You can't tell me that you been a cop for ten years and these cases are the worst you seen?"

"Probably not," said K.

"One thing you got to learn is not to take stuff personally. Not to take it home with you. You do, shik'is. You do. I can smell it all around here."

"Those are my socks," said K.

He felt shocked and hurt. He'd worked so hard not to let Robbie Begay see the new guilt that had joined his old guilt, his guilt about not having got there in time to save the Amazon. If only he hadn't lingered at Latep library ogling the temporary librarian.

"There's a time for joking," said Begay, "and this ain't it. What I think is that you are still feeling guilty for something that you could do nothing about. That kid killing himself. It wasn't you that killed him. But you got this damn thing about saving the world and now, instead of having learnt your lesson, you are going way extreme and try to save every damn body to make up for stuff."

"What would you suggest?" asked K coldly.

"Did you not listen? What I said just now: Do your work. Do it well. Don't take it personal. Don't hitch your own happiness to the cases you are working on, okay? There's nobody that would do that for you either, anyways."

"You brought me an eggplant," said K.

"And that, shik'is," said Begay, "is as good as it's gonna get."

CHAPTER TEN

Juanita Córdoba was carrying a bunch of sunflowers. Against the backdrop of the station it made for an incongruous albeit cheering tableau.

"Lovely flowers!" said K. Somehow he hadn't taken Córdoba for a flower person.

Córdoba looked uncomfortable, as if she had been caught out doing something untoward. "The girl—you know? At the hospital."

"How is she?"

"The same, I think," said Córdoba. "The consultant says they need some time to see if she has some damage. . . ." Córdoba pulled a petal off the sunflower. It shone bright yellow in the sunlight.

"These really are pretty," said K. "They are very bright."

Córdoba nodded. "They say you never know. There's people that are in a coma for twenty years, and then they wake up and you find out they heard everything. All that time they are awake and alert, but they can't let anyone know. They are trapped in their body, you know? Like that guy who woke up after nineteen years in a coma and asked for a tuna sandwich?"

The human condition in a nutshell. A body's out for nineteen years, floating in his own private galaxy, and when he wakes up what does he desire? A tuna sandwich.

It put K in mind of that thing about five hundred years of Swiss democracy and brotherly love producing the cuckoo clock. K wondered what he would ask for, were he to wake up after all that time:

Fifteen bottles of Bitter & Twisted IPA, a bong and The Doors' "Celebration of the Lizard" on full blast? Or a sleeping pill.

Then it sank in what Córdoba had said.

"Coma?" he said.

Córdoba had pulled another petal off one of the flowers and was rolling it between thumb and forefinger. The Amazon would be lucky if there was any flower left by the time Córdoba got to the hospital.

Córdoba dipped her head and chewed her lip: "You want to come along?"

The honest answer was "no, not really" or rather "no, really not."

He racked his brains for an excuse.

Then it occurred to him that the alternative to accompanying Juanita Córdoba to the hospital could well turn out to be discussing the Missing Child case with Gutierrez, or worse Maribel Alvarez.

Fire one way, frying pan the other.

"Sure," K said.

• • • •

At San Matteo General the charge nurse was reluctant to allow visitors.

"Has the patient had any visitors?"

The nurse shook her head.

"How is she?"

The nurse lifted her shoulders. It was an ambiguous gesture that could have meant that the girl wasn't doing great or that the nurse did not know how the girl was doing.

Córdoba said, "thank you," as if they had come to some agreement, and strode past the charge nurse. K followed. The charge nurse remained fixed to the spot. Perhaps she too admired Córdoba's chutzpah.

The Amazon looked pretty much as she had when they had last seen her. The bruises around her neck seemed to be growing fainter. Her hair looked lanky and greasier than it had last time. K wondered in whose domain of responsibility washing comatose patients' hair fell.

There was nothing in the room that gave any clue to the Amazon's identity, no personal effects, no get-well cards, no tender mementos left by visitors.

There was just the big, strong girl on the bed, lying under white sheets, a drip delivering who knew what and one of those machines with screens on which different colored lines dipped and rose and which, when shown in the movies, always spelled impending disaster.

Córdoba took one step into the room, looked around, turned and left.

Oh great. He had agreed to accompany Córdoba, not to be dropped off in the sick room by her. He had to summon all his willpower not to bolt and run after Córdoba. If survivor and savior were bound together for all eternity, what was the deal with a partial survivor?

He looked at the girl with her closed eyes. A small mercy. He did not think that he could stand looking at her empty eyes. Her far-away, empty eyes, and her being here in this hospital bed, all alone and nameless.

He owed it to her to bear her empty eyes. He owed it to her to be here and stand it and not flinch, because there was nobody else there for her.

"Hey," said K. "How are you?" If she woke up now and asked for a tuna sandwich he'd be ecstatic. But from the girl there was nothing that indicated that she had heard him or was aware of his presence.

Córdoba returned, carefully carrying a water-filled vase and the bunch of sunflowers. She walked to the bed, set the vase on the bedside table and began to arrange the flowers in the vase with the single-minded concentration of an Ikebana master.

You could work with people for years, form your ideas of them, come to believe that your idea of them was informed—and then they would do a small thing that turned everything you had thought about them on its head.

K hoped that his purely theoretical, headspace-confined lust for Juanita Córdoba wasn't about to turn into some kind of love-type emotion.

Lust was fun. Love was nothing but an energy-sapping drag.

Córdoba looked up and smiled shyly. "Is this okay?"

"Lovely!" K said.

Clearly it was a case of fiddling while Rome burned.

• • • •

"You the officer who found her?"

K credited his jaundiced lens for making all nurses today evoke auditions for the part of Nurse Ratchet.

"Yes, Ma'am."

The nurse cast a withering look at Córdoba, who was straightening the Amazon's bed covers.

"We need to talk to you."

K followed Nurse Ratchet through labyrinthine corridors, several hallways and waiting areas, some more corridors, through a key-card-operated glass door and from thence to an office whose occupant seemed to be excessively fond of passive-aggressive jokes of the "I am an acquired taste. Don't like me? Acquire some taste!" kind.

Ratchet motioned to a chair, muttered something inaudible and turned on her heel, leaving K to contemplate the manifold meanings and implications of "Telling a girl to calm down works about as well as trying to baptize a cat" and "Today I feel like putting an Out of Order sign on my head and going back to bed."

The longer K sat and waited the more pissed he started to feel. Feeling exasperated with your job was something he could empathize with, but this was a hospital, for pity's sake. And the last thing patients and relatives needed were these sour burps of discontent right in their faces at a moment when conceivably many of them were going through what might be a point of major crisis in their lives.

When the office's incumbent finally appeared the cheerful ambience had generated in K a simmering rage that Ms/Mrs or Miss Acquired Taste did nothing to appease. She wore a sequined top in a spectrum of neon colors that fractured and reflected light in a visual migraine-inducing manner. She took her place behind her desk and began clattering on the keyboard, eyes fixed on the screen.

If this was the way they treated patients and relatives, Milagro General Hospital merited to be dragged in front of an ethical tribunal and—hopefully—to be closed down pronto.

"What did you say?" Ms AT hissed.

Apparently he had once again said out loud what he thought he'd only thought.

"You heard me," K said and looked at his watch. "I give you five."

Having lost the following stare-down contest, the woman began to shuffle papers while holding forth in unrelieved monotone about what K eventually understood to be the Amazon's billable status, the point of contention being that this particular patient had no name, no identity and no Social Security number, which was why to Milagro General Hospital and in particular to Milagro General Hospital's billing department the comatose patient presented a problem, as an unidentified, undocumented patient did not have a billing address and there were no details on insurance status and financial solvency either.

Furthermore, the diagnostic limbo in which the unidentified patient was currently residing presented an obstacle to various pathways to identification that could be and would be employed once the patient had been conclusively determined to be in a permanent vegetative state, whereupon specific methods of identification such as facial recognition software could be and would be employed without seeking consent, as the conclusively diagnosed, permanently vegetative patient could be placed under the hospital's temporary legal guardianship which would then be able and entitled to fluidize assets and extract funds to settle outstanding and accruing medical bills, until such time when the patient's closest relatives had been located.

"Your five are up," K said, turned his back on the incredulous sequin-top and walked out, somnambulating through the maze of corridors until he at last happened on an exit and emerged into daylight, where Córdoba eventually found him. Córdoba, who would not be shocked or floored by anything, who had seen it all and knew it all, told him that was the way things rolled and that the girl would probably be transferred pretty soon to somewhere else, which K understood to be some local equivalent to a Mother Theresa's outfit. Not to worry, there was time still, said Córdoba, time and hope that they would be able to identify their girl and all would turn out okay.

And K, who damn well understood that Córdoba was saying all this to make him feel better about all of this mess and not because she could see any light at the end of this particular tunnel, felt that mixture of gratitude and despair that weighed on the soul like a hundredweight.

CHAPTER ELEVEN

Monitoring protests and breaking up demos wasn't a frequent ask for the cops of Milagro town, where folk generally held with the status quo, unless avarice and economic advantage beckoned, whereupon Milagro folk proved capable of surprisingly nimble ethical turns.

Which explained that these days there was barely any old boy who hadn't some stake in the booming recreational marijuana industry, while the federal gung-ho administration with its incessant warnings of an SOB invasion of rapists and pushers and *very bad hombres* had encouraged a mushrooming of Mom & Pop outlets specializing in the sale of semiautomatic assault weaponry, no need for background checks, natch.

K had volunteered for this particular callout with joy in his heart and a spring in his step. Outside San Matteo County's main economic hope and K's particular nemesis, XOX HQ, a motley crowd was waving makeshift placards fashioned out of cut-up cardboard boxes. Uneven lettering proclaimed opposition to XOX, covering all tactics from cunning reason to heartfelt pleading to militant outrage. On the highway pickups thundered past, drivers leaning on their horns, presumably not for the purpose of expressing solidarity.

On K's approach, the demonstrators waved their placards with renewed zest and amplified their chants by several decibels. As a cop you were always assumed to be on the side of The Man.

Showing sympathy to the cause would only be rejected as a strategic device to devious purpose, so K decided not to bother. He cast about for the organizers or head honchos or instigators of the demonstration. Despite the self-proclaimed egalitarianism of many of such gatherings it usually was easy to spot the alphas. There was however no apparent leader to this group. The age range of participants spanned several generations.

K sidled up to a no-nonsense-looking woman with closely cropped steel-grey hair and steel-rimmed spectacles.

"A spontaneous gathering?" he asked matter-of-factly.

"Why? Are you fixing to arrest us?" the grey-haired woman asked.

"Not as yet," K said gravely. "Are you planning to do something that might get you arrested?"

She looked at him speculatively. "We are planning to go to Quorum. There's a group there already."

"To Quorum Valley?" asked K.

"To the XOX plant at Quorum. For a sit-in. We're going to block off the entrance so their trucks can't leave!"

"Why?" asked K. After all, the XOX plant had been sitting there for a good while, spider-like extending the web of its enterprises; tolerated, if not positively fêted by the frack-friendly folk of Quorum Valley amongst whom the extractionist spirit ruled large.

"XOX vandalized some protected wilderness. Didn't you hear?"

The question was, how had they heard?

Barely any time had passed since the Amazon had chosen her lonely path of protest that had ended with her alone, unresponsive and unidentified, in a hospital bed. No one had been to see her. No one seemed to be missing her. And yet here there were all these folks joining in her cause.

The grey-haired woman was looking at him. Light reflected in her spectacles.

"Not an easy job, huh?" she said.

"Does it show?" K said lightly.

"Here," the woman dug in her pocket and produced a card. "In case it gets too much."

K nodded and put away the card. Pretty enterprising way of touting for her Reiki practice, he had to hand her that.

"How did you hear of the Quorum Valley situation?"

"How did we hear of the Quorum Valley *situation*?" She shrugged.

"Who organized this gathering?" asked K.

"You mean, did we get a permit?" asked the woman.

"No, that's not what I mean," said K sharply. "I mean: who organized this demo?"

"I didn't see the notice until late last night. It just was there, in my social media." She fumbled in her shoulder bag and drew out a phone.

"Here it is—it's a flyer—see." She stretched her phone toward K.

The flyer was a concise and seething call to action, impressive in its efficient brevity. It had to be, sent out late at night, at such short notice.

"Who sent out this flyer?"

The woman peered at the screen. "I don't think it says. Why? Is that important?"

K shrugged. "I don't know."

"Anyway," said the woman. "This is just the start. I'm looking forward to our sit-in at the Quorum plant. Last time I was at a sit-in must have been thirty years ago." She leant toward K. "Fancy coming along? The press is going to be there too. A touch of police brutality would help our cause." She honked merrily.

She looked around. "I guess I should go. I don't want to be accused of consorting with the enemy. See you in Quorum?"

●　　●　　●　　●

K mingled with the environmentalists. Most of them were, alas, less approachable than his steel-rimmed lady. More or less everyone

who would speak to him confirmed what she had told him: the flyer had arrived late at night and no one had paid much attention to
who had issued it. It was a worthy cause. They had turned up. They
hoped to make a difference.

Which, in K's book, made them a pretty gullible and naïve lot.
How come no one here had been able to tell him who had organized
the demo? How come the flyer had no contact information? No
details on origin?

Something stank. It wasn't the common cause. It wasn't the
protestors' righteous outrage. It was that a mass of people had been
summoned, directed by an invisible source that could be anyone.

The Sierra Club. The Downwinders' Association. The San
Matteo Environmental Alliance. The CIA. XOX.

Maybe XOX was hoping to incite a riot amongst protesters
that would lead to arrests and a vigorous law-and-order backlash,
that would generate outrage among the rapacious hydraulic fracturing cheerleaders of Quorum and beyond, and which would eventually lead to a full-blooded civil war between environmentalists and
extractionists. Partisan propaganda wars and dirty strategies being
back in vogue these days, it seemed a plausible plan for XOX to
hatch.

At the far end of the throng K spied Bachman Jr. the future
hope of the *Milagro Gazette*. As yet it hung in the balance if Bachman Jr. would decide to follow in his old man's footsteps as editor
of the Milagro Gazette or beat it to the bright lights, big city.

"Are you covering or protesting?"

Bachman Jr. was a likeable kid, trustworthy and nerdish with a
light sprinkle of idealism.

"Covering," said young Bachman. "XOX won't pay attention
to the demo anyways."

"Unless demonstrators get busy with some industrial sabo-
tage," K suggested.

Bachman smiled. "That'd make a great scoop."

"Who organized the demo?"

"I was supposed to do an interview with the organizers," said Bachman Jr., "but there's no contact details on their flyer. So far nobody I asked could tell me— everybody's got the flyer and nobody's responsible for it. I guess I'll just have to try to interview XOX."

"Try their CEO," K said genially. "Lucky Easton."

"Thanks, I will," said Bachman,

"Ask him about Goosewash Wilderness. And maybe you want to take a drive to Quorum and have a look for yourself how XOX is going about things."

K hung around until the protesters began to stow away their placards and pile into the people carriers that would transport them to Quorum wilderness, obeying an anonymous call to arms that might have been issued by friend or foe.

•　　•　　•　　•

"What happened?" asked Begay. "What did you find out?"

K shrugged.

"Did they have a riot?"

Begay did not seem to find K's hypothesis that the protestors had been summoned by an evil counterforce at all paranoid.

"You're talking to an Indian whose folks were sent to work in the uranium mines, because they were cheap and dumb and the companies didn't want to waste profit on safety," Begay said coldly. "I know there's nothing that these companies won't do for a dime. Did anything happen?"

"Not as far as I could see. I don't think there was a riot or anything. Don't you think it's strange that there was nobody taking responsibility for having organized the demo?"

"Maybe they were afraid they'd get blamed if things got out of hand?"

"Maybe," said K. "But all these folks had was a flyer that landed in their inbox late at night."

"And they all turn up like some kind of zombies? That what bothers you?

"That too," mused K. "But there's something that bothers me more. If someone called all those people out, that person knows about XOX and Goosewash Wilderness. And if that person knows about XOX and Goosewash Wilderness, they would know about our environmentalist too..."

"And—?" said Begay.

"And yet nobody's been to see that poor girl at the hospital. No visitors, no inquiries, no missing alerts. Nothing."

"Nothing, huh?" Begay clicked his tongue: "There's no nothing. Nothing is always something."

K found he wasn't in the mood for Robbie's cryptic pronouncements:"Whatever. That still doesn't get me any closer to nailing Mr. Lucky fucking Easton. I'm at least hoping the Milagro Gazette managed to get some dirt on him."

Begay regarded him incredulously.

"You don't get it, do you? Oh boy, do you still have some ways to go."

CHAPTER TWELVE

The Milagro Gazette had given one paragraph on page five of the newspaper to the demonstration, therein describing it as uneventful, mentioning the vicinity of XOX Energy Corporation as the location for the demonstration without specifying the reasons for said demonstration, thereby creating the impression that XOX HQ and Quorum Valley had been arbitrarily chosen for the pleasure of an obscure bunch of folks who just liked to gather and wave some placards for no particular reason.

The Milagro Gazette's page one and most of page two carried a lead article on Lucky Easton, CEO of XOX Energy Corporation, proud family man and concerned father of two daughters. Mr. Easton had submitted a generous proposal to donate to Milagro Municipality four dozen semiautomatic handguns inclusive of ammunition and lock boxes to the purpose of furthering the hardening of schools. The safety of Milagro's young was at stake. The accelerated implementation of the School Marshal Plan throughout San Matteo County was of primary concern. Four dozen semi-automatic handguns with the requisite ammunition and lock boxes would go some way to fulfilling that aim. In a short interview, San Matteo County's Superintendent of Schools, Ivan Fletcher, expressing his profound gratitude and paying homage to Lucky Easton's civic spirit, reiterated his own school hardening credentials, concluding with the hope that by the end of the year every school in the district would be fortified, bulwarked and hardened to military base grade.

K phoned the Milagro Gazette and demanded to speak to Bach-man Jr.

After three cycles of holding muzak Bachman Jr. came on the line.

"What's the deal with the XOX demo reporting?" K asked roughly.

The pause that followed was sufficient to solve a cryptic cross-word clue or two, had K been so inclined.

"There's a new reporter covering commerce and community," Bachman Jr. said carefully.

"Do you happen to vet your new reporters for bias?" K asked.

"You could address your concerns to the managing editor," Bachman Jr. suggested.

"Managing editor? Where's your dad?"

"On leave," Bachman Jr. said. "Sorry. Got to go. Good luck."

• • • •

The sheriff who read K's mind better than K was comfortable with pronounced an explicit embargo on further visits to XOX and to Lucky Easton by either Gutierrez or K.

"The guy's practically got himself local hero status. And now he's got the newspaper in his pocket too. Who is going to confront Easton on the mess XOX has made?" K demanded.

"It ain't gonna be you, Son," the sheriff assured him.

Who then? The evil-doers and destroyers of this world escaped their just deserts aided by the complicity of an inert majority and the misplaced scruples of the ethical few— a perfect conspiracy of enablers. XOX already owned the town and now Easton had the schools and the media on his side too.

All that seemed to remain was the hope that his nemesis would eventually catch up with Easton and bite him on the ass.

• • • •

K roamed the station's corridors seething, his mind flooded with unwholesome fantasies of punishments fit for the likes of Easton, mostly derived from his scant knowledge pertaining to medieval techniques of enhanced interrogation, when he nearly collided with Gutierrez, who was carrying a mug of coffee and hadn't, it seemed, been minding how he was going either.

"Hi," said K and shook a splash of coffee off his hand.

Gutierrez didn't look so hot, having been on night shift yesterday and back at work today, which wouldn't have given him a whole lot of time to kick back and relax. His hand trembled as he raised his mug. He took a draught of coffee and spilled some on his sleeve.

"Are you okay?" asked K, out of politeness rather than concern. He didn't wait for a reply. "The schoolgirl I mentioned yesterday—Luisa Alvarez, did she come back?"

Gutierrez shook his head.

"Did her sister come in?"

Gutierrez nodded and held up two fingers. No wonder Gutierrez looked so weary.

"Twice? She came in twice? Her sister still hasn't come back? Sweet Lord—that means she was right. I just thought she was being hysterical, trying to get us to file a missing person's after barely two hours." A terrible thought occurred to him. "They haven't found her? She isn't. . . ?" he couldn't bring himself to finish the sentence.

"No. No!" said Gutierrez.

"She's alive?"

Gutierrez lifted his shoulders. He bit his lip.

K's mind started to run riot.

"Óscar—what is it?"

Gutierrez made the kind of beckoning motion that one might make guiding Little Red Riding Hood to the bonnet-wearing Big Bad Wolf.

Gutierrez led the way, dragging himself along the corridor, shoulders slumped, head hanging. His dejection was contagious.

With every step K felt more anxious. On his forehead cold sweat beaded. He tried to recall the annoying counselor's advice, but couldn't remember a single thing except that his PTSD—according to the annoying counselor everything was his PTSD—and the persistent dread that resided in his bones was the residue of that stuff that had happened to him and he had to relearn that not everything that happened was bad. Expecting bad things all the time was just his PTSD.

K particularly loathed how the counselor had insisted calling it "your PTSD," as if PTSD—whatever that was—was a particularly clingy determined pet that just wouldn't leave his side. Though maybe visualizing *his* PTSD as an attention-seeking pet wasn't such a bad idea. Maybe there was a whole new treatment approach in there that he could make a mint of: PTSD Conversion and Pet Visualization Therapy perhaps. PTSDCPVT—the acronym needed some work.

The idea wasn't half bad though. What type of pet would his be? An irrepressible Jack Russell? An impish marmoset? A rabid komodo dragon?

At least the pet visualization had temporarily distracted K from his dread. Maybe hatching schemes to make money from self-help strategies was in itself curative.

Gutierrez opened the door to the cubbyhole that had been designated "Special Investigations Suite," switched on the lights and sank heavily into the chair behind the desk. Apparently he knew the password to the SIS computer. K did not. He wondered if the password was imparted to officers according to favor or merit. As far as he could remember he'd never even set foot in the coffin-sized Special Investigations Suite.

The screen illuminated Gutierrez' face and cast it in a ghastly greenish hue. The lines the frown had etched into his forehead were about a quarter inch deep and his mouth was set in the manner of someone preparing himself to be rolled over the Niagara Falls in a barrel.

"Get on with it," K implored. He'd not meant to say it out loud. Antagonism was getting him to where solicitous concern had not. Gutierrez' nostrils flared.

"You better come this side," he said.

K moved around the desk dragging his chair with him. He sat down beside Gutierrez.

For the longest time he did not understand what he was looking at. Slowly, like the eye accustoming itself to a lack of light, blurry patches of color tightened into shapes that morphed into bodies. Scantily clad bodies, unclad bodies, in a variety of poses none of which left much to the imagination. The bodies, or the body; K began to understand that these were not several, but one nubile female body offering itself or being offered to a camera that steadfastly focused on the body only.

"Why are you showing me this?" K croaked.

Gutierrez looked at him as if he couldn't quite believe he'd heard right. Whatever he saw in K's face confirmed that he hadn't misheard. Gutierrez scrolled to the top of the screen, clicked on 'Profile' and pointed to a headshot of an unsmiling dark-haired girl.

K still didn't get it. Weird as it was, he'd spent his life hitherto without ever seeing a porn-site. There was something at least that he'd been spared. "What is this?" he asked again.

Gutierrez sighed, allowing himself to display just the slightest hint of exasperation.

"Luisa Alvarez," he said.

"Luisa Alvarez?" echoed K.

"Luisa Alvarez," Gutierrez said. "It is her."

"What is her?" said K, uncomprehending.

Gutierrez snorted. His exasperation was pretty pronounced now. Almost aggressively so, in fact.

"This is Luisa Alvarez. I checked. Though here it says she is seventeen." Gutierrez shrugged. "She knows what she's doing. Seventeen puts her beyond statutory rape."

"You are not making any sense," said K.

"I wish I wasn't," Gutierrez said.

"What is this?" asked K.

"You don't know what this is? It's a hook-up site."

"What?"

"A hook-up site," repeated Gutierrez— as if repeating nonsensical verbiage would help making sense.

"It is a 'no strings attached' kind of site where people can find someone to get it on with," Gutierrez explained in a remedial teacher's aide voice. "This one's pretty hardcore. I'm surprised it's not been taken down. It's very . . . explicit. The good little sister," he said. His voice was thick.

K shook his head. "Where did you find this?" The idea that Gutierrez would have trawled through porn sites searching for a missing-fifteen year-old was pretty disturbing in itself.

"Dilger," Gutierrez said.

"Dilger? What's Dilger got to do with this?"

Gutierrez's face hardened. "Dilger saw Maribel Alvarez." He looked at K meaningfully.

Apparently he was meant to understand something. Gutierrez was plainly expecting some penny to drop. But the penny was stuck.

"Sorry," K said lamely.

"Maribel Alvarez came in three times, okay? Yesterday afternoon when she talked with you. The second time she came back was in the night," Gutierrez explained.

"Let me guess—2:30 am?" asked K.

"How did you know?"

"Because that is exactly twelve hours after Luisa went missing. Did you do a Missing Person's?"

"No," said Gutierrez. "I was due to clock off because I'm working split shifts this week—I told her to come back in the morning and sent her home. She came back first thing this morning and got everybody sore. Becky was pretty annoyed with her too. She says Maribel Alvarez is too pushy and no wonder her sister left. And

Dilger heard that and when he saw Maribel he said he was going to do some background checking," Gutierrez pointed at the screen.

"So Dilger sees Maribel Alvarez and goes off and finds this stuff on her sister? I don't get it."

"Maribel looks like a wild girl, no?" said Gutierrez.

K supposed 'wild girl' was yet another chauvinist euphemism, so he neither confirmed nor contradicted.

"Dilger said when he saw Maribel Alvarez he knew: 'If the little sister is hot like the older sister, I have a darn good idea where to find her,'" Gutierrez's rendition of Dilger's hillbilly drawl was pretty impressive, "—and so he did."

That a cop would effortlessly find his way through kiddy-porn sites and still manage to blame the exploited victim was beyond creepy. K hoped that what lay at the end of this road was a suspension for Dilger.

He peered at the headshot of the somber girl and tried to unsee the detailed shots of her nude body. He read the short and to-the-point text, detailing Luisa's sexual preferences, which pretty much included anything that dates or customers or suitors or whatever the term was could set their wormy, corrupted, perverted minds on.

"This doesn't make sense," K said.

"You don't want it to make sense," said Gutierrez.

"That too," admitted K. "But this isn't right. Where is she supposed to have learnt all this stuff? Her sister says she's at home all the time and real studious. This thing sounds like it's been written by a hooker. "

"A lot of kids now know stuff they shouldn't. Dilger said that's how she learns, from her sister," Gutierrez said. "Should we show this to the sister?"

"You can't be serious? You want to show this to Maribel Alvarez?"

"I don't want to. I'm asking if we ought to. Maybe she won't worry so much? Or she will worry about other things?" Gutierrez drummed his fingers on the desk. "Maybe it is better for her to worry about this, than worrying about Luisa being dead?" he offered.

"Not yet," K urged. "Don't tell her yet. Let's see what else we can find out first."

Gutierrez shrugged again. "As you want. But the others mostly have seen this. Now nobody is going to waste their time bothering about Luisa."

"Not quite nobody," said K.

CHAPTER THIRTEEN

"Easy!" K said. This was the second time Gutierrez had nearly bumped into the car in front. Gutierrez stamped on the brake. Sweat beaded on his forehead.

Apparently K wasn't the only one on the squad with nerves. Unfortunately this did not make him feel any better. "What are you worried about?" he asked. Of all the dumb things he could say.

Gutierrez nevertheless essayed to answer. "Everything. Meeting the family. I never like meeting the families. There's never anything that you can say to a family that's missing a child—or even a grown-up, you know?"

K knew.

"And with . . . Mexican families. . . ." Gutierrez left the sentence unfinished.

They were bumping along an ungraded road that climbed toward the foothills of the mesa. It was a part of Milagro largely unknown to K, although it was less than three miles from the center of town. For some reason the mesa foothills had been left largely undeveloped. Here and there were small homesteads, haphazardly located on the parched plain, noticeable from afar by the greenery that surrounded them. The green wasn't of the manicured and over-watered lawns of the landed gentry, but soil used judiciously and to maximum capacity. There were clumps of fruit trees, patches of corn, raised vegetable beds crowded with peppers and squash, beans climbing along structures erected for that purpose.

Something of the mesa slopes reminded K of Quorum Valley in years gone by. When all the land around him had been bought up by Californians, or bore-holed and drilled to Bejesus by the likes of XOX, K thought it possible that he might move here, amongst modest folk who tilled the soil and did not waste that most precious of natural resources on watering their lawns.

•　　•　　•　　•

The Alvarez home was a double wide on a private plot to which various extensions had been added. Trailer and extensions had been painted sky blue. The paintwork was well maintained and the color made K feel he was traveling in another country. There was a fenced plot where they grew vegetables and an orchard of fruit trees. It was a homely looking property.

"What a nice place," K said.

Gutierrez rotated his head in a way that made K think he had some doubts and indicated for K to go first. K was sorely tempted to insist on Gutierrez taking the lead, but found that he didn't have the energy. He went ahead, climbed the stairs and pulled the rope hanging from a brass ship's bell. To the right of the front door was a life-size terracotta spaniel proffering its paw.

"How are we going to play it with that website thing?" K began, when the door was opened by a middle-aged woman with short pepper and salt hair and a kindly face.

"Mrs. Alvarez?" K asked.

The woman nodded. She stood aside and motioned them in.

On the TV a telenovela was playing. The screen was populated with a number of meticulously groomed, fair-skinned folks preening, pouting and glowering and gliding along in gleamingly marbled and abundantly pillared palatial abodes. In the background one caught glimpses of white-aproned domestics scurrying about: handymen carrying ladders, gardeners raking leaves, whose skin tone tended to be of darker hue. The audience targeted by telenovelas in the majority were people whose lives resembled those of the menial extras, rather than that of the main players and their fortuitous circumstances. The complicity of the downtrodden and exploited in glorifying the status quo at least went some way to explain why the world was in the state it was.

K was getting to think that anything at all that helped alleviate discontent and unease was okay. Call it corruption of ethical standards or the grinding mills of time on social conscience—he was done with it all.

Life was short, ugly and brutish and one had to take one's distractions as they came. Maybe telenovelas were the reason Maribel Alvarez had sex with Lucky Easton. Maybe they had taught her that the only way to fortune and luxury was over or under a male body belonging to the dominant majority.

Mrs. Alvarez said, "My mother. She likes telenovelas."

She motioned to an area where three sofas were arranged around a glass-plated table. On the table were a bowl of fruit and a plate of cookies wrapped individually in cellophane. The room was verdant with potted plants, crowding most feasible spaces, some hung in planters from the ceiling, sizeable trees branching out of colorful terracotta pots, on the whole creating a feeling of sitting in a forest clearing.

"Lovely plants!" said K.

"Sit, please," said Mrs. Alvarez.

She went into the kitchen and busied herself with kettle and pot. She joined them bearing a tray and distributed glasses of mint tea.

They sipped their tea in silence and the silence seemed to be lasting rather long. K shot a sideways glance at Gutierrez, who turned and looked at him in a way that could be interpreted as expectant or deferential or challenging, K wasn't sure which, except that it damn well looked as if Gutierrez was expecting K to take the lead. Gutierrez produced a notebook and held a pen at the ready, as if he had merely come along as the stenographer.

K braced himself for an outburst of anguish, distress and fury by Mrs. Alvarez.

By now the kid had been missing long enough to give real cause for concern. As far as K was concerned the discovery of the porn profile made Luisa's disappearance even more of a worry. It seemed sneaky, even unethical, not to share with the Alvarez family all that they knew about their daughter's secret life. At least K assumed that she had kept this part of her life secret. Into the back of K's mind swam memories of cases where so-called normal families had pimped out their underage children for material gain.

Mrs. Alvarez spoke English in the halting manner of one whose seldom and reluctantly used second language it was, and it was clear that she did not have much confidence in her ability to express herself in the dominant majority's tongue. It was also clear that Gutierrez had no intention of relieving K of his coerced lead investigator role, despite increasingly obvious linguistic obstacles.

Maybe it was due to Mrs. Alvarez' limited English, her shyness or an overwhelming self-discipline, but in view of the harrowing circumstances she seemed remarkably collected, calm even.

The barebones facts that Mrs. Alvarez was able to give them pretty much tallied with what Maribel had told them: Luisa did not possess a cell phone. She cycled, walked or got a lift to school from a neighbor, depending on the neighbor's shift. The neighbor's name was Astrix Gonzalez and knowing that she was a woman made K less suspicious of her; although presumably women too were capable of abduction and ill-doing.

There was no indication that Mrs. Alvarez considered Astrix Gonzalez a possible culprit. But then there was no indication that Mrs. Alvarez nurtured any suspicious, anxious, negative or even pessimistic thoughts regarding her daughter's mysterious absence.

Mrs. Alvarez' view of Luisa cohered with Maribel's description of her little sister. Luisa was a "very good girl"; reliable, responsible, studious and punctual without fail.

Sitting here, opposite the hospitable mother Alvarez, sipping sweet mint tea, K found he could not push his imagination far enough to reconcile porn-profile Luisa with the home-loving, devoted and studious daughter that her mamá was portraying. Neither could he imagine that a caring, loving, sheltering home like the one they were sitting in had spawned a youthful jezebel who trawled the net for sexual suitors via explicit websites. Here in this wholesome, greened environment, these thoughts seemed obscene and almost sacrilegious.

Dilger might see as the source of Luisa's corruption her older sister, Maribel, but sleeping with your boss when you were twenty, however nasty a piece of work that boss might be, was a ways away from posting pornographic profiles when you were fifteen.

A simple test would be to probe Mother Alvarez on her perception of her older daughter Maribel. If she was similarly blinkered regarding her older daughter then they could assume they were dealing with one of those deluded mothers for whom their devil's spawn could do no wrong.

"Your older daughter Miss Maribel alerted us to Luisa missing," K said experimentally.

"Alert?" said Mrs. Alvarez.

"Miss Maribel told us that Luisa had gone missing," K explained. "About two hours after school had finished."

Mrs. Alvarez nodded. K busied himself sipping tea, while Gutierrez looked at the notebook on his knees.

"Does Miss Maribel live here too?" K asked eventually. He downed his tea. Strategic mistake—Mrs. Alvarez immediately got up to refill his glass.

K pondered how to repeat the question without making it seem conspicuous, when it occurred to him that he was well on the way of following Dilger, namely blaming Maribel's conduct for the straying of her little sister—the very same Dilger who had applauded a prominent politico's brags of "titty-grabbing" as the wholesome actions of a regular red-blooded guy.

K decided he wasn't going to ask any more questions about Maribel. "Do you have any ideas where Luisa may have gone?" he asked instead.

Mrs. Alvarez shook her head.

"A friend maybe?" asked K.

Another shake of the head.

"Does Luisa have a favorite place?"

"Her house," said Mrs. Alvarez and smiled happily.

It was uncanny, this woman's serenity. The mother's calmness just made no sense set against her older daughter's frantic worry.

"Does Luisa use social media?" K asked.

Mrs. Alvarez looked confused.

Gutierrez rattled off a list of monikers, most of which K had never heard of. Mrs. Alvarez' blank face did not indicate she had much of a clue either.

Gutierrez tried again, this time reciting a spanglified version.

K began to appreciate that contemporary colonialism did its magic via "el Facebook."

It didn't have much effect on Mrs. Alvarez, in whom K had found a fellow Luddite. No wonder he had warmed to her so quickly.

"Does Luisa have a computer?" asked K.

"You want to see?" asked Mrs. Alvarez, and showed them to a study nook in the far corner of the room, one of those convenient integrated desk cum bookshelf units that were practical and space-saving in one. There was a laptop sitting on the desk. Mrs. Alvarez opened it up. K looked at it like one would at the entrance to a dark cave that might turn out to be a dragon's lair. Of course they would have to take the laptop with them to the station. He tried to explain this to Mrs. Alvarez.

"Luisa needs to study," said Mrs. Alvarez uncertainly. She pronounced it "stowdy."

How long would they keep it? She wanted to know. They would be as quick as they could, K reassured her.

Still, he now understood why Mrs. Alvarez was so calm. She clearly expected her daughter to return at any moment.

"Do you know Luisa's password?" asked K. He was really starting to get with it. Mrs. Alvarez looked at him as if he'd asked her to perform the moonwalk.

"*¿Tiene usted el nombre de usuario y contraseña de Luisa?*" asked Gutierrez. Mrs. Alvarez looked confused.

"To open the computer," said K.

Mrs. Alvarez frowned and pressed the *on button* on the laptop. The laptop was a low-spec affair; even K could see that by the time it took the thing to come to life.

"Oh!" said Gutierrez. It took K longer to understand that he was looking at an icon-populated screen. Luisa's computer was not password secured.

"This is Luisa's computer?" asked K.

He could pretty much tell that it had to be by all the schoolwork folders on the desktop. What about internet access? asked Gutierrez. Luisa used the internet at the school library when she needed to, explained Mrs. Alvarez. At home they did not have internet.

Posting a hook-up profile from the school library's computers took some balls. Somebody who was capable of leading the perfect double life at so tender an age with such brazen determination deserved respect.

Maybe Luisa's double life was the result of some mental health condition like schizophrenia, psychosis or multiple personality disorder? People with multiple personality disorder often managed to alternate seamlessly and entirely convincingly between several contradictory personalities.

"Has Luisa ever been to see a psychologist?" K asked.

"*Psicólogo,*" Gutierrez translated.

Mrs Alvarez looked confused.

"Never mind," K said quickly.

It was bad enough they now had to make Mrs. Alvarez show them Luisa's room. Often grim reality only hit families when they beheld foreign bodies intruding into their child's private sanctum. There was something about cops in uniform in a child's room that really brought home to folks how desperate things stood.

The room that Mrs. Alvarez showed them into was either that of a child emulating her elders or that of a fully evolved grown-up.

Luisa too liked plants and hanging baskets. An impressive collection of ferns, ivy and air plants dangled from the ceiling, which made Luisa's room hell for someone of K's height.

The girl had apparently kept busy with intellectual pursuits, arts and crafts, and old-fashioned accomplishment. A half-finished quilt of elaborate pattern lay folded on a chair. Balls of wool were piled in a wicker basket. Spiral bound note pads and project books were stacked neatly on the desk; pens and pencils crowded a glazed terracotta mug.

Above the desk hung a verse in stenciled calligraphy:

Joy and woe are woven fine,
A clothing for the soul divine.
Under every grief and pine
Runs a joy with silken twine.

"Is nice, no?" said Mrs. Alvarez. She had come up and had joined him looking at her daughter's artwork.

"Yes," said K. "Very. Luisa likes poetry?"

"She loves," said Mrs. Alvarez. She stretched the "o" so that it sounded like "loafs." She smiled. A joyous smile, full of pleasure and pride—which K ruptured by asking for permission to search the room.

•   •   •   •

Gutierrez had contrived to escort Mrs. Alvarez out of the room, leaving K to search it on his own. Searching rooms of the missing and the deceased was another part of his job K did not rate. He could never get past the guilt of intruding somewhere he had not been invited. Also one often happened upon stuff that one did not particularly want to happen upon, so that even when the missing were recovered hale and hearty, one would find it difficult to look them full in the face ever again.

His priority would have to be to locate Luisa's secret computer from which she conducted the online aspect of her double life. Doubtless it would make their search much easier if they found her computer. There were bound to be clues to whom Luisa associated with that the IT folks could dig out of whatever kind of encryption she used. Perhaps she had run away merely to take her pleasure with whom K hoped was an honorable person of only mildly kinky inclination, rather than a fully fledged predatory pervert.

One thing was pretty clear: If Luisa turned out in her other life to be a "normal" if slightly wayward teenager, they would have the mammoth task of trawling through all of her social media content.

K still hadn't gotten over a case where they had had to comb through thousands of photos, thousands, no exaggeration, of a young woman, a girl really, barely older than Luisa, a murder victim. They had had to look at all these photos in the hope of finding a clue to her death and a clue to her murderer. But until they struck pay-dirt, there had been days, no, weeks, spent scrolling and scrolling and scrolling and zooming in and out and out and in.

K had tried to calculate the percentage of her short time on this earth the young woman, the victim, had spent on taking, tagging and posting these images, which presumably also entailed looking and evaluating—*THUMBS UP! SMILEY EMOJI!*—others' offerings. Eventually he had come to the conclusion that there had been nary a place that she had deemed unfit to "selfie" in.

There had come a point when all compassion had drained from K and he had entirely identified with the killer.

The visual virtual legacy she had left had itself become self-incriminating evidence, good enough reason as to why someone might have wanted to annihilate her. It was probably a Facebook friend not brave enough to unfriend her.

They had eventually found the murderer. Her murder had had nothing to do with her online life. It had been a case of real-life flesh and blood mistaken identity.

And nothing and no one would ever give K the time back he had spent looking at a dead stranger's selfies.

There was nothing in Luisa's desk drawers, nothing under her bed, in the bed, under the mattress. Nothing in the planters, nothing in the wool-basket, nothing under the quilt, nothing behind the books on the shelf, nothing on top of the shelf.

Luisa's wardrobe was a paneled and carved wooden affair, like something out of The Chronicles of Narnia. The wardrobe was so big that K allowed himself to hope for a moment that Luisa had simply changed rooms and moved into her wardrobe.

K turned the big brass key and opened the heavy doors.

The wardrobe was as neat, as sparse, as well-ordered as Luisa's room. Sweaters, T-shirt, socks, undergarments were meticulously stacked on their allotted shelves. Trousers, jackets and shirts hung in segments. The clothing in there was practical and gender-neutral. K found no hidden-away see-through lingerie, fishnet stockings, leather brassieres, bondage gear, gimp masks, strap-ons—nothing that the hook-up site profile had led him to expect to find.

If Luisa was "bad," she was very, very good.

He took out stacks of clothes, separated them, probed in the far recesses of shelves and pulled out drawers, turned pockets inside out, returned to the book shelf, took out books one by one, leafed through books; went to the desk, leafed through notebooks, peered behind picture frames, examined the ceiling for loose tiles, poked his head out of the window to examine the flowerpots beneath, sorted through the wicker laundry basket. . . .

This had to be the least incriminating room he had ever seen. Even a convent-bound nun might have a yellowing love-letter tucked away among her veils. There was nothing in this room that spoke of secretiveness, nothing that spoke of a need to hide anything. The room spoke of a wholesome self-containedness and therefore was entirely unnatural as a teenager's lair.

K picked a couple of T-shirts out of the laundry-basket.

That way they wouldn't have to make a special trip if it came to using the dogs.

They walked past the spaniel with his raised paw, through the small orchard and past the vegetable plot with its realistic-looking scarecrow that K only noticed now.

He wondered how he had managed to pass the scarecrow without noticing it. Dressed in a man's trousers, a jacket and with a broadbrimmed hat, the scarecrow was unusual in that it had been constructed leaning on a rake.

"Hang on a moment," K said to Gutierrez. "I want to have a look at that scarecrow over the there."

He walked to the vegetable plot and leaned over the fence.

Gutierrez coughed, which probably was his reticent way of indicating that he'd appreciate it if K hurried up.

Gutierrez' cough was becoming quite pronounced now. Reticent, verging on the passive aggressive. "We'll stop at the drugstore and get you some cough sweets," K called over his shoulder.

The scarecrow really was pretty realistic, though he didn't know how effective a scarecrow bent over a rake could be in terms of its primary purpose.

Scarecrows, as K had found out to his disappointment as a child, kept away birds not because they looked like people, but because the rags people dressed them in moved in the wind. Pieces of fabric fastened to ropes or branches would be just as effective at keeping away birds, as would be randomly tied strips of plastic.

The work that had gone into making this particular scarecrow was pretty impressive. This really was some scarecrow. Particularly how it raised its head and straightened its back and nodded at K.

Bloody Gutierrez really should have done more than coughing.

"Hello," K said.

"Hello" the scarecrow said.

It spoke with a Spanish accent and had a deeply lined face. It was hard to know if this was Luisa's father or grandfather. He could have been a younger man ravaged by a hard life or an older man, well-preserved.

"We came for Luisa," said K.

His sentences were getting shorter and not any more accurate.

The man nodded. It became clear pretty quickly that he wasn't going to say anything more and was not going to introduce himself. He did not seem hostile, just wary and as if he did not have anything to say or there was nothing to say. And so it seemed inconsiderate to prolong the encounter.

"Goodbye," said K with a little bow. The man nodded and went back to leaning on his rake.

K climbed into the patrol car. "Thanks a bunch," he said furiously.

Gutierrez coughed. "I thought you were joking."

"I was joking? What about?"

"The scarecrow."

"I was joking about the scarecrow?" asked K.

Gutierrez coughed again. Gutierrez cleared his throat. Gutierrez looked extremely uncomfortable. Gutierrez' squirming did not make K's mistaking a real live person for a scarecrow any easier to bear. Besides, he did not understand what there was for Gutierrez to squirm about. Surely the squirming was all his.

"I thought you were saying scarecrow as a description."

"As a description?" asked K. He was completely at sea now. It was like being made to solve one of those cryptic crossword puzzles that he had never been able to figure out.

"Óscar," said K. "Stop squirming and just tell me."

"Squirming?" asked Gutierrez.

"Just tell me," K said.

"Ithoughtthatyouarejokingaboutthemanisascarecrow," Gutierrez said very fast.

K's brain took a while to reconstruct and digest what Gutierrez had just said.

"You what?" he was outraged. "You thought I was calling an old man a scarecrow?"

"I misunderstood," said Gutierrez unhappily.

"How could you?"

"I misunderstood," Gutierrez repeated.

All K understood was that he had been misunderstood in a pretty awful way. If this understanding was an indication of how K came across, how Gutierrez perceived him, as some callous asshole that would disrespect an old man, this was terrible.

"I don't understand how you can think that of me," he said.

Gutierrez mumbled unhappily, "I misunderstood."

Gutierrez was chewing his lip.

"Look, I don't want to make you feel bad for making me feel bad," K said. He was getting to be quite the viper these days.

And it was this, his own dig at Gutierrez that solved K's cryptic puzzle. For Óscar Gutierrez to assume that a fellow cop was making a disrespectful comment about a Latino was a matter of routine acquired through experience.

It was not a personalized assumption, so to speak, it was merely that in Gutierrez' radius that was how people behaved. That was what he braced himself for every day.

What K had been on the receiving end of was Gutierrez' personal prejudice that all Anglos were prone to behaving like assholes. Fair enough.

"Do you think that was Luisa's father?"

Gutierrez shrugged.

"Or her grandfather?"

Gutierrez shook his head. "It's hard to know. I think he was some relative. Could be the father, or grandfather, or uncle."

K realized something. "They did not mention any men. Maribel Alvarez did not mention any men. Just that Luisa would help mamá and abuelita with house chores and cooking. She did mention the brothers . . . but they are kids."

Gutierrez nodded. He had begun to squirm again.

"Is there something else grinding on you?" K asked sharply. His patience was starting to run low.

Gutierrez said hoarsely, "Maybe some of them don't have papers."

"You mean they are illegal?" As soon as he said the word he really did hate himself for it. "I meant to say: they are here without papers?"

Which is exactly what Gutierrez had said.

"Just the men? Or is that why we didn't see anything of abuelita?"

"It is possible," said Gutierrez. "There are families that always lived here when all this was Mexico. And they were divided between here and South of the Border. Some came to visit. Some stayed. It could be that some of the Alvarez are legal, and some don't have papers."

"It must be stressful to live without papers."

K himself had contemplated this option a long time ago, when the question had arisen of whether to return to the UK or whether to keep running. But K had neither wanted to return nor to continue running. By getting papers and becoming a small-town cop in a small southwestern town he'd come as far from his old self as was possible. Which was a kind of running, after all.

It was safe to assume that the great US of A made it easier for some than others to acquire permanent visas and citizenship.

"The family is going through a real bad time," Gutierrez said.

"Yes," K agreed.

"We don't have to bother about their status now, when the little girl is missing," Gutierrez said.

So Gutierrez took him for an asshole after all. This had to stop.

"Did you think I would rat them out because of their papers?" K asked. He had a hard time keeping his voice calm.

Gutierrez turned and looked him straight in the eye. His chin was set. "I have to make sure."

"If it turns out I am bothered about their papers, what then? What would you do then?"

Gutierrez did not answer. K did not really see what Gutierrez could do. Warn them? The men knew how to stay away anyhow. And if Gutierrez really thought that K snitched on illegal aliens, would his plea for clemency not have the opposite to the effect he desired?

"I get the feeling that you take me for a racist," said K.

"I take every gringo for a racist," spat Gutierrez.

"Whoa!" said K.

At least now there were quits.

Gutierrez looked as if he was going through a monumental internal conflict.

"Truth be told I'm kind of glad you got off your mature high horse," said K.

Gutierrez opened his mouth.

"I hope you are not going to apologize," said K.

• • • •

"All this used to be Mexico," Gutierrez said after a while. He said it quickly, as if uttering an obscenity.

"I know," said K.

Maybe Gutierrez had forgotten that he'd just told K that or maybe he thought that, given the opportunity, this fact couldn't be stated often enough. Gutierrez had a point. After all, the other side with their SOB terrorists and racist cant weren't coy about repeating themselves either.

"My aunt, my father's oldest sister—when Tia Araceli was growing up, everything was segregated. In summer, when it was real hot they didn't even let our kids swim in the outdoor pool with the Anglo kids. There was just one day, the last day before they drained the pool, that everybody that wasn't Anglo was allowed to swim in there."

K was conscious of Gutierrez' quick sideways glance.

He wants to check out how I'm taking this, K thought unhappily. We know each other, we have some sort of friendship going and yet he can't trust me to agree that there is discrimination here still, as there always was. He thinks he might offend me if he mentions it.

"There's families here that have been living here since 1650, you know? Mexico sold the land to this country and they were never asked if that was alright by them. And now they're treating Mexicans as if they don't belong."

K was starting to feel offended by Gutierrez' furtive sideways glances.

"Is that why you let me do all the talking in there?" he asked waspishly.

"Yes," said Gutierrez calmly. "I wanted them to feel that they are getting the best."

Ding-dong-ding, the witch ain't dead.

"'Best' meaning that an Anglo-looking cop is a better deal than a Mexican-looking one?"

Gutierrez nodded.

K considered and discarded the impulse to ask how a Catholic family that had flower-garlanded pictures of the Holy Mother Mary and altars with crosses and burning votives dotted about would view a Jew cop.

Which way exactly did the dysfunctional hierarchies of this vainglorious melting pot run?

Gutierrez had the grace to break the silence just before it settled at proper awkward.

"When I last visited with Tia Araceli we got talking and she said the way things are now is the way they were when she was a little girl when nobody thought it was wrong discriminating against Mexicans. Even the Mexicans themselves thought there was nothing wrong with being discriminated against. Tia Araceli said things have gone back to how they were, but now they are even nastier because people know how to find reasons to justify their nastiness. They can find a bunch of other nasty people on the internet and learn from them how to defend their nasty ideas—and how to spread them."

"Maybe that is why Luisa left? Because she couldn't bear how things are going?"

It was a possibility. How would the relentless onslaught of hostile culture-based defamation affect a sensitive kid? How did it in fact affect this whole battered, bruised and maligned generation who were growing up in a land that did not want them and turned them stealthily into objects of mandatory mistrust?

CHAPTER FOURTEEN

The star shimmered, soft and golden; morning star; evening star; Jupiter; Saturn; Betelgeuse; an emblem of hope; a guiding star; a little sun, sown on the lapel, that he had to follow, that he must not lose sight of, through blood-red poppies, radiant buttercups, hemlock, swaying grass, humming bees and whirring hover flies, dragon flies too, the craw of crows and screech of hawks from the fir, spruce and pine-covered slopes beyond, and up there an eagle, gliding, current borne in wide circles against azure skies, the sun so warm. And he had lost his star because he had been distracted by the eagle and there was no Grandpapa, the golden six-cornered star on the lapel of his dark woolen coat, he could not see Grandpapa and he needed Grandpapa to guide him out of this high-growing meadow which wasn't a meadow anymore but a red-earthed, boulder-strewn wasteland and the sky had changed too, was glowering Martian-red now, scorched earth, red sky and he was running, the air smelt of burning, breathing was painful, smoke filled his lungs and burnt them up and he could feel them turning black from the inside, but he knew that he had to run, run, run and was stopped by the edge, by the crevasse and stood and looked down and all those bodies, naked bodies, a mount of corpses that grew out of the abyss.

At night things came out of the shadows and fell into place. It would have been convenient to have one of those dreams while he was still seeing the annoying counselor, because this dream would have given him something to talk about, though he wouldn't have told the annoying counselor about his dream, because he had never told anyone about these dreams, not even Lili, but maybe Lili had them too and did not tell anyone either, and if Lili had them too it would mean that it was true what K believed—knew—to be true: that these dreams were messages from Grandpapa, not Grandpapa as they had known him, because Grandpapa as they had known him had never spoken about the yellow star and all that had come with it; and if K hadn't seen the number tattooed on Grandpapa's arm one day, he'd never have known.

The dreams had started after Grandpapa had gone and K had concluded the dreams were a "those who do not remember the past are condemned to repeat it" kind of deal, which was fair enough; the least he could do was to carry a burden in dreams that others had borne in reality. And maybe—pity that this thought hadn't come to him in time for his meetings with the annoying counselor—it wasn't just *his* damn PTSD he was carrying, it was PTSD for the whole damn of history and the future yet to come.

●　　●　　●　　●

Begay had a good instinct when to keep out of K's way and had left him mooching around the kitchen in the early hours. Now he joined him on the porch steps, offering a cup of freshly brewed coffee.

They sat side by side listening to the birds conferencing.

"Hey!" said Begay. "Did you see that yellow thing?"

He pointed at a yellow bird of almost clownish brightness.

"Goldfinch, I think," said K.

Every few weeks the bird population in the orchard changed according to some mysterious micro-migratory system.

"I think they negotiate a schedule for their migration so they don't get in each other's way."

"Smarter than people, huh?" said Begay.

On cue, a stunningly bright copper-headed hummingbird chased off a rival who had descended on the feeder.

"That's a rufus," said K. "They pretty much have a human mentality."

Sometimes he wondered if, like a colonial overlord, he was upsetting the natural balance with his hummingbird feeders. Certainly all these damn birds seemed to do was fight about who ruled the feeder. They expended more energy fighting about the feeders than they could possibly get from the cane sugar solution it dispensed.

"So," said Begay. "What's eating you?"

"Nothing in particular," said K.

"Come on!"

"Or everything," said K. "For instance I had a weird situation with Gutierrez and a scarecrow yesterday—"

As he listened to himself talking K understood that, far as he could remember, this was the first time that he had addressed the elusive ethnic dividing line. Certainly it had been the first time he had fully understood where he was perceived to stand.

Begay nodded thoughtfully.

"'Chief.' When I was a kid, sometimes an Anglo would call my father 'Chief.' Sometimes they would speak to my dad about his 'squaw.' It took me a while to get they were talking about my mom. My dad never got to explain the 'chief' and 'squaw' thing to me. I guess he couldn't find the right words. When I got older I learnt to listen real careful to how Anglos speak to us Indians. When you listen real close you get to hear a lot of chief-like crap."

"But I. . . ." K started to protest.

"I'm not saying you did—or didn't," Begay said ambiguously. "I'm just saying you learn to listen out for these things when you meet the dominant majority. Sometimes you might be wrong. Often you will be right. That's what your Hispanic buddy said: He takes every bílagáana to be racist."

"Gringo," muttered K. Oh what joy to be gringo to one group and bílagáana to another and racist to both.

"Besides: the guy don't know you well enough to understand

that you ain't got a real strong hold on reality. There's not that many cops that go around hallucinating scarecrows. Just let it go. See how you go with your buddy. My guess is he'll be okay about it. Coz most of the others are even worse."

Something occurred to K: "Do you think that is why the mother was so stoic? Is it just that she doesn't trust authorities and didn't want to show how she really feels about her daughter missing?"

"Stoic, huh?" said Begay, "Could be. Leastways that's how we Indians deal with bílagáanas that get in our face."

All that did not, however, explain why Gutierrez had felt he was doing the Alvarez family a favor by letting pseudo-Anglo K deal with their case. Wasn't that a gold-standard case of identification with the aggressor?

"Identification with the aggressor? You mean preferring to be Anglo?" Begay interrupted K's paltry attempt at elucidating the matter. "You got it wrong dude! We don't prefer to be Anglo, we prefer to play at being Anglo, That way you got the best of two worlds and you get to game the Anglos."

"That all sounds very jolly," said K, who could not make himself believe that it was all that easy to play at being Anglo, appearances being what counted most.

And it was appearances that were getting Luisa and the Alvarez family a raw deal. It was appearances—apparently—that made Mother Alvarez feign serenity vis-a-vis an official she naturally assumed to be prejudiced towards her. It was appearances that had made Gutierrez take a back seat during their visit with the Alvarez family, despite his indisputably greater cultural competence. It was in particular Maribel Alvarez' appearance that had furnished Milagro PD's finest with the excuse not to take Luisa's case seriously. If Maribel had been Anglo, would Dilger & Co have been similarly dismissive of her younger sister's disappearance?

"When are you gonna learn that *whats* and *ifs* get you nowhere? There are exceptions to every rule and rules to every exception, that's all you got to remember. Else we wouldn't be sitting here together, watching these damn birds making each others lives a misery, dig?" said Begay, warding off a rufus intent on impaling a rival.

●　　●　　●　　●

As soon as K entered the break-room, the braying began.

Predictably Dilger had lost no time telling everybody about the Alvarez hotties. There was much mirth about K's gullibility and jokes galore about Maribel Alvarez' apparent penchant for police uniforms and how exactly Milagro PD could endeavor to afford this particular customer the fullest satisfaction.

K decided to forgo his coffee and to pass on confronting bigotry, and made his way to reception where he found out that not taking Luisa Alvarez' disappearance seriously did not mean that Milagro PD wouldn't be going through the motions of taking the case seriously. And the person appointed to demonstrating Milagro PD's dedication to the Alvarez case was K, who had been delegated to pay Luisa's school a visit.

School visits were a task for which Juanita Córdoba plainly would have been the better choice, what with her women's refuge work and all this domestic violence intervention and family mediation stuff she always did.

K guilelessly shared his constructive thoughts on case load distribution with Becky.

Becky's reaction made him want to go home and recline on his imaginary chaise lounge with a phial of smelling salts and a cold compress to the forehead.

K hadn't known that Becky was a militant feminist, as much as he hadn't known that he was a despicable sexist. And all because of his sincere conviction that Córdoba was the better qualified to deal with teenagers and teachers.

K gave it another try, treating Becky to his theory of schools being seething cesspits of conformist pressure; throwing in as freebie his thoughts on families as boiling cauldrons of dissent, built on decades if not centuries of neuroses wherein resentment and injury simmered away in a toxic stew. . . .

There was no negotiation and no escape. Becky informed him steely voiced and stony faced that an appointment had been made for him specifically with Luisa Alvarez' grade teacher. And after meeting Luisa's grade teacher, K was to meet with the school's janitor for purposes of accessing Luisa's locker.

"Give the guy a receipt for the stuff in Luisa's locker," Becky snapped, "and make sure you don't lose anything."

K couldn't remember exactly how he had been treated before he had begun to decompensate, but he didn't think it had been quite like that.

"Didn't we use to get along?" he asked.

Beholding Becky's expression, he decided it was unwise to stick around for an answer.

He capitulated, doffed his imaginary cap and made off.

•   •   •   •

Milagro's combined Middle and High School, with its inspiring acronym MMHS, was a cluster of nondescript concrete buildings fronted by an expanse of dusty playing fields located on the southeastern boundary of Milagro city limits. For once K detected something like social justice in the school's awkward location. MMHS was in convenient walking distance of Vista Perdida, a trailer park notorious among cops and social workers.

From Córdoba he knew that both Milagro Elementary and MMHS operated a kind of crèche and daycare for kids who needed a refuge and of whom there were more in Milagro than any town could afford to be complacent about.

K watched small groups of middle-graders trickling in and out of the main building. Several panes on the glass doors sported cracks possibly inflicted by accidentally misdirected balls, or judiciously aimed boots.

The appearance of a cop on the schoolyard had an enlivening effect on the vandal hordes. A glimmer of interest flickered in deadbeat eyes and wan little faces lit up with the prospect of witnessing mayhem, the misuse of structural power and maybe even a bona fide shoot-out—preferably with a couple of fatalities.

K's progress through the school passed smoothly and without obstacles, if he ignored the reverberating jostling, catcalling and jeering that seemed to be the pervasive mode of interaction amongst students.

Corralling middle-graders with high school students was a recipe for creating trauma if ever there was. On one end of the hallway snot-nosed kids, barely out of diapers, prematurely scarred by life's cruelties, shuffled; on the other, hormonal teenagers swaggered and sashayed toward each other in parodic premating ritual.

On K's approach the smelly throng parted like the Red Sea for Moses and he arrived at the appointed classroom a couple of minutes early.

•　　•　　•　　•

The hallway was hung with photos of the year's grade 11 students. The photos had been arranged alphabetically, so it was not hard to spot Luisa Alvarez, who came second, right after Hillary Abbott, who gazed owlishly through thick-lensed glasses.

On the photo Luisa Alvarez had a somber face, unadorned by either makeup or affectation, with a promise of beauty in it. K nevertheless felt uncomfortable looking at it, because in this photo here Luisa looked exactly as in her photo on that *site.*

K worked his way along the photos. He lingered on two photos next to each other. On first glance it looked like the same photo twice over. Maybe whoever hung the photos hadn't paid attention. Maybe they had wanted to max out the number of blonde girls. Eventually he understood that the photos were not of one girl but rather of a pair of identical twins—twins in any case. If they weren't identical then nature had made a pretty good fist of creating them very similar.

Being a twin himself, the younger twin by twenty-two minutes to an overbearing older sister, K identified with twins and their plight.

He looked at his watch. It was time.

•   •   •   •

"Officer Kafka?" the teacher asked.

K produced his ID. "Ms. Davies?"

"Siwan Davies," Ms. Davies introduced herself. "Grab a chair."

Ms. Davies was sitting behind her teacher's desk or podium or lectern or whatever they called it nowadays.

K lifted a chair from the front row and set it down opposite Ms. Davies.

"How is your search going?"

It was a question K found hard to answer.

"Not so well?" Ms. Davies was looking at him intently. She looked like a person who didn't miss much.

"I'm hoping you can help us shed some light on the situation," he said. "Do you happen to have any thoughts on Luisa's missing?"

"Atypical," said Davies without hesitating. "Completely out of character."

"You think Luisa's missing is out of character?" asked K. "What is Luisa's character?"

"She is a joy and a delight," said Ms. Davies. She leant towards him. Her eyes were a striking cobalt blue with yellow rays like a sunflower's petals fanning out from her pupils. "Luisa is one of those kids who drink in poetry; who feel the magic of words; who you can see transforming when they learn something new— kids that give meaning to the word transformative. One of those kids I went into teaching for."

"'Joy and woe are woven fine, A clothing for the soul divine. Under every grief and pine Runs a joy with silken twine,'" quoted K. "Luisa has this in her room. She copied it out in calligraphy and illustrated it. Did you study Auguries of Innocence with the class?"

126

"Blake?" asked Ms. Davies. "I wouldn't dare to. This is not that kind of class. Mostly they sit out their time here because they believe it's easier than math or science. On the whole it is the kind of class that you try to protect what you love from, rather than sharing it with them."

She clasped a hand over her mouth. "That sounded awful. Maybe I should stop teaching—with that attitude." Her face had clouded as if she had only just realized something. "I'm guessing you're not here to discuss the vagaries of my career, Officer Kafka. Luisa's disappearance—it is extremely out of character. I can't imagine where she has gone. She . . . didn't mix so much with her peers, you know."

It sounded as if Ms. Davies thought that was all for the good.

"Did she—does she have a boyfriend?" K revised: "Did she have a romantic interest in anyone? Was she dating someone?"

Ms. Davies shook her head. "Not that I know or noticed."

"Was she—is she a secretive person?"

"Secretive?" Ms. Davies frowned. "What do you mean by secretive?"

"Could you imagine her leading a double life?" K asked.

Ms. Davies' frown deepened. "Double life? Very cloak and dagger. What kind of double life?"

K cleared his throat "Ms. Davies—" he began and stumbled helter-skelter into the matter of Luisa's hookup profile.

He stopped. His mouth was dry and he felt as embarrassed as if he'd been talking about his own virtual proclivities.

Ms. Davies shook her head. "No."

This seemed less like manic denial than like dead certainty.

"You seem very sure," K observed.

Ms. Davies nodded. "I am."

"How come you are so sure?" K inquired.

"Because as a teacher you acquire a certain knowledge of character."

"But you are not infallible," posited K.

"No," admitted Ms. Davies. "And there are some students that I can't be sure about. There are a few that I am. A hundred percent. And Luisa is one of them."

It was definitely a view of Luisa that K preferred.

"But how do you explain. . . ?"

Ms. Davies frowned and her eyes clouded. She pondered and eventually said, "Why don't you talk to Cuauhtémoc? Cuauhtémoc Rodriguez. He and Luisa have a kind of friendship going,"

"Cuauhtémoc," said K. "Brilliant. Did his parents call him that or did he adopt this name for himself?"

There were few compensations for having to live in the 21st century. Encountering a Cuauhtémoc in Milagro, smack on the route that Vázquez de Coronado had taken in his quest for the Golden Cities of Cibola, was one.

Ms. Davies' cobalt eyes sparkled. "It's great to see Franz Kafka being so enthusiastic about Cuauhtémoc. What about you? Did you choose your name or were you given it at birth?"

"I did not choose it."

"What a great name to be born with. You are very lucky."

"You like Kafka?" K asked.

"Who wouldn't?" asked Ms. Davies. Her voice was vibrant with enthusiasm.

In K's opinion, people who enthused about Franz Kafka's work led lives that weren't sufficiently Kafkaesque. His own reality emulated Kafka's imaginings to an uncomfortable degree. K tended to regard Kafka as a realistic writer.

"I don't know whether to laugh or cry," said Ms. Davies when he'd shared his thoughts on Kafka. She burst out laughing. She had a dimple on her left cheek. Her hair was dark red, the color of autumn leaves, and she had the milky skin of a true Celt.

She must have noticed him checking her out. A faint blush crept from her neckline up to her face. K understood now what they meant when they spoke of a milk and roses complexion.

K wondered whether, when Ms. Davies had been speaking

about Luisa's otherworldliness, she had not been speaking about herself also. He was beginning to find her quite irresistible, though he was pretty sure that he wouldn't get the chance to try to resist her.

Ms. Davies shifted her body as if she was shaking something off. When she looked at him again her face wore an expression of affable neutrality. "Do talk to Cuauhtémoc," she advised. Her voice was businesslike. "I'll go and find him for you."

At the door she hesitated and turned back. "Your main purpose is to look for Luisa?"

"Yes," said K. "Would there be another purpose?"

Ms. Davies approached and sat down again. Her cobalt sunflower eyes bored into his as if she was hoping for access to his brain.

"You are not concerned with other matters?"

"What matters are you referring to?" asked K.

"Our main concern here is to provide education. We try to give all of our students the opportunity to learn and to develop their abilities without having to worry . . . about other matters," she said rapidly. "Matters that have nothing to do with them, failures and oversights that aren't their fault at all and that still may jeopardize their future. . . ."

"I'm not affiliated with Homeland Security," said K woodenly.

This was the second time in two days that he'd been suspected of being with The Man on matters of documentation and legality.

On balance he'd rather be accused of being a meth-cooker.

"Sorry," said Ms. Davies. "I just have to make sure."

Did she really believe that all you had to do was ask and you would be told? With such gullibility, no wonder that the dark forces were winning out.

•　•　•　•

Cuauhtémoc Rodriguez was neither deferential nor boisterous; handsome without seeming aware of or attentive to his looks; an altogether appealing young man—as far as K could determine. But then he wasn't a specialist on teenagers. He rather tended to avoid them, unless he wanted to see his lack of procreative enthusiasm confirmed.

K was somewhat surprised by young Cuauhtémoc's comeliness, however. He had expected a nerd; a bespectacled, awkward boy with bad skin forever condemned to play best friend and confidant to damsels who inevitably fancied someone else.

"Do you know where Luisa has gone?" Cuauhtémoc asked him. K detected a faint Hispanic accent. Not really an accent—more the hint of an inflection.

K asked, "You were—you are friends?"

"Were?" asked Cuauhtémoc. His eyes widened and he looked frightened.

K shook his head and repeated, "You are friends with Luisa?"

"You haven't found her—or anything?" Cuauhtémoc asked.

K imagined that "anything" meant if they had found Luisa dead.

"No, we haven't found her—yet," he said. Looking at the boy's stricken face, he added, "We will. Don't worry."

From Cuauhtémoc's expression it was pretty obvious that he very much wanted to believe K. Despite the absence of forensic evidence K was 99.3 percent sure that this kid wouldn't have harmed Luisa.

"Ms. Davies said you and Luisa are friends? You spend time together?"

"We can talk together." Cuauhtémoc hesitated. "Luisa, she is very . . . deep."

"Deep?" asked K.

"Luisa—she thinks about many things—the world . . . injustice . . . pollution . . . the way they treat the planet, you know . . . politicians. . . ."

The boy hesitated and looked at K. Maybe to check out how K would take that roll call of radical ideas, or maybe because he had realized that put like that, Luisa's concerns were not that outré after all, but widely shared teenage preoccupations.

S*hould* be widely shared teenage preoccupations, as far as K was concerned.

"Was something troubling Luisa?" asked K, "except for the state of the planet and politicians?"

"Troubling?" asked Cuauhtémoc.

"Was there something that Luisa was worried about? Something that made her unhappy?"

Cuauhtémoc looked excruciatingly embarrassed. His eyes scanned the room as if he was looking for an escape route.

"Look," K said sternly. "I need your help here. Luisa has been gone for three days. Every moment counts, okay, Cuauhtémoc? Cuauhtémoc—you have a great name!"

Cuauhtémoc smiled shyly. "Cuauhtémoc was an Aztec king." He raised his head and his smile vanished. "He was tortured and killed by the Spanish. *Conquistadores* they call them. *Cobardes!*" he spat.

It was good to meet young people who still had a sense of history.

"Cuauhtémoc," said K. "I need you to tell me anything that you can think of about Luisa, okay? Don't worry if you don't think it is important. Tell me, even if it is embarrassing. Nobody will find out from me what you have said."

Unless Cuauhtémoc decided to confess. . . .

"You don't tell?" asked Cuauhtémoc. His English seemed to be getting more Spanish. "Students here are bad. If they don't like somebody they show them. They don't mind hurting somebody. They want that people are scared and unhappy."

Cuauhtémoc's English seemed to be deteriorating rapidly. K wondered if this had drawn the bullies. He certainly was a handsome young man. K would have thought that girls favored him. But maybe even teenage hormones obeyed the ethnic divide.

"Was Luisa bullied?"

Cuauhtémoc drew his head down to his shoulders.

K looked at the clock. Ms. Davies would want her room back.

Classes were due to start soon and here they were, getting nowhere.

"Can you come along with me to the police station?"

It was primarily a matter of practicality. At the pace this was going they would need at least a couple of hours where they wouldn't be interrupted. At the station there would be a slight chance of getting Córdoba or Gutierrez to join in and help this whole mess along.

"Police station?" The kid looked really frightened now.

K began to measure the distance to the door, calculating the angle at which he had to hurl himself at Cuauhtémoc to rugby-tackle him.

"Cuauhtémoc," said K. "All I want to do is find Luisa. There's nothing else I'm interested in. I just want to find Luisa. Do you understand? I hope that you can help me, okay? Help me to find Luisa."

Cuauhtémoc looked around as if he suspected the walls had ears.

"They are bullies—there are many bullies here. They do not like people that are not white. They do not like Indians. Especially they do not like Mexicans."

"You think Luisa left because of racism?"

"No," said Cuauhtémoc impatiently. "When everybody is prejudiced—why go now? For us it is normal that people are prejudiced." He lifted his head, his expression proud and contemptuous, and he shrugged his shoulders. "Let them be prejudiced." He made an expansive gesture with his arm. "Everything was Mexico. We got an old civilization. The Aztecs. The Mayas. They think we are peasants. They are ignorant. We don't mind what the ignorant people think of us."

Right on! thought K. "Are you saying that racist and prejudiced bullying is not the reason why Luisa left?"

Cuauhtémoc shook his head. "We don't care about these stupid people."

"Glad to hear it. So what else was going on?"

Cuauhtémoc lifted his shoulders again. "I don't know for sure."

"You have some ideas though," said K.

The kid was prone to self-censoring. K wondered if this was related to Ms. Davies' concerns related to documented status and Homeland Security. He did not think reassuring Cuauhtémoc about not being concerned with his settled status would put him at all at ease.

"There are some people really mean to Luisa. Really mean. It is like—war." Cuauhtémoc said eventually.

"Who are these people?"

Cuauhtémoc hesitated. "The cheerleaders," he said after a while.

"Did Luisa want to be a cheerleader?" asked K.

Cuauhtémoc flared his nostrils. It made for an impressive expression of contempt. "No,"

"Did something happen with the cheerleaders that might have made Luisa decide to leave?" asked K.

Cuauhtémoc shook his head. "I don't know. She never told me. But she was kind of closed, you know? She didn't tell me everything. We just hung out. We got along. We are two Mexicans. We are outside—" he made another sweeping gesture with his arm. "We are outside all of this."

He frowned and ran his finger along the table as if following an invisible trail "Luisa never said she wanted to run away." He reconsidered. "She never said something to me."

"You said she was kind of closed," K said.

"Closed?" said Cuauhtémoc, as if trying to recall. "Sure. She wasn't like other girls that—" He raised his hand and rapidly brought thumb and fingers together in a "yak yak" gesture. "She wasn't like other girls."

"She wasn't like other girls?" asked K

"No," said Cuauhtémoc.

"You like her?"

"Sure." said Cuauhtémoc.

"You like her a lot?" Meet Kafka, king of Subtle Interrogation Technique. Weismaker would have to give him a bonus.

He might just as well yell, "You are a suspect now!" and be done with it.

The boy blushed. His forehead was slick with sweat.

"You like Luisa, Cuauhtémoc?" said K sternly.

"I don't like Luisa in that way," the boy whispered.

"You are sure you don't?" In K's experience teenage boys whose raging hormones demanded to be obeyed weren't too choosy as a rule and tended to fancy anything that possessed the requisite primary and secondary sexual characteristics.

"No." The boy seemed to be going through a tremendous conflict that was all but tearing him apart.

"You better tell me," K said firmly.

The boy whispered something. It was so low K couldn't hear.

"Tell me so I can hear you," K said harshly.

Cuauhtémoc mumbled something. Still K did not understand. "What?"

The boy drew a deep breath: "I am GAY!"

The yell damn near burst K's ear drums.

The door opened and Ms. Davies appeared.

"Are you okay, Cuauhtémoc?" she asked worriedly.

"Yes!" shouted the boy and dashed out of the door.

"Oh dear," said Ms. Davies. "Did you say something to him?"

"What do you mean?" said K tersely.

"Did you say something to upset him?" she asked fiercely.

She was blushing again. K guessed that this time her blushing had nothing to do with sex. It was pretty sexy anyway, the deep blush spreading on her milky white skin. . . .

"Do you have a school counselor?" asked K.

"We used to. They cut the funds," said Ms. Davies.

"I think Cuauhtémoc could use some counseling," said K.

"Something to do with Luisa?"

"No," said K. "Just make sure it's not a Christian counselor."

"Not a Christian counselor?"

"Non-denominational. Non-judgmental. Open minded," said K firmly.

"Did you get all you needed?" asked Ms. Davies.

"I think I should talk to some of the students," K said. "Specifically I should talk to the cheerleaders."

Ms. Davies nodded.

"You think it is a good idea to talk to the cheerleaders?" It hadn't been a good question. Any teacher would be reluctant to rat out their students to the cops, however unsavory their students' behavior. "How many cheerleaders are there?"

"Now there are seven cheerleaders," said Ms. Davies. She studied him once again as if trying to assess his attitude. She had one of those open faces and clear miens that one didn't have to be a thought-reader to understand.

K decided this time he wasn't going to help her out by asserting his integrity and trustworthiness. Besides he quite enjoyed locking eyes with Siwan Davies.

"One left," said Ms. Davies. "LaRaina Cuthair."

"She's Ute?" asked K.

"Yes," Ms. Davies said.

"Would her ethnicity have anything to do with her leaving?" asked K.

Wow and if he wasn't going for it.

"Yes," said Ms. Davies. A pretty unequivocal answer to a pretty complex question —

"That was a pretty unequivocal answer to a pretty complex question," K said.

"Complex?" said Ms. Davies, raising her eyebrows. "I'd say it was a straight answer to a pretty straight question. I knew it was going to be problematic when LaRaina joined the cheerleaders, but I hoped, you know. I hoped it would be a new start—the beginning of some real change." She leant towards K. "Do you think that failure exacerbates crisis?"

"What do you mean?" asked K.

"If you try to change something, if you try something different to make a bad situation better and it fails, does that make the bad situation worse?" she asked.

"What are you going to do? Sit around and do nothing? There comes a point when you need to take a risk, don't you?"

"Thank you," said Ms. Davies. "I do hope you are right. I'm just worried that LaRaina was a victim to the cause."

"Did you push her into being a cheerleader?" asked K.

"Of course not." She sounded offended. "But I didn't try to dissuade her either, though I did anticipate how it was going to go."

"That ferocious, huh?" said K.

"That predictable," said Ms. Davies unhappily.

"How did LaRaina and Luisa get on?" asked K.

"I don't think their paths crossed that much. They had very different outlooks. Luisa would never go for being a cheerleader." She considered. "Except maybe for a certain solidarity based on being members of —" she raised her hands and made an air quotes gesture— "'minorities.'"

"Do you think I could talk to LaRaina?" asked K.

"She's away. I think her grandma is very sick. Besides I don't think she would talk to you—or anyone. She's just keeping her head down and pretending that whole cheerleader interlude never happened. And probably is hoping that everyone else forgets about it too."

"It sounds like a right witches' cauldron." As soon as he had said it he realized the sexist implications. "A pretty unhealthy environment," he added hastily.

"No more unhealthy than other schools." Ms. Davies protested.

"No," said K.

It was merely a mirror of the whole of society. That was what made it so grim.

•   •   •   •

The fetid hallways, chipped linoleum floors and stained walls hung with photos of youngsters whose sum of future disappointments would fill an ocean with misery, wasted promise and unfulfilled hope were getting to K.

The janitor didn't lift his heart either. He was standing at a distance, jangling his keys and huffing in a manner that could be due to asthma or impatience.

It was distracting K from his onerous task of clearing out Luisa's locker. Now and then a group of youngsters filing past would stop, gape, snigger and speculate as to the purpose of his visit. K was beginning to comprehend that the majority of these young people were not possessed of a wholesome imagination. Sticking his head into Luisa's locker in an ostrich reflex offered welcome relief from the morass of their depraved projections.

Luisa's locker was like Luisa's room: clean, organized, orderly. There was a neat stack of textbooks and another of exercise books, an oblong box holding pens and pencils, a three-quarters empty water bottle. Otherwise—nothing: No friendship mementos, stickers, keepsake fan-fare, nor photos tacked to the locker door, makeup, mirrors, hairbands, sanitary products or candy.

K transferred the locker's content into a cardboard box. The janitor huffily signed the receipt.

"This must be keeping you pretty busy," K said. "Your job," he added, lest the janitor took this as a caustic comment on the burden of issuing a signature. "There's a lot of talk about hardening schools," he added conversationally.

The janitor growled, "Vet."

"You're a vet?" asked K.

The grizzled man of few words nodded. K decided this wasn't the moment to make a wise-ass comment favorably comparing the challenges of the battlefield to the vicissitudes of a school campus. "The School Marshal Plan—is it a good idea?" he asked.

The man made a noise that was hard to interpret. He coughed, slid open a window and spat out of it. The audible plop that followed damn near made K say hello to his breakfast.

"You were saying?"

"Bullshit," said the janitor. "I been on three tours. I didn't take this job to do some more shooting."

K's heart soared as it did when he encountered sense in un-expected places—unexpected places because he was just as preju-diced as the next guy, and had assumed this taciturn individual to be the stereotypical free-ranging, unconditional arms-enthusiast.

"Did you tell them that?"

"They didn't ask me," said the man. "Doubt they will."

"If they require you to be armed—what will you do?"

The man shrugged. "I'm working on getting my MED license," he said slyly, "My MED Marijuana Retail License—Tier 2. Then I'm outta here."

"And who could blame you," K said heartily.

If nothing else, he was coming away from this school visit with a brand-new careers idea.

He lugged the carton on to his shoulder and waved a cheery and grateful good-bye.

CHAPTER FIFTEEN

A jolly crowd of Marshal Plan enforcers, secondary beneficiaries of Lucky Easton's largesse, were debriefing in the break-room.

Happily, the hours immersed in a school environment had steeled K's nerves and infused him with a Zen-like fuck-it mindfulness.

Besides, the janitor's corroboration of the cosmic yin-yang principle, whereby the number of schools recruited to the School Marshal Plan boosted the number of commercial Marijuana retail license carriers, had acted as balm on K's unquiet soul.

"Betcha next school shoot-out we get called to is gonna be that Miss Caulfield," Smithson chuckled.

"Regular hellcat," Young guffawed.

"Hell, yes," Dilger said. "If I was those kids I'd make sure I behave real good."

"I can't believe she has no prior experience. She sure caught on quick how to handle a gun," said Young appreciatively. "Almost never saw anyone get the hang of a semiautomatic that fast."

"Maybe Miss Caulfield can't wait to get shooting?" K suggested.

"Oh boohoohoo," Dilger snorted. "Let me guess: You don't want teachers to defend their kids. You prefer some random shooter walks in from the streets and guns down a bunch of innocent kids?"

"No. Much better to have them gunned down by a Miss Caulfield they know," said K, turning his back on leaden silence.

•   •   •   •

"There's a profile for Luisa on a hook-up site?"

K had eventually succeeded in escaping the break-room, after becoming embroiled in an argument on the merits of the School Marshall Plan versus the Guardian Plan via an appraisal of the Second Amendment as the Constitution's crowning glory, during which he had been called and had cheerfully accepted the epithet "pacifist" spat at him by Young, which for some reason had enraged Dilger, who had waylaid K waving a spatula encrusted with burnt egg and apparently had not appreciated K's suggestion of a suitable anatomical repository for said spatula and had instead threatened to loosen K's teeth for him, which seemed a somewhat quaint threat, considering the subject matter that had brought them to this point.

K, in need of an oasis of sanity in this madhouse, had sought refuge in Córdoba's office. Besides, he needed an ally because his orneriness had vanquished for good the tiny chance there had been of garnering the squad's help in the case of Luisa Alvarez.

It was a fact little appreciated amongst civilians that the amount of care and attention any given case received depended primarily on the dynamics of socio-political alliances amongst the cops, making any case that K championed in principle a lost one.

Córdoba, he had to hand her that, was nothing if not patient. Or perhaps she was daydreaming, imagining a workplace populated by competent, professional and efficient co-workers, while she role-played fathoming K's rambling narrative. He always found it difficult to explain something he did not fully understand himself.

In no particular order K told Córdoba of Luisa's confidant Cuauhtémoc and his "coming out," Ms. Davies' assertion that Luisa's disappearance was completely out of character and Cuauhtémoc's hints at bullying and racism, confirmed rather than denied by Ms. Davies.

When he finally got to the subject of Luisa's porn profile he began to empathize with Gutierrez' squirming and stammering. Having been furnished by his so-called career choice with plenty of

evidence of the human condition's seamier aspects, K didn't strictly understand why describing a teenager's medium-core web-pro-
file should embarrass him quite that much. He shared this thought
with Córdoba for good measure, just so she wouldn't think that he
was some kind of bigot.

Córdoba shrugged and said maybe he couldn't accept that people had different faces. If Córdoba had meant to reassure him, her
remark had precisely the opposite effect. What was she trying to
tell him? That he would do well not to trust appearances? That
she herself led a nefarious double life? Maybe the serious and sober Córdoba, advocate of abused women, sole female warrior in a
squad of throwbacks, spent her leisure time in leather corset, thigh
high boots, whip. . . .

"How did you find the profile?" asked Córdoba.

Maybe suspicions went both ways and Córdoba imagined
she'd rumbled him as a secret internet porn-fiend who'd been suc-
cessfully feigning technophobia all these years. At least K now had
the opportunity to point a fat finger at Dilger, which, as he realized
belatedly, forced him to mention to Córdoba the suspected dalli-
ance between Luisa's big sister Maribel and Mr. Lucky Easton.

Córdoba had taken out her phone and was scrolling about. K
thought she could have chosen a more tactful way of signaling that
time was up.

He duly fell silent mid-sentence.

"Thursday afternoon work for you?" asked Córdoba. "Before
we go see those cheerleaders I want to look at that profile of Luisa."

K couldn't even remember having at any point asked Córdoba
to come along to question the cheerleaders. What a great comrade
Córdoba was, the best.

"Sure," he said. "As long as I don't have to look at it again."

●　　●　　●　　●

"The contents from Luisa's locker," K said. "Fancy going through
them with me? Two pairs of eyes see more than one."

K set the carton on Gutierrez' desk. He trusted that Gutierrez' ingrained courtesy would prevent him from turning down his request.

"Sure," said Gutierrez and sighed.

"At least she's got good handwriting," K said.

They were leafing through Luisa's exercise books looking for messages, secret notes, cries for help, coded diary entries . . . who knew. There were people who kept work and pleasure apart, and young Luisa seemed to be one of them. She didn't even doodle on the margins.

"Maybe she really is too good to be true," mused K, whose own schoolbooks had been covered in cartoons depicting teachers in fitting zoological incarnations engaging in grotesque acts—and not all that ineptly as he remembered, His art certainly had been a girl magnet, for all that had been worth.

"We know that she's too good to be true," Gutierrez muttered.

"There's nothing we know for sure," K said.

He relayed Siwan Davies' 100 percent certainty that Luisa really was what Luisa did seem, namely a spiritual, philosophical, thoughtful, entirely wholesome, highly creative teacher's pet.

"A teacher's not going to know a student's private life," reasoned Gutierrez. "The time that a teacher sees a student is just a little part of their lives. And it's in a classroom with all those other students. What is a teacher supposed to notice in a classroom?"

"Luisa's teacher seemed very sure," K posited. "Her view of Luisa matches how Maribel described Luisa."

Gutierrez did not seem impressed. "People see what they want to see. I have dealt with a bunch of runaway kids and I never met any family that wanted to believe their kid did that. They always put the blame on somebody else." He leafed through an exercise book marked "Mathematics." Not "Math." Mathematics.

"I can't see anything here," Gutierrez said, stacking exercise books on a pile.

"How come we're not finding anything?" said K. Maybe everybody was wrong and Gutierrez was right and the kid really had perfected the art of the double life. "Do you think this is weird at all?"

"Not really," said Gutierrez. "I was like that."

"Like this?" asked K incredulously. "No doodling? No scribbling? No comments? No notes to your friends?"

"I was a serious student," Gutierrez said.

Serious? Creepy more like. K was beginning to appreciate one thing: going through a blameless person's effects was pretty boring.

He took a textbook, upturned it holding it by its spine and shook it. Gutierrez watched him working his way through shaking the text books.

"You're cheating," he said.

A strip of paper fluttered out of the Biology textbook and landed on the floor.

K picked it up.

"What is it?" Gutierrez asked.

"Just some web-link," K said and passed it over to Gutierrez.

"I'll just call up the link," suggested Gutierrez and got busy on his keyboard. "Oh."

"What is it?" asked K.

Gutierrez face was burning.

"You okay?" K asked. He got up and looked over Gutierrez' shoulder. "Oh—"

Gutierrez shut down the page. "I told you she is too good to be true."

K packed Luisa's possessions back into the carton. He sat down and drummed his fingers on the table.

"What are we going to do?"

"What we are doing anyway," Gutierrez said. "Nothing has changed except for your opinion of that girl."

"I find her quite intriguing," said K. "Perturbing, but also intriguing."

Gutierrez shook his head. "She's going to come back. That's

what happens with these kids. They run away with somebody and then they are fed up and come back."

"Unless they run away with the wrong person."

"I went ahead with the missing alerts and posters and the info-line. Every station has our alert and the newspapers and radio stations too. The community channel's going to run the alert too. It's going to come up every hour, so Luisa's missing is really out there."

"You did all this?" K asked.

"I wanted to get on it quick, before anybody changes their mind and tells me not to," Gutierrez mumbled.

"You think the sheriff would change his mind on us trying to find Luisa?" K asked.

"He's under a heap of pressure. We haven't got the resources. Something's got to give," Gutierrez said unhappily. "I have not seen the sheriff like this before."

Of all the terrible things Gutierrez could have said, this was the worst.

CHAPTER SIXTEEN

Today Becky Tsosie's fury stood at the 85th percentile. K's acquired survival skills did not, alas, include appeasing or averting Becky Tsosie's temper.

"Hey!" hissed Becky. "Your woman's here. AGAIN. She's been here like . . . half an hour."

"What woman?" scowled K on the off-chance of provoking Becky into a physical assault, which might yield a couple of days' sick leave—if the sheriff happened to be in a charitable mood.

From Becky came a guttural snarl that wiped the scowl right off K's face. If one dispensed with highfalutin notions like pride, swift gear changes from mutiny into meekness were surprisingly efficient tension de-escalators.

"I put her in the supply room," said Victor Becky with glinting eyes.

"Supply room" was a fancy name for the space where Lorinda stored her cleaning supplies.

K found Maribel Alvarez perching on a stepladder in the dark and cramped supply room that smelled of bleach and cleaning products, which now mingled with Ms. Alvarez' scent.

"The Interviewing room is free now," said K. He had decided against apologizing for the wait or anything else.

"Please," she said, as soon as she had sat down on the proffered chair. And then she stopped. Her "please" hung in the air between them so heavily that it felt almost tangible.

"Miss Alvarez. . . ," said K. He didn't know why he had relegated her from "Ms." to "Miss"; maybe it was to acknowledge how helpless she felt—or how much she needed help.

"Miss Alvarez. Rest assured that we are doing everything we can to find Luisa. We have put out alerts to every police station in the county; we have alerted the newspapers; the local radio is broadcasting an appeal; we have an info phone line running. Everyone is looking for your sister."

It wasn't strictly a lie, this "we are doing everything we can," because there wasn't that much they could do. Considering their resources and the priorities that ruled the day, they had done most of what they could do. Considering too that Luisa wasn't perceived as a girl of unblemished character, but a teenager suspected of unwholesome interests and pursuits, they had indeed done more than they needed to.

"Have you got anything? Any information from the other police stations?" Maribel Alvarez cut through K's reverie.

"We are doing everything we can."

"Did you get something from the call line?"

"Everyone is aware of your sister," said K.

"Did you get some phone calls about Luisa?" pleaded Maribel.

"We are sifting through the calls." He wasn't going to tell her that all they had so far was a handful of pervy crank calls and that he was the only one doing the sifting.

"What about Luisa's social media?" K asked. "Have you checked out her posts?" For someone who understood approximately 17 percent of the content he had just issued, he sounded pretty damn convincing—to himself.

Maribel shook her head. "She does not like that stuff. I told you!"

K couldn't remember that she had.

"Did you tell me why Luisa doesn't like social media?"

"She doesn't like these things. She doesn't understand what they are there for. She is a private person." Oh sister, if only you knew.

"What about you?" asked K, "Do you use social media?"

"Why does that matter to you?"

Why indeed. It was difficult arguing for something that you didn't understand.

"It may be a way for us to look at Luisa's friends—her net-work—and give us some clues to where she is," K ventured brave-ly.

"She does not have friends like that."

To begin with K had found Maribel's description of her young-er sister a little curious; then touching, then neurotic; and now he found it disturbing, as if Luisa had been confined, like a latter-day Rapunzel, in the ivory tower of her older sister's wishful imagina-tion.

Would it not be plausible, if not likely, that little sister had learned off her older sister how to advance her prospects via the favors of old white men?

"Friends like that?" K repeated. He considered and decided against calling her out on this rather pithy dismissal of around 98.5 percent of contemporary adolescents. "What about your social me-dia network, Ms Alvarez?" he asked.

He never could remember the names of the endless permuta-tions on the theme of embellishing vacuous communication with frivolous gimmickry: Zapshnat; Instigawp, Fratbloc—whatever—that the post-millennial free-market economy was throwing up like a bulimic hurling institution-sized vats of M&Ms.

"I'm not on social media," Maribel said.

"Quite unusual these days." For K, this was a compliment.

Maribel however chose to take his remark as accusation. Fury and exasperation displaced anxiety and despair.

K resolved to consider, at a free moment, the curative potential of Replacing Anxiety through Anger Therapy, RATAT for short.

Anger was much preferable to anxiety. Anger, particular-ly righteous anger, was cathartic, empowering and frightening to the beholder, as K himself could attest, confronted with Maribel's seething fury and undisguised contempt.

"You share Luisa's attitude toward social media?"

"I closed down my accounts," Maribel said after a pause.

This seemed quite a radical thing to do. K had always thought of such virtual participation as a life sentence. Once opted in you were in it forever and beyond, as evidenced from the multitude of the deceased who endured as the undead of cyber space.

"Closing down your accounts—that's quite unusual, isn't it?" K tended to repeat himself when under stress.

"What would you do when you are trolled?"

"You were trolled?" When in doubt just repeat back what you've just heard. That was the one thing K had learnt from the annoying counselor. Although, come to think of it, it had been the counselor's self-same habit that had driven K away. "It must have been pretty bad if it made you close down your accounts?"

Maribel nodded curtly.

"Did you file a complaint? Get help. . . ?"

He didn't even know if you could file a complaint about things that happened on the internet. He didn't know who would be responsible for sorting that kind of thing out. God forbid it was the police.

At least, K found, he was acquiring some immunity to Maribel's withering contempt. Indeed he found he didn't ruddy care.

Instead, he found that Maribel's orneriness created in him an urge to call her to task about her relations with Lucky Easton; to let her have a piece of his mind about the destructive and immoral machinations of her lover, amongst which fornication and adultery whilst selling himself to the public as family man and proud father of two was the least of his peccadilloes.

"I am here because of my sister," Maribel rasped.

And then, suddenly, Maribel's defensive glaze cracked and fell away, revealing a fragile, frightened and deeply distressed young woman, faced by one helpless cop whose cool hadn't lasted longer than a gnat's hiccup.

"Please," she said. "Please! You have to find her!"

"We will," K said with as much conviction as he could muster.

Maribel Alvarez began to cry. She made no attempt to hide that she was crying; she did not dab her eyes or try to prevent her make-up from running. She sat blinking through the veil of tears coursing down her face. K stayed silent as long as he dared to.

"I know how worried you feel," he said eventually. It wasn't true of course— he didn't know how worried she felt.

He and Lili had grown up semi-feral, the offspring of feckless parents who were "wild children" themselves, hedonistic, wanton, self-centered and thoroughly irresponsible. The first couple of times Lili didn't come home and evening stretched into night and night into the wee hours, it had been K who had insisted on reporting her missing. He remembered a ginger-haired, thick-necked copper with a lilting Southern Welsh accent. "Give it a bit of time," said the copper. "If she's not back by tomorrow night we'll have a proper look, I promise."

"We told him not to worry!" trilled K's mother, who was working on one of her projects—priming terracotta pots, tie-dying T-shirts, knotting macramé plant holders, decorating bongs with cannabis leaf motifs, mashing up "energy balls" for some hippie festival. "He likes to worry. Don't you, Franz?"

The copper looked at him with a strange look in his eyes, something that could have been compassion or even pity. "His sister is a lucky girl." Lili had returned the following night. Her absences had become longer and longer, and K eventually had stopped worrying.

Maybe Luisa's mother was like K's mother and didn't know how to worry.

If he suspended his doubts for a moment; if he chose to engage with Maribel's idea of her little sister as pure as the driven snow, Luisa as a studious homebody—it was possible, wasn't it, that she'd taken off of her own volition? Wanting to experience autonomy wasn't just the preserve of unhappy teenagers. Even well-adapted teenagers might want to experience the world outside their family home. The Alvarez matriarchy's self-contained, nurturing coziness might well be a factor in Luisa's leaving.

It was plausible, wasn't it, that a perceptive and sensitive young person like the Luisa that Maribel, Cuauhtémoc and Siwan Davies knew and vouched for had become aware of the jarring discord between the cruel world outside and the idyll within, and had decided that she needed to conduct a field trip to reality as it was.

"Is this the first time Luisa has left?" he asked, just to fill the silence.

Maribel Alvarez looked at him incredulously. "The first time! I told you before!" Her voice was pitched to just below a scream. Her eyes were desperate.

"I'm sorry," K said sincerely. "I misspoke. I do remember you told us that Luisa's never gone missing before."

The problem was that Maribel Alvarez hadn't been made aware of the sinister hinterland of their paltry investigation. Somehow he didn't think she was going to be able to bear it. She would blame herself, her own lifestyle, her choices for impacting on Luisa.

"Whenever a young person goes missing," he said in his best counselor manner, "their family are always worried. Worried to distraction."

Which wasn't true at all, because there were plenty of callous bastards out there who hardly noticed when a kid or two went missing; who were perhaps even glad for the lightened work- and aggro-load, and the reduced grocery bills.

In fact, the proliferation of parental neglect these days possibly directly fed into the police's trending laid-back attitude toward missing children cases.

"Miss Alvarez, we've had many, many young people going missing and many, many worried relatives, and so far . . . so far they've all come back." He thought that was true. If someone really had stayed missing, he assumed he would have remembered. Unless the case had been so horrendous that his unconscious had chosen to suppress the memory.

Maribel Alvarez had begun to shake again. The intensity of her shaking disconcerted K.

"You are not giving hope a chance," he urged.

Her whole body shook.

"How is your family? How are they holding up?" He hadn't been able to think of anything else to say. Now he'd opened the gate wide for her to heap all the sorrows and worries of the Alvarez family on him as well.

He watched the shaking slowly subsiding, like a whirlwind that had been shaking up a tree letting go and continuing on its path.

She regarded him through narrowed eyes as if she was considering how to answer. She lifted her chin. "They're doing okay—I guess."

"They are doing okay?" echoed K. So the Alvarez family were still calm, still collected. Of all the possible answers, he hadn't anticipated that one. He had been pretty sure that by now they would be worried, really worried.

Apparently the Alvarez family was, on the whole, doing better than he was. Why were they though? How did they manage it? Had K been in their place he'd have been sectioned by now. Well, they had the advantage of not knowing how little of a shit the Milagro squad gave for the disappearance of their kid.

"That's reassuring . . . isn't it?"

"I don't know," whispered Maribel. "Mamá is . . . I don't know how she feels. I think she's okay. My grandmother . . . she is in her own world," the girl said softly.

K had so many questions and no idea how to ask them. To question Maribel on why her family were doing okay would imply that he did not share their optimism or faith or denial or whatever it was that was buoying them.

And what about the grandmother? Often "being in their own world" when speaking of old people implied a deteriorating mental state or dementia. Well, whatever fueled the Alvarez matriarchs' optimism, they were lucky.

K wished for them that their hope would endure as long as they needed it to; preferably until this case came to a happy end—even though K could not feel in himself much hope that it would. But maybe that was just him.

Best to wrap up the meeting now, on this particle of a positive note.

"We will keep you informed. We'll be in touch. . . ."

"Can you come and speak to my grandmother?" Maribel interrupted.

"You would like me to speak to your grandmother?"

"Yes!" Maribel Alvarez had reverted to her initial state of pique, which had to be a good sign. At least she wouldn't leave the station crying.

K wondered what good she thought his visit would do, as clearly all he did was annoy and exasperate Maribel.

"How do you think my talking to your grandmother will help?"

The girl had regained her composure. She shrugged. "I don't know."

Great vote of confidence there.

"Sure," K said. "I'll be glad to."

Doing anything, anything at all, had to be better than doing nothing.

CHAPTER SEVENTEEN

They say the path to hell is paved with good intentions.

K's feeble attempts at acts of altruism inevitably brought with them punishment in the shape of obstacles swiftly fashioned by whoever's path he happened to cross.

"Why do you need to see them again?" the sheriff growled.

These days Weismaker tended to treat him like a wayward schoolboy given to truanting. Maybe Weismaker had to make up for all the paternal concern, patience and tolerance he had shown K on his long way back to so-called normality.

K mumbled something about family liaison, keeping the channels of communication open, the importance of maintaining citizens' trust in the force. . . .

"Glad you remember something of that motivational course I sent y'all on at City Hall," the sheriff said.

The "motivational course" was to accustom San Matteo County police to public presentation and representation and had been delivered by a prematurely self-satisfied youngster, encased in an expensive suit, whose downy cheeks had yet to experience the chill gusts of reality.

"The missing girl's sister is very distraught," K said.

"It ain't your job to comfort folks, Son," the sheriff said.

"It's not my job to have ideas. It's not my job to comfort people. What is my job?" In K the old mutinous spirit was stirring.

"Your job today? You're gonna be helping out Dilger with the School Marshall Plan."

"The Marshall Plan? Dilger?" K yelped.

"If you got some spare time later you can visit your family," said the sheriff generously.

•   •   •   •

Dilger had insisted they park behind the building. Then he spent a good twenty minutes stealthily circling the building with set chin and furrowed brow. Dilger had not thought to enlighten K as to the exact purpose of their visit, and K hadn't asked.

Now he was leaning against the patrol car and enjoying the passage of clouds reflected in the school building's windows, leaving Dilger to creep about.

Eventually, and much too soon for K's liking, Dilger was done with his reconnaissance.

Imperiously snapping his fingers, Dilger summoned K to a side entrance where he had taken position. Having learnt the hard way to pick his battles, K trotted over. Waggling his eyebrows meaningfully, Dilger depressed the door handle.

"Aha!" he crowed triumphantly. "Open! Unsecured! Anybody can just walk in from the street and do whatever they put their minds to."

They found themselves in the echoing hallways of Elm Street Middle School.

"C'mon! We need to show 'em. C'mon now! Hurry!"

K trailed after Dilger, who did the whole cop-show prime-time shtick, sliding, his back pressed to the wall along the hallway, arms outstretched, gun clasped with two hands, digits trigger-happy. When the sheriff had gang-pressed K into this excursion he hadn't quite made it clear that the deal was going to involve a military grade maneuver.

"Are we auditioning for Blade Runner?"

Dilger hissed "shhhhh," tiptoed round a corner, stopped at a door, listened, beckoned to K, tore open the door, stormed through, leapt on the bespectacled woman of middle age sitting at the desk and held his gun to her head.

"Bang! Bang! You're dead!"

Teacher and students screamed as one. K hadn't known that terrified humans could scream so loudly and in such coloratura cadences. His eardrums throbbed.

He snatched Dilger's Glock, opened the magazine, dropped the ammo into his palm and pressed the gun against Dilger's stomach.

"And now Officer Dilger will continue his school safety training for your benefit," he said, and smiled winningly. "I'll be outside—securing the exits."

He found his way to the exit door, aimed his foot at it and kicked it open. There was a yelp and a thud. K looked down at the young person on the ground, struggling to his feet.

"Oh gosh—I am so sorry," K said. "Are you okay?"

The kid nodded and wiped dust off the knees of his pants.

"Did you kick open the door?" the kid asked.

"It's been one of those days," K said.

"Cool!" the kid said, wide-eyed.

"Don't take me as a role model," advised K. "By the end of the day I'll likely have a disciplinary and be unemployed."

The kid fumbled in his shirt-pocket and produced a crumpled pack of cigarettes that he extended toward K.

"Are you making a point about lambs and sheep?" asked K.

He accepted the cigarette and the kid produced a lighter. They leant against the sun-warmed wall side by side and looked out on the deserted schoolyard, smoking companionably.

K drew the smoke into his lungs and exhaled, blowing smoke rings toward the sky. The kid blew smoke rings too. He was better at it.

"I don't usually smoke," K said. "But I needed this. Thanks."

"Sure," the kid said. He took a drag, dropped the cigarette and ground it out. He collected the cigarette-end and wrapped it in a tissue. "Pick up the butt when you're done. See ya," he said and vanished through the unsecured door.

K inhaled deeply. He was getting the hang of blowing smoke

rings. The secret was slow exhalation. He watched with pride as a halo-sized ring drifted toward the clouds.

The door opened and Dilger thundered through. "Where have you been?"

K dragged on his cigarette, exhaled through the nose, stubbed the cigarette out on the wall and wrapped up the stub. "What's the plan?" he asked. "Going to take some hostages?"

Dilger clenched his jaw and stabbed an index finger at K. "You are going to tell those teachers about school safety."

"Am I?" said K.

"And I'll be sitting at the back, watching you all the way."

•　　•　　•　　•

The vibe K was getting from the assembled teachers was hostility tempered with gratitude for the respite this session afforded them from their charge of youthful terrors.

Dilger had made good his threat and had taken a seat at the back of the room, from where he was eyeballing K.

Damn if K hadn't forgotten what he was supposed to talk about.

"What am I supposed to tell you?" he asked the assembly.

Interesting how teachers shared their students' class room etiquette. They did as K imagined their kids would do when asked a dumb question: they stared at him in mute disgust and remained silent.

"Anything in particular you would like to hear?" He hoped for a resounding "nothing," which he would take as implicit permission to bring this farce to an end and exit with a residue of dignity.

"School safety! You are supposed to tell them about school safety!" Dilger hollered from the back row.

K looked out at the sea of frowns, the legion of sour expressions, the aggregation of disapproving, pursed mouths bearing uncanny resemblance to cats' assholes. Well, the sheriff should have known better than to trust him with making a silk purse out of this particular sow's ear. He was going to pass on to these folk the yield of his expert five-minute Google search that he had meant to share with Milagro PD's Marshal Plan enthusiasts.

"I always like to start with numbers," he said disingenuously. "Who doesn't like numbers? So here are some numbers on school shootings: This year to date, there have been sixty-nine fatalities as the result of school shootings. This year the total number of children enrolled in school nationwide from pre-kindergarten to Grade 12 stands at 50.7 Million students. Do we have a professor of mathematics here? Would you give us the percentage of fatalities based on number of students, please?"

Practically everybody produced a phone and began hacking numbers into it. Muttering; incredulous exclamations; heads moving together conferring; phones being swapped to scrutinize and confirm results. It was quite the lively crew.

"Anyone care to share?"

"Zero point zero zero zero—" said a voice from the back.

K turned to the white board. "How many zeros?"

"Zero point zero zero zero one three six zero nine four," a basso profundo read out.

"0.000136094," K wrote. "Have I got this right?"

The assembly muttered an affirmative.

"I'm sure we are all agreed that the death of even one student is a death too many. I'm sure we all agree that we need to try our best to prevent these tragedies. In trying to find a way to prevent these tragedies, we owe it to our kids and to ourselves to explore and consider all available options and their possible consequences.

"We all desperately want to prevent school shootings. But we need to understand that by hardening schools and arming staff we are engaging in a Faustian pact. We are making a deal with the devil. What is our pay-off to the devil? It is that by implementing the School Marshal Plan we are agreeing to bringing up and educating our children in a siege atmosphere.

"By opting for a paramilitary solution to keeping our schools safe, we are condemning our children to spend the most formative years of their lives at a place we have taught them to associate with danger and death.

"We do this for a zero point zero zero zero one three six zero nine four percent chance of a child falling victim to a school shooting.

"So I am asking you: what do you prefer? Would you rather your child spent ninety-nine days in cheerful oblivion or a hundred days in dread and fear?

"I have a dream, ladies and gentlemen. I have a dream of investing the money we are going to spend on securing doors, installing metal detectors, surveillance cameras, armed guards, and in training and arming teachers, instead in school counselors to support struggling and disaffected students; in visionary teaching staff; in a broad curriculum; in extracurricular activities to develop students' creativity and interests; in educational field trips to broaden the mind. That is my dream.

"You all drive carefully now. Remember: your chances of dying in a vehicle-related accident are a few thousand percent higher than those of your child dying in a campus shooting. Thank you."

K began to shoulder his way to the door. A mob of teachers surrounded him, barring his way.

"Any questions regarding arms training are best answered by Officer Dilger," K said. He was wondering whether to save them the trouble and refer them directly to Weismaker for their complaints.

"That was great," said a man with a mustard-colored tie and a great mane of silver hair.

"It was?" asked K.

There was a general murmur of affirmation.

"We need to stop this madness!" said an athletic woman, the PE teacher, probably.

"Thank you," said a guy with old school horn-rimmed spectacles. "You said what we needed to hear—we knew it, but it especially helped that a police officer said it."

K hadn't the heart to tell him that what they had witnessed had been an act of defiance, not an officially sanctioned message of common sense delivered by a committed representative of Milagro law.

•   •   •   •

News traveling fast, K's triumph was short-lived.

He had barely got back to the station when Young blocked his way. "I hear you want our kids shot? That right? You want any bad guy that has a mind to, walk in the school and just pick off these kids, and blow them to hell? You don't want teachers to save their kids? That what you want?"

"The sheriff asked to see you," Becky called.

Young bared his teeth in a sinister scowl. "Yeah! You try and explain just what you did over there to the sheriff. Good luck, buddy."

Never mind.

Whatever.

Plenty of fish in the sea. Loads of jobs to choose from. Busboy at Barbie's dive-bar. Customer Service Associate at the Green Light Marijuana Dispensary. Principal Shampooer at Bella Wow!'s Dog Grooming Salon. Bestselling Author of "A Thousand and One Crafty Tips on How to Survive Selling Your Soul."

The sheriff didn't even ask—he just handed K a steaming mug of his ghastly potion. This had to be bad.

"Thank you, Sir," mumbled K. Under the sheriff's glare he gulped down three mouthfuls in rapid succession. Speed was of the essence here. He felt Weismaker's coffee, unrelieved by sugar or creamer, making short shrift of his esophagus on its caustic way to destroying his stomach lining.

"What am I going to do with you?" Weismaker growled.

What indeed.

K met Weismaker's eyes and held them. A man who could swallow half a mug of the sheriff's coffee could do anything.

"I suppose you could fire me."

The sheriff nodded. "That doesn't bother you?"

K considered. "I don't know. I guess it bothers me more to represent stuff I don't agree with."

"Stuff?" said the sheriff.

"Stuff like that School Marshal Plan," said K. "Not only don't I agree with it, I think it's the most fuckwitted idea that anyone could ever come up with."

"Just let it all hang out, why don't you?" said the sheriff.

"I probably should—it might be my last chance," said K boldly. Better to go out with a bang than a whimper. "It's not just that I don't believe tooling up schools is a good idea. I believe it is a positively, proactively bad idea that in the long run won't protect students, because it will lead to more school shootings by creating a generation of paranoid, disturbed, gun-fixated kids. And while we're at it: Lucky Easton is buying his way into respectability by sponsoring arms for schools, so there's no way anybody is ever going to make him pay for what XOX did to Goosewash Wilderness. And there's our young woman over there in the hospital, who we can't identify—" K paused for air.

The sheriff sat down, sighed and ran a hand through his graying bristles.

"How do you think your talk went over there at the school?"

"It went swell," said K. "Though I don't think Dilger especially appreciated it."

"That there is my problem," said the Sheriff. "Thanks to you we got ourselves a gap in opinion about wide enough to hold a cruise ship. I got all these—" he pointed at a pile of message slips— "congratulating me on my great cop with common sense. Seems they especially liked the 'I have a dream' bit. Matter of fact they liked it so much, Bachman is going to run an article on it in the Milagro Gazette."

"Oh," said K. This he had not expected.

"Well," said the sheriff. "I reckon it's my problem now. Just do me a favor and keep your darn opinions to yourself. I don't want a civil war to break out. Just do your thing quietly. When it is APPRO-PRIATE. You get me?"

"Yes Sir!" said K. Though in truth he didn't get the sheriff at all.

He doubted that in this lifetime at least he'd find out where exactly the sheriff stood.

"And now go and visit your missing girl's family," said Weismaker.

CHAPTER EIGHTEEN

As soon as the door opened K regretted having agreed to the visit.

Mrs. Alvarez' eyes widened. She gasped. Her hand flew to her throat as if warding off an invisible strangler. It seemed that Maribel had somewhat overestimated her family's optimism and good faith.

"There's no bad news, Mrs. Alvarez. Please, don't worry," K said rapidly.

"No bad?" Mrs. Alvarez said uncertainly.

No bad news. No good news either. No news at all, in fact. And this was the second time today that K stood before civilians not knowing why he was there and what he was supposed to do.

"I just wanted to see how you are," K said. "How are you?"

"Come! Come!" Mrs. Alvarez now looked so happy to see him that her beaming face almost made his visit worthwhile.

She ushered him in, escorted him to the kitchen table where a very old lady was grinding corn in a very old-fashioned way, by means of a stone corn grinder.

"She likes doing that," Mrs. Alvarez explained, as if apologizing for the lack of state-of-the art gadgetry. The old woman ground a smooth oblong stone over a pile of maize kernels in a metate. K settled on the seat appointed to him and watched the hypnotic transformation of kernels into smooth yellow-speckled cornmeal. The age-old skill displayed before him evoked in him a sense of wonder and awe.

So this visit had already yielded two positives. Admittedly the first positive, mother Alvarez' relief at the bad news he wasn't bringing was, strictly speaking, might be cancelled out by the terror that his visit had provoked.

The old woman barely looked up when he joined her at the table, just a swift raising and dipping of the head, a fleeting glance out of deep black eyes, and back to grinding maize.

The heady aroma of cloves, cinnamon and boiling milk filled the air. Mrs. Alvarez set three steaming glasses on the table, sat down and motioned for K to drink.

The drink was hot, aromatic and very sweet. K sipped slowly, buying time. It was pretty excruciating to be sitting here in the absence of new developments, in the absence of a brief, in the absence of a plan.

"How are you keeping?" It was a feeble opening that nevertheless had cost him ample deliberation. The only thing that he had been able to think of asking was "how are you coping?" To ask how they were coping had seemed a bad idea. K was relieved that the less loaded "keeping" had occurred to him. But maybe the Alvarez matriarchs were not that well versed in the subtler nuances of English.

"Miss Maribel asked me to drop by," said K. "Just to see how you are and if, you know, anything new has come up, or if you have remembered something or—"

"You talk to my mother," said Mrs. Alvarez.

"Would your mother like to talk to me?" asked K.

"She is in her own world," said Mrs. Alvarez.

Most families did their best to keep a doddering old relative out of sight and mind. The Alvarez family seemed markedly keen on promoting their grandma, which K found oddly endearing but also perturbingly odd.

K wished he had had the guts to ask Maribel what "her own world" meant. It was a question, he felt, that Mrs. Alvarez would struggle to answer in English, and his Spanish wasn't up to existential ponderings either.

"Is it a nice world?"

Mrs. Alvarez considered the question earnestly. "I think," she said after a while. K assumed that Mrs. Alvarez deemed her mother's world a largely nice one. Way to go Officer Kafka, with intercultural interpretation skills so sketchy that he couldn't tell confirmation from hesitation, and asking questions so vague and wide they were practically unanswerable.

"My mother she comes from the . . . how do you say—*la selva*? My mother, she belongs to pueblo lacandón. . . ."

The old lady sitting here, grinding corn on a matate, really did come from another world. She was a Lacandon out of the rainforest.

The Zapatistas and "el Subcomandante Marcos" were what K associated with the Lacandon people.

Were the Zapatistas and el Subcomandante still out there in the Chiapas rainforest, fighting the good fight, standing up for indigenous rights, resisting capitalism and undermining the neo-liberal agenda?

Or had they been paid a king's ransom to write their memoirs and then promptly relocated to Switzerland?

The fêting of the Lacandon people's secluded existence by explorers, anthropologists and adventurers had drawn into the depths of the rainforest an ever-increasing volume of travelers suffering from civilization fatigue who brought with them the delirium of progress, like the blankets saturated with smallpox that had made America great.

"*¡Encantado!*" K said. The old lady ground her corn and did not look up.

"Your mother must have seen many things in her life," said K.

"Many different things," Mrs. Alvarez agreed.

"So you would like me to talk to your mother?"

"I would like my mother talk to you," corrected Mrs. Alvarez.

"Certainly," K said, "it is an honor. Thank you."

Mrs. Alvarez smiled.

"Is there something special you want your mother to talk to me about?"

He was moved, he was intrigued, he enjoyed the hospitality, but he was damned if he knew what he was supposed to be doing here.

Mrs. Alvarez had one of those expressive faces that spoke across linguistic barriers, and what it said was that she wasn't sure either.

"My mother has many dreams," she said. "She sees things in her dreams. She knows things."

K tried to look as if soothsaying, clairvoyance and dream interpretation were all part of the job description. Mrs. Alvarez launched into an explanation that he could only follow partially, namely that dreams were part of her mother's people's tradition, their dreams were real and spoke to them and so they knew things that other people did not know, and she hoped that by telling her dreams to a new person, abuelita would remember new things and then she would be able to tell them when Luisa would return.

"Your mother has dreamt of Luisa?" asked K.

Mrs. Alvarez looked briefly nonplussed, as if she couldn't quite believe his question. "Of course, all the time."

That's why there wasn't a question *if* Luisa was coming back. The only question was *when* Luisa was coming back. So this was how the Alvarez matriarchs managed to keep calm and positive.

It was confidence not hope that blossomed out of the old lady's dreams. Maribel had perhaps ventured too far from the family home to be able to reap the full benefit of the Lacandon tradition. But traditions apparently needed new blood to flourish, and K began to comprehend that he was being recruited to boost the audience and thereby increase the chances of accurate recall.

Mrs. Alvarez topped up their glasses with the hot, fragrant milky potion and laid a pile of colorful wool and crocheting needles in front of her mother. She collected the bowl with maize meal, matate and mano and carried them to the kitchen counter. From the pile of wool the old woman picked a bright orange and began to crochet. Her daughter, Mrs. Alvarez, drew a chair to the table and settled.

Are you sitting comfortably? thought K. Then I'll begin. . . .

CHAPTER NINETEEN

"Have some jalapeno poppers!" urged Magnusson. "On the house."

It was a quiet afternoon at Barbie's.

"Why are you so keen on getting me to eat jalapeno poppers?" K asked.

"I have a new supplier," said Magnusson. "You'd be helping me out."

K had long believed that if Gunnar Magnusson, retired economics professor turned dive bar owner, could run a business, then could anyone.

"Go on then," said K.

"You look happy," said Magnusson.

"Do I?" asked K.

"Are you?"

"Oh, I wouldn't go that far. . . ," said K.

Magnusson laughed. "I hope I haven't offended you by insinuating that you might be happy?"

"Happy is a pretty strong word," conceded K. "But I suppose I am . . . intrigued? Enlivened. . . ?"

"That's good enough—almost as good as happy. So tell me what it is that has enlivened and inspired you?"

"I wish I knew," said K. "No, Actually I don't need to know. Better to just go with the flow."

"Way to go!" said Magnusson delightedly. "Maybe you are learning after all!"

"Learning would be good," K said. "I visited a family whose teenage girl disappeared and I spent the afternoon listening to a grandmother's dreams."

"Dreams?" asked Magnusson. "Interesting dreams?"

"I didn't understand them," said K.

"Cryptic dreams?"

"I didn't understand them because the old lady was speaking Maya."

"You hung out and listened to people tell dreams in Maya?" asked Magnusson.

"The old lady's daughter translated—she tried—but her English isn't that great. It didn't really bother me that I didn't understand. It was like listening to birdsong across the canopy. I went into a kind of trance. After a while I started to feel that I understood everything they said, as if it had entered my bloodstream. Of course I didn't really understand anything," K added hastily, "but I felt like it. I felt like I belonged."

"Sounds like an afternoon well spent," said Magnusson

"On a personal level—maybe. Professionally—I'm not so sure. It's a complicated case. Nothing is like it's supposed to be. And I can't make any sense of it at all. . . ."

"An ambiguous case?" asked Magnusson when K had sketched out the case.

"Most of the squad have made up their minds. And so has the sheriff. The majority says we don't need to bother."

"I didn't know your job included morality policing." Magnusson took off his glasses and started polishing them on his sleeve. "I do hope you'll forgive me for saying this—your view of the girl seems a bit skewed too."

"Skewed? What are you saying?"

"Your squad judges the girl for being precociously promiscuous, while you are not allowing yourself to consider that she might be precociously promiscuous. Together you are making her into a yin and yang deal."

"You mean the Madonna/whore thing?" asked K.

"I mean your duty as a police officer is to protect citizens. It shouldn't matter who she is or what she is. She and her family are entitled to your help and support regardless."

"Funny," said K. "I think I said something like that to her sister. The sister loathes herself and idealizes her little sister. She reacted as if I had slapped her, when I said her little sister needn't be a saint to deserve being loved."

"A lot of projection going on. . . ," mused Magnusson.

"Then there's the mother and the grandmother—it's like they live in an oasis or on their own little island, there's something so peaceful and wholesome, so apart from this world—they are enchanting."

"You are smitten," said Magnusson. "Maybe you found your ideal world? Maybe this family has opened a door for you?"

"Doors—don't they say dreams are the backdoors to our conscious or something? I was definitely hoping for abuelita's dreams to open a door and show me some clues."

"You were hoping to find clues in cryptic dreams?" asked Magnusson.

"Why were the older sister and her mother so keen for the old lady to talk to me? And all she talks about are her dreams. You know what's weird? As long as abuelita kept talking everything made complete sense to me. Now all I'm left with are jaguars and spider monkeys and bees, a shed-load of bees, good bees, sweet bees, bad bees, biting bees—they really like their bees, those Lacandons—and rivers and ocelots. . . . What do you think?"

"What do you want me to say?"

"Give me an idea how I should look at those dreams," said K. "There's hardly anyone I can talk to about this stuff. It makes me feel lonely and like a crackpot."

"Dreams. . . ," mused Magnusson. "Dreams are about the only space in our lives where we aren't seduced into confusing the tangible with the truth. How are your poppers?"

"Not bad," said K. "Though I think the oil could have been hotter."

"Argh!" said Magnusson. "I got this kid in the kitchen. He's a good kid, but he's got the attention span of a gnat."

"As concerns your new supplier, these poppers are good," K said. "What did you mean by 'confusing the tangible with the truth'?"

"Did I say that?" Magnusson asked.

"You should listen to yourself sometimes. If you can't remember what you said, you probably won't be able to explain what you meant by it either?"

"Confusing the tangible with the truth. . . . It seems to me you got a lot from your visit?"

K nodded.

"I think I probably meant that you should accept your experiences for what they are." Magnusson regarded K sternly over the rims of his glasses. "I do hope your fixating on clues isn't going to take away from the validity of your experience."

"There's the small matter of going there as a cop on duty."

"So? You went in there as a cop and what you found touched you as a human. Are you going to discount it because it doesn't fit your schedule?"

"I didn't know you were so spiritual." K was being disingenuous. He found Magnusson's metaphysical excursions slightly disturbing. As usual they'd come to a point where K couldn't tell if Magnusson was very wise or if Magnusson was seriously losing his shit.

"I once had this Icelandic girlfriend. Sigrun Ólafursdóttir," said Magnusson dreamily. "They believe in allsorts—huldufólk— elves I guess you'd call them here—for the longest time I thought she was having me on, you know, but it turns out she wasn't. They really do believe in huldufólk. The bluest eyes she had. . . ."

K suspected that most people felt, when having a conversation with him, like he was now feeling having a conversation with Magnusson. The old boy was rather prone to going round the houses, diverting from dream interpretation to Icelandic elves and a long-lost-love's blue-blue eyes.

"It wasn't only Sigrun Ólafursdóttir," said Magnusson, savoring the name. "I got to meet this couple. They were both professors—tenured professors—and they had bought a plot of land to build a house on. They had it all set up, all ready to start building, when they discovered an elves' mound just where they had planned to build their house. So they couldn't go ahead—they had to set it in a different part of the plot and of course that made all the plans go awry. They'd designed the house around the trajectory of the sun, and all that didn't work out anymore."

"Whoa," said K. "They must have really cursed those elves."

Magnusson shook his head. "Not at all. They had respected the elves and so the elves looked after them. It was a very happy house they lived in."

"Is there a moral to this story?" K asked.

Magnusson cocked his grizzled head and pondered. "I suppose so. Respect elf mounds would be one. Conversely, if you happen to have a belief, respect it. If you happen to come across someone else's belief, respect that too. The same goes for someone's dreams."

"Uh," said K.

"I sense some resistance," Magnusson observed astutely. "I know damn well that when you say 'spiritual' you mean 'unhinged.'"

"Unhinged is a bit harsh," K amended. "I prefer 'away with the fairies.'"

"Since you are so keen on finding clues in your Mayan grandmother's dreams and since you insist on a so-called rational explanation for everything, how about this as a hypothesis: because the dream state catches us undefended, our dreams are often clearer than our 'rational' thoughts while awake."

"Do you mean that dreams weave together stuff that we know, but that we don't know that we know?"

"You are becoming so American," chided Magnusson. "'Stuff that we don't know that we know.' It rather takes the magic out of it, don't you think?"

"Whatever," said K. "Is the crux of what you are saying that our missing girl's grandmother's dreams might be true? The stuff about the bees, and the jaguars, and the spider monkey, and the ocelot?"

"What is the matter with you?" asked Magnusson. "You're not usually this literal-minded."

K winced. "Maybe I'm just doing unto you what others are doing unto me. But honestly: What about the jaguars?"

Magnusson shrugged. "What about the bees? Just find your equivalent for whatever your grandma's jaguars stand for. It's unlikely that jaguars mean anything to you. But what is your particular equivalent to the jaguar? That's what you want to ask yourself."

K doubted his dreams would yield any equivalents to abuelita's jaguars. He rose to leave.

"I'm just saying that because you are insisting on exploiting those dreams for your police work," Magnusson called after him. "Personally I hope that you go back to valuing what you found there—clue or no clue."

As usual K left Magnusson not knowing if he'd been confused even more, or had become extraordinarily wiser.

Maybe it was a bit of both.

CHAPTER TWENTY

"Whatever you want, you can have. Just take it. The less there is, the less I'll have to pack up."

"You really want to sell up?" K regarded the maze of bookshelves stacked to the ceiling, and tried to calculate their combined length. There had to be a couple of miles at least, holding how many books? Fifty thousand, a hundred thousand?

"It is time," Agnes Prohaska said.

Agnes Prohaska's face was crisscrossed by a myriad lines that spoke of a life lived to the full; thoughts thought without boundaries; and pleasures taken without fear.

"You got ages to go!" protested K.

"It's not my age," said Prohaska. "It's the Age that's driving me out."

Agnes Prohaska was Milagro's last living communist.

She'd got out of Czechoslovakia during the Prague Spring. Upon becoming a naturalized US citizen she had rapidly revised her erstwhile critique of the Czechoslovak regime. The freedom touted as the Western world's main achievement was just so much hooey and applied only to the freedom to choose what to consume— if you could afford it, that was. According to Agnes Prohaska, the main difference between the Western and the Eastern bloc was the class of opium they used to sedate their people.

Without Agnes Prohaska, Milagro would lose its one and only bookstore.

Once upon a time this very bookstore had achieved something like national fame—or notoriety. Thanks to Prohaska's limitless knowledge and diligent sourcing the store had built up a reputation for stocking every book that readers of a certain sensibility, outlook, philosophy and political persuasion could imagine. It was said that during the bookstore's heyday Alan Ginsberg and Jack Kerouac traveled all the way to Milagro and that Agnes Prohaska and Kerouac had embarked on a passionate, albeit brief affair.

K wished this was true, but doubted that it was. According to his calculations Agnes Prohaska had barely entered the United States when Kerouac died. But he didn't doubt Prohaska and Kerouac would have made a great couple.

Personally K carried an almost magical belief that no matter how rare or far-fetched the book he needed or desired, Agnes Prohaska would have it. The store was an inexhaustible Aladdin's cave of wonders and how Prohaska managed to keep track of her stock was anyone's guess.

"I thought if anyone can help me, it's you." K said.

"You are so very old-fashioned, Kafka." Prohaska pronounced his name as it would have been in the old country, which made it sound gruff and decisive and somehow more authoritative than the various pronunciation outrages that were committed against his name in this land. "Why not go online like everybody else?"

She led the way through the store in which the least feasible amount of space had been left between miles of corridors of shelves buckling under the weight of the complete inventory of the global print output.

After a mile or so Prohaska stopped, peered at a shelf and retrieved two yellowing volumes. "Here," she said. "These could help you."

It was so dark here in the recesses of the store that K wondered how Prohaska had managed to find anything, let alone make out the titles of her stock.

He followed her back through the maze of shelves to the front of the shop. His nose tickled and his throat ached from the dust. Prohaska held out the books to him.

"*Lacandon Dream Symbolism*? Where do you get all this stuff?"

Prohaska shrugged. "That's not so far-fetched surely? Have you forgotten where we live? I just tried to get my hands on what I could that I thought mattered."

K regarded the books quizzically.

"It matters to you, doesn't it?" Prohaska pre-empted K's question. "Besides my maxim is: whatever matters to the least number of people is the most important."

"You are a one-person preservation society? Preventing cultural heritage from dying out?"

"Trying to," corrected Agnes Prohaska. "It's a big job."

"I bet it is," said K. "And a noble undertaking it is too."

"I have done my bit," said Prohaska. "So you believe in dreams now? That's how you solve your cases?"

It was anyone's guess how dreams fitted in with dialectical materialism.

"We work with what is there. In this case a family member's dreams." K surprised himself by sounding firm and plausible. "So you really are going to sell up?"

Everything he liked about Milagro was going, or in decline.

"There are these young people that want to open a 'Fusion Sushi-Tapas' place. I don't know what that means."

"That means we lose our bookstore. Appleton's Book*ish* has closed up too. It's only a matter of time until Karolina's in Delgado folds," K said.

"There wasn't anyone who wanted to take over," said Prohaska. "I tried. Nothing. So I thought better go—how do you say? When the going's good?"

"There's also a saying: when the going gets tough, the tough get going," K noted.

"I did that too—" Prohaska halted and regarded K speculatively.

"Why don't you take over, Kafka? You like books. You understand what this place is about. You can run it part-time. Even just open it a couple of days a week—an evening or two? You could stay being a policeman—" she barely bothered to disguise the disgust in her voice.

K coughed.

Prohaska held up her hand imperiously. "Don't say anything. Think it over when you have time. No hurry. It's all paid off. I have what I need to live. So you could run it for a while as a trial. There'd be no risk for you. And no more risk to me than I can afford. The only thing you have to invest is your time. And—who knows? Maybe a bookstore owner named Franz Kafka will give this store a whole new lease on life."

CHAPTER TWENTY-ONE

"Must have been a good day, huh?"

Begay was sprawled on the couch, phone held aloft and Wittgenstein rolled into a ball on his chest. "I been making friends with your puddytat," he said.

The good day was starting to sour. That's how little it took. "He's called WITTGENSTEIN," K said sharply.

"You don't think I'm gonna bother with Wee-wee-steen?" said Begay. "I'm gonna keep calling him what he is: puddytat."

"I thought he'd have more pride," K said sorrowfully.

"Puddytat! Puddytat!" crooned Begay and pulled the cat's ears. Wittgenstein got up, shook himself and stalked off.

"And all of a sudden you're looking real happy again," observed Begay. "I bet you'd be even more happy if he'd clawed me, eh?"

K's ideal self was offended, while his honest self knew that Begay had a point. "There's always a next time."

"So: when you came in just now you were almost smiling—not smiling exactly, but leastways you weren't looking as if they'd made you suck on a lemon for eight hours straight."

"That's what I normally look like?"

"Did something good happen?" Begay insisted.

"I visited the Alvarez family," said K. "Nothing's happening and nobody thinks we need to do anything to find her, because she's a wild girl. I don't even know why I went. Just to show them that we do care, I guess."

"And that made you happy?"

"I saw Magnusson and he thought I looked happy, and now you are saying the same, so I guess it must be true," K said sarcastically.

"I'm waiting," said Begay.

"They are lovely people and I'm glad that I visited them."

Had it not been for Begay's gift for listening he would have dried up there. As it was, he felt compelled to share his enjoyment of the melodious Maya language; the reviving powers of hot, fragrant, milky drinks; the joys of communal meaning making; the healing power of family bonds—

Something in Begay's face made him stop.

"What?" K asked.

"Maybe you want to pay more attention to what you rate," Begay said softly, "and work to get something of that into your own life, too."

"Thanks for the sucker punch," said K.

Begay shook his head. K began to regret his ill-tempered response.

"Anyways, I spent a couple of hours with two lovely ladies listening to dreams in Maya. Maybe I should move to Mexico and learn Maya?"

"Maybe you should stay right here and grow up," Begay said.

How much easier it was to sour a mood than to keep it buoyant.

"What about Diné dreams? Do Diné believe in dreams?" K asked evasively.

"Old women do," Begay said after short contemplation. "When I was a kid I remember shima sani and shinálí asdzáán and shima yazzie and all those aunties always going on about their dreams. But shima sani was the worst. She used to dream a lot and it was all bad."

"So Diné do believe in dreams?"

Begay shrugged. "I don't know if everybody believes it. Dreaming is more of an old ladies' thing."

"I dream," K said.

"Figures," said Begay.

"Seriously, do you know about the meaning of dreams for Diné? Like some dreams having a special meaning?"

He'd barely had a couple of minutes leafing through the Lacandon dream symbolism books that Agnes Prohaska had given him and already he was on the way to becoming a fully committed cross-cultural dream-researcher.

"You mean like the stuff about coyotes? If a coyote crosses the road you stop, coz crossing a coyote's path is bad luck?"

"That's not dream symbolism," said K. Curiosity got the better of him. "So when you're in your car, let's say, and a coyote crosses the road, what are you supposed to do? Turn around?"

"You wait until another car comes by and then you follow it. You're okay once the coyote path's been crossed."

"What about the other car? Won't that get the bad luck by crossing first?"

Begay shrugged. "I don't know. That's just what they tell you to do."

K thought through the implications of a superstition that encouraged you to avoid bad luck at the expense of others.

"I can see what you're thinking," said Begay. "There's worse things you can do to somebody, believe me. I'm going to show you in a minute. Are you hungry?"

"Do you plan to poison me?" asked K.

"We'll have to wait and see," said Begay. He rolled off the couch and walked to the stove with the stiffness of someone who'd spent too much time in one position. "Come here!"

If K hadn't known Robbie better he would have interpreted his expression as nervous and excited.

"I hope you are hungry," Begay said.

"Sure. Very hungry. I haven't eaten all day."

"So you'd probably just about eat anything?" Begay sounded disappointed.

"You cooked!" said K, looking at the skillet on the stove. "What is it?"

Begay made a face as if he was about to call "tah dah!" and lifted the lid off the skillet.

"Smells great," said K. He wasn't just saying it. "What is it?"

"Rat-tat-oil," said Begay.

"Wow!" said K, "You cooked that?"

"I ordered it in from KFC," Begay said testily. He held a spoon out to K. "Better try it. I never done this before,"

"Let's hope it tastes as good as it smells!" said K.

Begay nodded. He really did look nervous now.

K popped the spoon into his mouth and savored the medley of vegetables that had just the right consistency. Each one had been cooked to develop its aroma to its maximum, and they complemented each other in a symphony of flavors that was more than the sum of its parts. He made to sink his spoon into the pot again.

"Hey!" said Begay. "No double dipping! You like it?"

K nodded. "I really, really do. Wow! Who would've thought."

"Whaddaya mean 'who would have thought'?" demanded Begay. "I make mean ribs, just ask my folks,"

"Sure," said K, "but that's meat. But this is all vegetables! And a couple of days ago you didn't even know what an eggplant was."

Begay had started laying the table. He produced a Baguette—"Gotta have some carbs"—and set the pot with a ladle on the table.

K brought out a bottle of red wine and rinsed out a pair of wine glasses that had been sitting around gathering dust.

"Honestly, how did you do this?" K dipped a hunk of bread into the unctuous stew. "Ratatouille is not an easy dish."

"Let me just show you what you are missing," said Begay, reaching into his pocket and producing his phone. "All the secrets of the universe in one handy object."

"Surely not all," said K.

"Damn near all," insisted Begay. "What I done is look in your refrigerator for what is there. My heart sank right to my boots when I saw what was there—I mean what wasn't there, which is all the stuff I like to eat, practically. And then I get this." Begay held up his phone. "I put in the names of all the vegetables that are there and that I know what they are called—and this rat-tat-oil thing was practically the first thing that came up."

"You cooked this from your phone?" asked K incredulously.

"Where you been, dude?" asked Begay. "Practically everyone does this."

"Not just a pretty face then," said K.

It was turning out to be a pretty good day after all.

•   •   •   •

After they had washed and dried the dishes, Begay went back to the couch and his phone, while K settled down with his Lacandon Dream Symbolism volumes.

They offered a well-written, thoughtful, at times almost poetic account, despite the author somewhat underestimating the true menace that so-called progress would ultimately present to these remote people.

But maybe the Lacandon had known all along.

"Hey," K called to Begay, "Listen up! The Lacandon term for foreigners, 'ts'ul,' originally *'appears to have been something to the effect of "plague, punishment, invader."* [1] What do you make of that?"

"I hope understanding what bílagáana are like helped those people. Did it help them?"

"Probably not in the long run," said K.

"How come the bílagáana can go everywhere and ruin stuff?" asked Begay.

"Because they like to shake hands?" said K. "Here it says: *'the Occidental handshake is represented in dream symbolism by touching something sticky which adheres to the hand. . . . The Lacandones have learned to shake hands as a foreign custom—used in dealing with foreigners—but they do not practice it amongst themselves and consider it a disagreeably familiar custom.'"*[2]

"Are you gonna read the whole book to me?" asked Begay.

"Why? Don't you like me reading it to you?"

"It's okay. I was just wondering why you picked that stuff about the hand-shaking?"

"I don't know . . . I suppose because it says a lot in two short sentences. It puts the dynamics of cultural misunderstanding in a nutshell." K realized that seemingly mundane activities could carry a lot of depth. "Do you think that people from different cultures can ever really understand each other?"

"I don't even think that people from the same culture can understand each other," said Begay.

"So you're basically saying that there's zilch chance that I'll be able to understand the old lady's dreams?"

"You don't really believe you're gonna solve that case by looking at dreams?"

"It would be neat though, wouldn't it? I'm going to read some more in this book. Who knows. . . ?"

The more K read, the more he appreciated the Lacandon. One could not but admire a people so immune to illusion that "good fortune" to them was simply a "lack of misfortune" and in whose world view fatalism and free will mingled anarchically.

The prophecies the Lacandon received in their dreams were generally negative. Life was precarious and fraught with danger. It was ruled by a conspiracy of natural forces, dangerous predators and malicious strangers in multitude.

As far as K could determine, with a Lacandon dream you always stood a chance—provided you were a deft hand at dream interpretation, understood precisely what dangers and vagaries awaited you and did your damndest to avoid them.

K liked the idea of avoidable, not inevitable, prophecies. To the Lacandon, dreams were guiding messages in a dangerous world. There was no hint of a shepherding lord; making beds in green pastures, being guided to still waters. As Lacandon you were alone, but you stood a chance if you understood your dreams. As an additional bonus, the Lacandon, according to the author, had a disdain for community living. Their term for those who did was *kah*, derived from *"mashing something into an amorphous mass."*

K decided he had found his soul-brethren.

But what about abuelita's dreams? According to this book, those dreams saturated with ocelots, bees, jaguars, hornets and snakes could be taken at face value or could be understood to indicate a precise opposite. Great was small, and small was great, a rope might be a rope or a snake. Dreaming of your *Onen* or anything that was a whole or partial or related or inverted representation thereof could be particularly revealing, but when K visited the old woman he hadn't known about the significance of the Onen, which was a bit like, but also wasn't at all like, a clan totem. He didn't even know which one of the four Lacandon Onen abuelita belonged to.

The closer you looked the more complex things became—just a short while ago he had hoped that it would be a case of listening to an old lady's dreams and looking up their meaning in a second-hand dictionary.

Now it seemed that not all bees and ocelots were equal.

●　　●　　●　　●

"It's a pity you don't want to hear about my Lacandon people here. It really is a great book," said K, making another doomed bid to kindle Begay's interest. "I got the book in a great store too. Have you ever been to Agnes Prohaska's bookstore?"

"Bookstore? Nobody reads books anymore. Old books?" Begay wrinkled his nose. "They have this moldy smell. Like the school library. Boy did it stink—that's why I don't like reading. I think it's all that boarding school misery clinging to those old books."

"I didn't know you went to boarding school," said K.

"I didn't," said Begay. "But my school was where the boarding school was before. I don't think they bothered getting in some new books for us. They just let us get on with these really old, moldy, yellow books that had those tiny bugs running around in them."

"These books don't smell. It's too dry. I didn't notice any smell." said K.

He thought it wiser not to mention that it would take a few weeks to vacuum the dust of ages off miles of shelves. Instead he casually mentioned Agnes Prohaska's proposal.

"Ask yourself why your old lady wants to get rid of the store," Begay said.

"She didn't make any bones about it. She's run it for more than fifty years and times have changed. And they are after her place to open some Sushi-Fusion-Tapas thing in it."

"Sushi-Fusion-Tapas?" asked Begay. "I don't know what that means."

"She's got tens of thousands of books in there. Rare books. Like this book here that I'm trying so hard to share with you." K waved the Lacandon dream volume at Begay. "Don't you think it's great that I found this Lacandon dream dictionary in a bookstore in a small town in the middle of nowhere, where folk aren't all that keen on reading? That's because of Agnes Prohaska's lifelong mission to preserve books like this as a cultural archive. And she knows every last one of the thousands of books she has got and where to find it. That's damn near a miracle. "

"You pretty much made up your mind to run it," Begay said.

K shook his head. "I don't know."

"So when did you get this whole idea about running a bookstore?"

"I didn't get the idea. The idea was given to me. When I got the Lacandon dream dictionary."

"So those dreams got you somewhere already, eh? How much you pay for the book?"

"Nothing. Agnes gave it me. She'd have given me any book I wanted."

"See!" said Begay triumphantly. "What kind of business is that? Just throwing stuff at folks for free?"

In K's brain something ignited—like a prairie fire taking hold.

"What? What did I say?" asked Begay.

K spoke slowly and deliberately. "It think it might be the kind of business I would like to run."

1. Bruce, Robert D. Lacandon Dream Symbolism; Vol 2; 1979; p.323.
2. Ibid.

CHAPTER TWENTY-TWO

Weismaker squinted at K and sighed. "So the grandmother is from some tribe and they believe in their dreams and the grandmother had some dreams? That what you are saying?"

K had thought it wise to report back to the sheriff. As so often, he had thought wrong. His Lacandon dream excursion wasn't going to get him any kudos with Weismaker, never mind secure him the sheriff's blessing.

"The grandmother is Lacandon. Up to a few decades ago her people had barely any contact with so-called civilization. They live in the rainforest. . . ."

"Yes, yes," said the sheriff impatiently. "And they dream. And they believe in their dreams."

K nodded. "Luisa's grandmother had some dreams of. . . ."

"Spare me," said Weismaker.

"What I'm saying is," K continued soberly, "there's a case to be made for taking a Lacandon's dreams more seriously than. . . ."

"My grandmother's, for instance?" Weismaker said.

"Your grandmother dreamt?"

"Oh boy, did she dream. Every darn breakfast we had to listen to her dreams. Then we had to listen to all the warnings that came with the dreams. There wasn't a day that didn't come stuffed with warnings about this, that or the other. Made for a real positive outlook, that," said Weismaker.

"Maybe that's why you joined the police force," K ventured.

"You lost me," said Weismaker coldly.

"Where was your grandmother from, Sir?"

"Transylvania."

"Really?" K asked, intrigued.

"No," said the sheriff.

• • • •

Suitably chastened, K set off to look for Córdoba. He found her ready and holstered, having arranged for them an appointment at the school.

"Where were you yesterday? There were some things I wanted to check out before we do the interviews."

"What did you want to check out?" he asked.

"Just some preparation," said Córdoba. "Never mind. Too late now. The sheriff said you went to visit the girl's family?"

"I did. Do you happen to know anything about the Lacandon?" K asked.

"The what?"

"The Lacandon? A rain forest people from Yucatan?"

Córdoba shook her head. "Why do you want to know?"

K took the opportunity to launch into another eulogy on the Lacandon, but today, it seemed, was not his day for turning skeptics into believers.

Córdoba looked less than impressed. "There are still some primitive people in Mexico."

"Traditional people," K corrected prissily.

"Backward," said Córdoba. "But Mexico is modernizing real fast."

She said it as if that was a good thing.

K decided this was neither the time nor the place to start chasing his Lacandon dreams. More the pity, as he had gotten quite a lot of interesting information on their dream interpretation from his book. Even if Robbie had rudely rebuked any of his further attempts at sharing his newly gained insights.

And here he was, in the glaring light of harsh reality, and reality, he suspected, didn't come much harsher than in the guise of an American high school cheerleading squad.

•   •   •   •

They made it to MMHS in time. Córdoba seemed to know her way through the school's sprawling campus to the sports hall.

The sports hall was a huge building and somewhat in need of repair. In the hall a rank fug of sweat, floral deodorant and teenage hormones hit them. It was not a good mix.

The cheerleaders clustered at the far end of the arena, twirling batons, performing warm-up stretches and practicing shimmying moves—or whatever they called it. The girls observed the cops' approach blankly and without apparent curiosity. The aura of detached disinterest did not leave them as Córdoba announced the purpose of their visit.

At a glance all girls were light of hair, long of limb and honeyed of complexion.

A strawberry blonde girl practicing twirling dropped her baton to the sneers of two of her peers lounging halfway up the staggered seating. They looked very alike and K recognized them. They were the two blonde girls whose photos on the school corridor had caught his attention. He was pretty sure now they were identical twins.

"Why are you here?" said one of the twins in a drawl that might have been insolent or perhaps was merely due to a lack of practice constructing whole sentences. Below her the cheery cluster sniggered.

Córdoba shrugged. "We have to start somewhere," she said, making it sound as if she was sharing a valuable insight into efficient police procedure.

A man emerged from a side door and introduced himself as Coach Daner Hansen, while feasting his peepers on Córdoba's comely proportions.

"You here about the Alvarez girl?" the coach asked. "There's not much we can tell you here. Right, girls?"

"We'll talk to you last," K said affably, "as you have to be here to tidy up after everyone."

He could see that the manly Hansen really loved the allusion to tidying up. His mouth had become a grim line over which moustache bristles hung like the quills of a skinned porcupine.

• • • •

The coach showed them to a cramped and stuffy office at the back of the sports hall, smelling of must and dust, which K preferred to the historical layers of bodily secretions and body-odor-combating products that the sports hall hummed with.

Córdoba was scrutinizing a list.

"You got a list?" asked K.

"I talked to the teacher, Ms. Davies," said Córdoba casually. "Did you know that Lucky Easton's twins are cheerleaders?"

"The blonde girls are Easton's daughters?" K asked.

"One of us should sit behind the desk," Córdoba decided. "It's more. . . ."

"Intimidating?" said K.

"Official," said Córdoba.

"Whatever effect it's supposed to have, I'm pretty sure you'll be better at it." Which wasn't any less than the gosh-darn truth, but Córdoba still gave K a look that said she suspected this was his cheap way of trying to weasel out of his duties. Which was the other part of the gosh-darn truth.

"We'll take them alphabetically," Córdoba decided.

"Do we have a strategy for this?" K asked.

"Let's just play it by ear and see how it goes," said Córdoba.

"Shall I get the first one?" asked K.

By now Córdoba would have understood that he intended to play gofer to Córdoba's lead investigator. He did not think she would mind that much. Córdoba was one of those people whose pace did not slacken when marching toward responsibility.

The most notable thing about cheerleader number one, alphabetically speaking, was the way Seenthyia Breenhauser spelled her name—or presumably the way her parents had chosen for her name to be spelled.

Ma and Pa Breenhauser had certainly bequeathed to their daughter an abundance of misspelling opportunities. Maybe, in a world whose population was growing and where the desperate scramble for attention was becoming an increasingly elaborate strategized quest, this was a cunning ruse to secure for Seenthyia attention she didn't otherwise merit.

As soon as K thought that he felt ashamed. She was just a young kid, at the beginning of her life, her future. It was just that he did not much like anything she represented. And, he told himself, what she did represent was lauded by the dominant majority, so not liking her was redistributive justice—his usual free pass for biased judgments.

Seenthyia's answer to Córdoba's opening question, "What can you tell us about Luisa?" did not do much to improve K's opinion.

"Luisa? Not a lot. At all. Because, you know, we don't hang out. We are— different people—you know? And, like, we are cheerleaders, so we are, like, really busy? Yeah? We got all these games coming on and we are, like, due to merge with Trinity High's cheerleader team, because, like, we are a small team, right? So we are planning to merge, like, because, then we are a bigger team. Like almost twenty and that's way more, spectacular, like. . . ."

Córdoba agreed. "Seven is a small team. How come you're so small?"

"You need to be real dedicated," said Seenthyia. "Like. Real. Dedicated. You need like—A. Lot. Of. Commitment. Right?"

"Isn't it real expensive too?" K couldn't control himself. "The costumes and everything? They say it can be almost a thousand dollars?"

"Way more," said Seenthyia Breenhauser proudly. "You got to be able to afford it."

"You used to be eight, right?" Córdoba asked.

Seenthyia Breenhauser shrugged. "There was one girl left a while back."

"A while back?"

"Like. . . ." Seenthyia counted on her fingers. "Three weeks back?"

"Three weeks? That's not that long?" enquired Córdoba.

Seenthyia shrugged.

"Three weeks . . . that would have been right in the middle of term?" calculated Córdoba.

"I guess," said Seenthyia.

"Cheerleading's a real special thing," Córdoba said vibrantly. "To be a strong squad, to be really good, you really got to get each other. That's what cheerleading's all about, right? You got to be a crowd leader, you got to be a spirit raiser, you got to be an athlete, you got to be an entertainer, right? You are ambassadors for your schools. . . ."

Seenthyia Breenhauser was drinking in every one of Córdoba's words. Her face lit up with an enthusiastic glow that made her almost bearable. Her eyes were shining, as if gazing to the far horizons and spying there a Shangri La. She nodded vigorously. "Ambassadors. . . !" she said.

"It must have been real difficult to lose a team buddy," Córdoba said.

Seenthyia, still starry eyed, shook her head. "Not really," she said.

"No," said Córdoba softly, in a tone that was somewhere between statement and question.

"No," confirmed Seenthyia. "Not everyone fits in, you know? You gotta fit in, like . . . because of the—" She furrowed her brow. "Team dynamics," she issued, and looked at Córdoba as if she'd just split the atom.

191

Córdoba nodded: "Team dynamics," she repeated. "There's a whole science behind it, huh?"

"Yeah! It really is . . . like . . . you know. . . ." Seenthyia had found a new best friend.

"So now the squad's running better? The team dynamics have improved?" asked Córdoba.

Seenthyia looked confused.

"When LaRaina left the team," Córdoba said. "Did the team change?"

"You really got to fit in, you know. You gotta integrate. You gotta want to integrate," Seenthyia explained. "My mom says they don't really want to integrate. They don't really want to make the effort."

"Whose decision was it for LaRaina to leave?" asked Córdoba. "Was it the team's decision?"

"Like . . . we talked to each other and then we went to Coach Hansen, and I guess he told her," Seenthyia shrugged. "And she left."

The poor kid really wasn't the sharpest tool in the box. Lucky she at least had her pernickety name to lend her some gravitas. She hadn't registered the significance of Córdoba knowing the gone cheerleader's name. Maybe she thought all cops were omniscient.

"Was LaRaina friends with Luisa?"

"Luisa?" asked Seenthyia.

"Luisa Alvarez," said Córdoba.

"I don't know. Maybe," said Seenthyia. "What's that got to do with. . . ?"

"Luisa disappeared," said Córdoba. "You know that Luisa disappeared?"

"Sure," said Seenthyia. "Most everyone knows."

"LaRaina and Luisa?" Córdoba repeated.

"They were kind of friendly, I guess. LaRaina was kind of mad at. . . ." She stopped and bit her lip.

"At you?" Córdoba asked, her voice razor-sharp.

"No, no. Not me," stammered Seenthyia.

Juanita Córdoba's eyes were coal black and ice cold.

"No," pleaded Seenthyia. "I didn't ever have anything going on with her really. I mean I didn't really know her. I didn't mind her. She didn't bug me. At all. Really. We were just like . . . different people, right?"

Córdoba fixed her with a basilisk glare.

"Somebody was mean to Luisa and LaRaina got mad at you? That it?"

"She didn't get mad at me . . . I mean she didn't get mad at me especially . . . just all of us I guess . . . she thought it was all of us. . . ." Seenthyia stammered.

"Was it or wasn't it all of you? You are a team, right? Team dynamics? One acts mean and y'all pile on and run along? That what happened?" Córdoba's voice was cold with contempt.

Seenthyia shrugged helplessly. Her lower lip trembled. Just a couple of minutes ago K would not have thought it possible that he'd end up feeling sorry for her.

The girl's eyes swam with rising tears. K busied himself watching the slow progress of a small black beetle wobbling along the edge of the wall.

"I didn't like it really," Seenthyia whispered. "I didn't think it was right either. She wasn't a person that got in anybody's way . . . you know? She was just quiet, like, she kept herself to herself. . . ."

The use of the past tense in reference to Luisa was beginning to creep K out.

"But everyone else thought it was okay to bully Luisa? Everyone, except La Raina and you?" Córdoba's tone had softened somewhat.

"Not everyone. . . ," said Seenthyia. She frowned and made a counting motion with her fingers. What she counted seemed to surprise her. "Most everyone did not like it," she confided.

"But it felt as if most everyone did?" asked Córdoba.

"Yes," said Seenthyia. She looked bewildered.

"Group dynamics," said Córdoba. "They can be weird."

Seenthyia nodded.

"So somebody minded Luisa and pulled you all along?"

Seenthyia chewed her lip.

"Must be a real strong person to have that much of a hold on y'all," said Córdoba contemptuously.

"I got my own mind!" Seenthyia said defiantly.

Córdoba arched a brow.

"I do!" Seenthyia insisted.

"Tell me about it," Córdoba said.

K thought her phrasing a trifle ambiguous.

Seenthyia chewed her lip.

"Tell me," said Córdoba.

Seenthyia raised a hand to her mouth. For a moment K thought she was going to start sucking her thumb, surely an admission of guilt if there ever was one. The girl fastened her front teeth around a hangnail and began tearing at it.

"I thought you have your own mind?" asked Córdoba.

The girl's eyes darted from side to side. Her teeth worried the hangnail.

"If you realize you've been doing wrong and continue doing it, that's about ten times worse than doing something wrong because you are not realizing it's wrong," Córdoba said. "This is your chance to put some things right. Luisa's disappeared. How will you feel if something bad has happened to her?"

Seenthyia's teeth tore at her thumb. The hangnail gave.

"Tell me," Córdoba said.

"I didn't mind Luisa," the girl said.

"You say you didn't," said Córdoba.

"What?" said the girl.

"You said you didn't mind Luisa," Córdoba said.

"I didn't," said Seenthyia.

"Why use the past tense?"

"What?"

"You said 'I didn't mind Luisa,' not: 'I don't mind Luisa,'" Córdoba said. "Do you think something happened to Luisa? Do you think Luisa is dead?"

"Dead?" the cheerleader asked hoarsely. "Dead?" Her voice had a hysterical edge to it.

"She's been gone for a pretty long time now. One thing everybody that knows her agrees on is that her disappearance is pretty much completely out of character. I think it's time we got worried. Real worried."

The girl whimpered.

"Is there something you need to tell us?"

"I don't know. I don't know. I don't know anything," Seenthyia sobbed. She drew her legs to her chin and buried her head between her knees. Tears rolled down her shins and dripped to the floor. They watched in silence.

Eventually Córdoba sighed and reached into her pocket. "If you do remember something, if you hear anything, I want you to call us, Seenthyia. You did wrong. You went along with some real bad behavior. But you can still make it right. Okay? Just think of Luisa's folks. How they are feeling right now."

Seenthyia bit her lip and took Córdoba's card. The girl's face was a mess of red welts and streaked mascara.

Córdoba got up, walked across the office and flung open a door K had not even noticed was there. The door led to the back of the parking lot.

"Go straight home. Don't hang about. That way you can help us help Luisa, okay?"

Seenthyia nodded.

They watched her walk unsteadily to a bashed-up Ford pick-up, hoist herself into it and drive off.

Córdoba closed the door.

"Next!" she said.

•   •   •   •

Ava Byrone entered the room showing none of the defiance or defensiveness that Seenthyia Breenhauser had displayed. She wore a glaze of self-possessed cool that would be hard to shatter.

Ava demanded to know what had taken them so long. Was every interview going to take that much time? She had stuff to do. Like: important stuff.

Córdoba said that "the first girl" was long gone, something had come up that they had to sort out in between, apologies for the wait.

Ava Byrone noted the apology. They were dealing with someone primed to gauge nuances in behavior; adept in noting others' weaknesses; expert in computing micro-behavioral minutiae into socio-metric ranking.

What could she tell them about Luisa Alvarez?

Not a lot. In fact Luisa Alvarez was pretty much entirely unknown to Ava—this was a big school with many different groups; Ava was incredibly busy with school work and the cheerleading squad; there wasn't anything she could tell them that would be useful for understanding Luisa's disappearance. Maybe Luisa had gone away and was staying somewhere in a cabin, studying? She had jumped a grade after all. That took a lot of studying. Anyways, there wasn't much to say as Luisa Alvarez had pretty much kept herself to herself. Though, and now Ava allowed herself a tiny smile, didn't they say still waters ran deep? Maybe Luisa had a secret life? She looked at Córdoba meaningfully.

Córdoba fluttered a hand in a "whatever" gesture.

Ava noted the gesture and was not pleased. She regarded Córdoba with undisguised antipathy. Had they talked to Luisa's friend—that boy with the weird name? she wanted to know.

Córdoba distractedly glanced at her watch and idly aligned a stack of flyers at precise right angles.

The Hispanic boy? Ava said, her voice rising sharply. Had they talked to that guy Cuauhtémoc? That boy that hung around Luisa—maybe he could tell them something? The Mexican guy. They really should talk to him. There was something about him that was weird. Maybe he was trying to avoid them because he was afraid? Could be there was some problem with his papers. Maybe . . . maybe Luisa's disappearance had something to do with Cuauhtémoc's papers?

Córdoba checked her watch again, suppressed a yawn, slapped her palm on the desk, and said "thank you."

Ava Byrone's eyes narrowed. Córdoba pointed her chin at the door to the sports hall and turned her attention to aligning the next pile of leaflets before her.

Ava shook her head incredulously, paused at the door and looked back at Córdoba, who was absently leafing through one of Coach Hansen's *The Cheerleaders' Drill Thrill* 'zines.

Ava Byrone tossed her head and strutted off.

"What was that all about?" asked K.

"We'll see," said Córdoba.

• • • •

Like Seenthyia Breenhauser, the next cheerleaders on their list, Ashleigh Curtis and Destiny Drake, were obviously foot soldiers, not leaders. It was almost shocking how transparently teenagers wore their status. K wondered if Seenthyia, Ashleigh and Destiny guessed how quickly they'd been weighed and judged as inconsequential.

Unlike Seenthyia Breenhauser, however, Ashleigh and Destiny's bland obstinacy could not be swayed or shaken. Each girl gave them a cookie-cutter spiel about the degree of dedication demanded of cheerleaders and the consequent lack of time this left for anything that wasn't cheerleading. So uniform were their answers that K decided they had to be either rehearsed or regurgitated renditions of Coach Hansen's motivational cheerleader speech. All the girls agreed that with their boundless, ceaseless, relentless dedication to the awesome cause of cheerleading there was no time to get to know, socialize with, never mind make friends with, anybody not belonging to the set.

Córdoba gave each girl a perfunctory couple of minutes' attention, then sent them away via the parking lot exit. After dismissing Ashleigh, Córdoba decreed they should wait ten minutes before calling the next girl in.

"Why?" inquired K, who wasn't too keen on stretching out the sorry task.

"The longer we make them wait, the more antsy they're going to get," Córdoba said.

After Destiny Drake left, Córdoba made them wait a full seventeen minutes.

"Why seventeen?" asked K.

"Because it makes us unpredictable," Córdoba said.

"Why not seven?" suggested K. The afternoon was stretching like chewing gum and he'd had as much as he could stomach of this vicious, vacuous bunch.

"I want the next one to sweat," said Córdoba.

Chelsea Easton took a seat and crossed long, smooth legs. Her eyes were of a peculiarly light blue that reminded K of the photos Victorians took of the dead, in which they were positioned, festively attired, seated in chairs as if alive. The only way one could tell that these photographs were of dead people was by their strangely pallid irises, the absence of reflection of light therein.

K didn't think Córdoba's strategically apportioned total of nineteen and a half minutes' wait had had the desired effect on this girl.

Chelsea kept her pale eyes fixed on Córdoba, who ran through her intro shtick as if being slightly bored—no, as if definitely bored. Whilst speaking she looked listlessly at a piece of paper, shoved it under a used coffee mug, stifled a yawn and surreptitiously glanced at her watch.

Having finished what she had to say—K assumed that it was what she had said to all the others who had come before, though at some point he had switched off, so contagious had been Córdoba's demonstration of boredom—Córdoba lifted her shoulders and spread her arms in a "whatever" gesture.

All that was lacking in this congenially sanguine tableau was Córdoba starting to file her nails while whistling Dixie.

Chelsea untangled her lissome limbs and crossed her legs the other way. Córdoba leant back in her chair and looked at Chelsea Easton as if trying to recall a recipe for flaky pie crust.

By now an internal conflict had begun to erode Chelsea Easton's studied indifference. There was certainly some relief at not being put through the mill, but also a considerable degree of the piqued narcissism of a teenager who had primed herself for her ten or nineteen minutes of notoriety.

"Anything you can tell us?" Córdoba droned.

Chelsea Easton opened her mouth.

"About Luisa," Córdoba added.

Chelsea Easton closed her mouth.

"No?" said Córdoba.

Chelsea stayed silent. Her eyes were hostile.

"No?" asked Córdoba.

The girl did not speak.

"Okay," said Córdoba, "You can go." She pointed not to the exit door, but to the door leading to the sports hall.

"How many have we got left?" she asked K before Chelsea had even reached the door. "Just two? Oh good."

The door clicked shut.

Córdoba glanced at her watch. "Let's give them a couple of minutes' hand-over time."

•　　•　　•　　•

Taylor Easton walked, nay, strutted in, sat down and crossed her legs much in the same manner as her twin had done. Cool and composed and with a palpable aura of contemptuous entitlement.

Córdoba's ennui seemed to have transformed itself in some indefinable way into sensual indolence. She had one arm draped over the back of her chair, her wrist dangling languidly; her splendid breasts were accentuated by her pose thrusting against her starched white cotton shirt; on her lips played the subtlest of mocking smiles.

Taylor Easton mustered Córdoba with cold eyes.

With Córdoba in siesta mode K did his robo-cop version of the preliminaries—Luisa Alvarez—disappearance—routine procedure—blah-blah-blah.

The girl shrugged golden shoulders.

"Luisa Alvarez? I don't really know her," she said.

"Her family is very worried," K said.

Taylor Easton shrugged again. "Like I said: I don't know her."

"Luisa's top of your class?" K asked.

K didn't think that his lame questions would get them anywhere, but with Córdoba languidly lounging in her chair like a Cheetah basking in the sun, he had better do something. "She's a very good student, your teacher told us."

Taylor raised her head. She smiled contemptuously, cold blue eyes holding K's.

"I'm sure she's a very good girl," Taylor said meaningfully. "A very, very good girl."

"Where do you think she might have gone?" asked K, ignoring the sarcasm.

Taylor stifled a yawn. "I don't know her. She's in my grade, that's all."

She uncrossed her legs and seemed ready to get up and leave.

Córdoba's voice, dripping honey and promise, filled the room. "Maribel Alvarez, Luisa's sister, you know her?"

Taylor's sneer froze.

"Maribel Alvarez, she works for XOX?"

The girl's eyes seemed to leach color; pinprick pupils fixed on Juanita Córdoba.

"Maribel—she works for Mr. Easton?" Córdoba repeated.

The girl's body tensed. Her eyes became slits.

"Maribel Alvarez. She works for your daddy?" Córdoba asked sweetly. Her voice seemed to have taken on a South of the Border timbre.

Taylor Easton's eyes charged with an electric light. Primal fury oozed out of every pore. Her voice was sharp as a whip. "That wetback whore."

Córdoba parted her luscious lips. "Pardon?" she said.

The girl paused. Her eyes bore into Córdoba's.

"Wetback whore," she enunciated carefully.

Córdoba's indolent smile lingered. "Thank you," she said huskily.

The girl looked fixedly at Córdoba.

"We are all done," Córdoba said, widening her smile.

Taylor Easton remained seated, staring at Córdoba in a way that began to worry K.

"Time's up," he said and pushed back his seat. He tapped on Taylor's shoulder.

The girl slowly rose from the chair.

K led her to the parking lot exit and opened the door. Taylor Easton stalked past. In the doorway she turned and looked back at Córdoba with a depth of hatred that made K want to get into his bullet-proof vest.

CHAPTER TWENTY-THREE

K wandered the corridors of Milagro PD like a ghost in search of a medium. Their concluding interview had been with Daner Hansen, who, in terms of attitude toward his nubile charges, walked a fine line between motivational vocation and salacious self-gratification.

Apart from the somewhat perturbing evidence of Daner's questionable outlook on females in general and cheerleaders in particular, they hadn't gotten much from the coach.

As to LaRaina Cuthair quitting: sadly, La Raina hadn't been a fit for the team. This happened from time to time. It was very important that the team gelled, because everyone needed to rely on each other—like 200 percent.

"Do you mean to say they cannot rely on each other at all?" K had asked. Hyperbole asserting itself via fictitious percentage conjecture was one of his many pet-hates and one trivial enough to call out pronto, as it occurred. Nevertheless he felt Córdoba's elbow digging into his ribs—a not altogether unpleasant sensation.

If K had looked forward to a debriefing and further analysis of what just had happened, had perhaps even hoped to find out what lay behind Córdoba's cryptic interviewing strategy, he had been disappointed. They had barely set foot in the station when Córdoba got called out to a domestic crisis situation.

"What now?" K called after her. She turned on her heels and hurried out, pulling on her shoulder holster.

"Later," she promised and was gone.

Gutierrez was nowhere to be seen; Becky's work station lay empty and deserted—and the sheriff wouldn't want to know anyway.

Córdoba's cheerleader interrogation had thrown up at least as many questions as it answered, and her technique had been as masterful as it was confounding, and now there was nobody to mull it over with.

When K spied Young and Dilger, returning from yet another Marshal Plan mission, climbing the stairs to the station in the peculiar, bow-legged manner of those whose pants sat too tight on their scrotums, K decided it was time to make like a banana and split.

•　　•　　•　　•

"Back for some poppers?" Magnusson called cheerfully.

"You need to change the dish-towel from time to time," K suggested ungraciously.

Magnusson looked at the smudged and streaky glasses he was drying. "You think so?"

"You need to hold them up against the light to see the smudges."

Magnusson held a wine-glass toward the light. "I see what you mean. Neat! I didn't know that."

If someone so imminently unsuited to his trade as Magnusson was to bar-tending could survive and even thrive, there was hope for every damn body.

"I just wanted to show you this."

"*Lacandon Dream Symbolism.* So you really are doing your homework, eh?"

"It seems I really am." K had just remembered the dream that had awoken him in the middle of the night. "I'm even dreaming."

"Interesting dreams?" Magnusson set a mug of coffee in front of K that in terms of aroma damn near challenged the sheriff's rank brew. K muttered his thanks, took a sip and worked on controlling his facial muscles.

"Weird dreams."

"Come on then," said Magnusson.

"I was walking with this old man. A very old man. He was wearing a white robe—like a hermit or a Greek philosopher. And he seemed very fragile. Pale. Unsteady on his feet. I had to help him along and he kept saying he needed to relieve himself. And there was no bathroom anywhere, we were walking through—I think it was a forest. Then we got to a bathroom and there was a long line of people waiting. All the while he is complaining and I am getting worried that he is going to have an accident, and I'm a bit annoyed with him too. When it is our turn I take him into the bathroom and it's this big room, almost a hall, with grey concrete walls and in the middle is a round basin, actually it's like a huge well, with a concrete knee-high wall running around it and this body of water is really deep—sixty feet deep or so. The water is clear and very deep, but my old man, he insists that is the toilet and he gets ready to squat on the wall and relieve himself into that clear water. And I am in a complete panic. What am I supposed to do? How am I supposed to clean up after him? The whole well is going to be contaminated, and then I see at the other end of the hall a whole busload of—I think they were young people—and they were disabled, and they were going to swim in that water—there was a channel or a river leading to the basin—and they are getting in, one by one, and they all look- contemplative, reverential, as one by one they get into the water. I see them swimming under water and—I woke up."

"Do you often dream like this?"

"Not like this. This one's a new one," said K. "This one seems like it is trying to tell me something, but I have no idea what that could be. Don't worry, I'm not going to ask you to interpret."

"It is a weird dream," Magnusson agreed. He leafed through *Lacandon Dream Dictionary*. "I wouldn't mind borrowing this. Where did you get it?"

"Agnes Prohaska's, where else?"

Magnusson shook his head. "That's one great bookstore. Do you know when I moved here, I almost bought that store?"

"You almost bought the bookstore?" K asked.

"Yeah, Agnes was fixing to sell it—and then she changed her mind," said Magnusson. "Why are you pulling that face?"

K shrugged. "Just can't imagine Agnes Prohaska wanting to sell her store."

"Ever since that time Agnes and I have been friends. We talk, you know?" Magnusson said. "We talk, Franz. Agnes told me that she offered you to take over the bookshop."

K's cheeks burned. He heaped sugar into his mug, stirred furiously and took a gulp of the tooth-shatteringly sweet concoction.

"Stop behaving like a kid that's been caught doing something wrong."

"Do you still want the bookstore?" K croaked.

"No," Magnusson said. "I'm okay with what I got here. Agnes knows that. What about you?"

It took draining the entire mug of coffee for K to regain a state approximating composure.

"I'm not usually a liar."

"You aren't one now," Magnusson said. "You really have to stop inflating your minor glitches to major moral failings. You got to stop beating yourself up, Franz."

"So you and Agnes talked about her wanting to give up the bookshop?"

"Agnes thinks you and the bookshop would be a good fit. Think about it. By the way—we're both real proud of you."

"Proud?" Besides Prohaska not being the kind of person to cultivate pride for herself or others, K could not think of a reason that would unite Magnusson and Prohaska in feeling proud of him.

Magnusson slapped down a copy of the Milagro Gazette.

"You made Page One! Look at that headline: '"I Have a Dream" Milagro Police Officer Galvanizes Teachers to Resist Marshal Plan.' Pretty impressive."

"Oh God," groaned K.

"What now?" There was an edge to Magnusson's voice.

"It was just something I said—a spur of the moment thing. Dilger made me talk to those teachers and I hadn't prepared anything."

"You don't like what you said?"

"I don't like that I used Dr Martin Luther King to make a trivial point. These are revolutionary phrases. We should save them for when we really need them."

"I wouldn't say a call to educating children wisely and peacefully is making a trivial point. Agnes told me she's already had some teachers in her store, looking for books and debating active resistance, just like in the old days. That's not a bad result for a made-up speech, is it?"

"My successes, for all they are worth, are mostly unintended."

Magnusson laughed. "Well, keep on going—without intention, if need be. Don't forget your newspaper!"

CHAPTER TWENTY-FOUR

"That'll get you a load of hate mail," said Begay, folding the newspaper.

"You think so?" That there could be consequences to his rabble-rousing speech hadn't occurred to K.

"Maybe even worse," said Begay darkly. "You are lucky I'm here to look out for you."

"Who'd be interested in a little speech to some teachers?"

"Practically all the people you don't want to be," said Begay. "Anytime anybody says something about guns, that's not totally about how guns make us all free and keep the world a place for the good guys, the NRA becomes the least of your problems. There's bunches of crazoids that even the NRA doesn't rate. Vigilantes that like to take the law into their own hands. All these guys sitting in the boonies off the grid trying to clone Hitler from a shoelace—those are the folks you gotta worry about."

"Those aren't going to read newspapers," K said hopefully.

"You better prepare yourself for some trolling, is all I'm saying."

"Well unless they roll up here, there's not a lot of ways of getting at me."

The general unpleasantness conjured by Begay's warnings brought to mind the cheerleader interviews. "Hey, fancy doing some online sleuthing?"

"Legit?" asked Begay.

"I didn't know you are bothered. Besides, I don't know what you are allowed to do and what you are not allowed to do. I just want to get an impression of what these girls are really like. And how they operate. Is there a way of doing that?"

"So you just want to snoop on them? How come you're interested in what goes on in social media all of a sudden?" Begay had started to fiddle with his wonder-machine. "Where do you want to start?"

"How should I know? I don't even know what I am asking you to do."

"You just fancy a little recce round their social media to see what they are like?"

"I suppose so."

"Who's the weakest link, would you say?"

"The weakest link? What a terrible question."

"Don't go all moralistic on me. It was your idea. Besides we aren't going to do anything bad. We're just going to get an invite to the party and see what's going on. I need somebody that's kinda easy to impress, and eager to make friends, and insecure. You got anybody?"

"I suppose . . . you could try Seenthyia Breenhauser," K said. "Is there a risk she'll rumble you?"

"It ain't me, it's Tiffany." said Begay.

Tiffany, it seemed, had a long and successful track record of cyber-communication with drug cartels, pedophiles, money-launderers, meth-cookers, an impressively comprehensive, eat-your-heart-out rogues' gallery of social menaces.

"How come you never mentioned Tiffany?" K felt like Alice in Wonderland, falling into a hole and emerging in an entirely different world he'd never suspected existed.

"I don't feel I owe Redwater anymore," said Begay. "I don't mind who knows what they are doing over there. Anyways—they are all up to their necks in dirty deals, so I don't care."

Begay sounded just as disillusioned as himself. K felt a mixture of relief and sorrow, which, coming to think of it, might be his default state.

"Are you burning your bridges?"

"What bridges?" said Begay. "There ain't none."

"Maybe we should get together and open a PI agency?" suggested K. "Bumble and Co?"

"Bumble? Bumble-be-you. With Robbie Begay they get the best there is. I'll do the sleuthing and you can make the coffee and sit in a corner with your pussycat on your lap like Blofeld. Yep—I can see that working. Anyways—should Tiffany make friends with just this cheerleader buddy here? How about we send out a bunch of requests to all of them? You got their names?"

K consulted his list. "Seenthyia Breenhauser, Ava Byrone, Ashleigh Curtis, Destiny Drake, Chelsea Easton, Taylor Easton, Madison Zinzendorf."

Begay typed rapidly. "Just sending out some friend requests and then we sit back and wait 'til we get a response. It's a good time now, downtime, plenty of time to check your notifications and make some new friends. How about you get me a beer?"

•　•　•　•

Begay was staring at his phone like a raptor watching a burrow.

K was on his second beer. He felt relaxed and sleepy.

"These kids ain't playin' ball," Begay muttered.

"Friendships take time," K said woozily.

Begay shook his head. "Dude! Where have you been?! With teenagers friend requests are like boomerangs—you barely get them out and caboom! They are returned."

"It can't be that easy?" asked K.

"It surely can," said Begay. "It's the numbers that count, see? Whatever media you're using, you want to max out on the number of friends or followers or whatever there is. How d'ya think these folks get to three thousand friends, five thousand friends? It don't pay to be choosy."

"But what do you do with five thousand friends? How do you keep track?"

"It's not so much about keeping track of them. You're hoping they keep track of you and give you loads of likes."

"But what for? What do you do with the likes?"

"You count up how many people rate you," Begay said.

"A short circuit for narcissists," said K, picturing ever-expanding circles of navel gazers laboring under the illusion that whatever they did was of interest to others, while all that was of interest to others was their potential of being interested in them.

It was a peculiar type of stale hell, and one that K did not understand at all.

"The fact that none of your cheerleaders has answered Tiffany's request—could be we got ourselves a clue," said Begay. "Usually with kids it don't take more than a couple of minutes until your request is returned. They don't care who you are. That's why it's so easy for those pedos to groom kids—it's just no hassle at all to get into a cyber relationship with a young person. But none of your gals has answered yet—and it's been more than an hour already. So I gotta ask myself: why ain't nobody interested in being my friend?"

"Why?" asked K obediently, though it seemed far more plausible to him that a body would choose NOT to answer a friend request than that they would. Why the hell would anyone?

"Coz they are being cautious. Why are they being cautious?"

"Because they are more sensible than I gave them credit for?" K said.

"Unlikely," Begay said. "C'mon, Sherlock! Work those little grey cells!"

"Not a fucking clue. Why don't you just get on with it and tell me before the suspense knocks me cold?"

"I just told you. They got something to hide. If you put your mind to it, there's barely any info on anybody that doesn't jump right out at you in a nano-second. Nowadays it's harder to *avoid* knowing things about people than knowing everything about them.

For everything that's not out there, you betcha folks have taken darn trouble to hide. You still not getting it?"

K put some effort into masking his uncomprehending mind by a keenly appreciative expression. "Sure I am!"

"All you need to get is: there's a reason that there's nothing. If there's no tracks, that's a track in itself. No tracks? Could be that the mountain lion is crouching on that tree right on top of you, watching."

"How did the mountain lion get up that tree?"

"Everything's a clue. That's all you need to understand. Now . . . I just need one. I need just one body to accept Tiffany as a friend. How come nobody's interested? C'mon, lil' mousey, c'mon. . . . Is there anybody else we can try? We got to get in there somehow."

Begay's being mad keen on bagging some cheerleaders, K guessed, had more to do with some atavistic hunter's instinct than his commitment to the issue at hand. It was likely an alternative to playing those games with the gnomes and dragons and magick swords that K didn't get either.

"Dilger's just got his nephew working at the station as an intern. The kid's supposed to be some kind of wiz at computer stuff. Dilger's the one who dredged up Luisa's profile. I think the guy went to same school as Luisa and the cheerleaders. The guy's a football player, so could be he knows these girls?"

"What's that jock's name?"

"The intern? I don't know. I just know he's Dilger's nephew. I call him the Odious Intern."

Begay was back on his cell. Screens made for short attention spans.

"Hunter Denning," said Begay.

"What?" said K.

"Hunter Denning, Your jock. That's his name. Graduated MMHS a year ago. Coaches the junior football team," Begay scrolled down the screen, soundlessly lip-reading his way through whatever there was. "One hell of an all-rounder. Great guy. I'm surprised he ain't over there at one of those ivy-schools on a full scholarship. Boy, y'all should be grateful to have him, ya hear?"

"Where did you get all this?" asked K.

"You really are remedial! It's right here, on your Milagro PD website."

"He's already on the website? He's barely started. Gosh. He does have a lot of teeth, doesn't he?" said K, looking at the Odious Intern's exposed ivories.

"You ain't gonna forget that smile in a hurry," said Begay. "Look at this one too—"

It took K a beat to recognize himself, set jaw, haunted eyes and hair that had obviously been hastily finger combed.

"Ugh, where did they get that?"

"Probably from your file. I bet they asked you to update your profile for their website and you didn't, huh?"

"Can't remember," said K. "I probably didn't understand what they meant."

"So now you got basically no profile—just the year you started at Milagro PD and your name- that's all they got on you. Look at your jock. Half your age. THAT's a profile!"

"Not half my age," protested K.

"Damn near half your age," said Begay. "Your high-flying jock ain't gonna be some dead-beat cop in some dead-beat town. No Siree. You want to know how it's done? That's the way: Four thousand eight hundred and seventy-seven friends and now Tiffany's one of them."

"You're already in there?" asked K.

"Yessir!" gloated Begay. "Now we are going to make friends. Tiffany's going to put herself out there. Let's see. . . ." Begay scrolled, squinted, scrolled. "That guy's your lost twin. He's your wotsit—alter ego. He practically digs everything you don't. Look here: Family cookout. Big plate with a nice big steak, rare. Don'tcha dig how the blood's running into the sour cream? Attaboy. And here. Look what he's posted:

If Guns Kill People
I guess PENCILLS misspell words
CARS drive drunk
& SPOONS make people fat.'
D'ya think it was him or his pencil that spelled 'pencil' wrong? Anyways, he posts this right after that school shooting. Great guy. That dude knows how the world rolls. One hundred twenty-seven likes. Shall I like that? Uh . . . no. I need to keep Tiffany neutral— she needs to get on with everyone, not just NRA jocks. So . . . let me see—what am I gonna like? It needs to be recent. . . . There's about a million photos there. That dude sure rates himself. And he's showing most of his teeth in most all of 'em."

"Evolutionary speaking grins are grimaces of fear. It's how primates avoided fights. You show your teeth. The other ape knows you are afraid."

"And doesn't want to pick a fight with a pussy?" asked Begay.

"I suppose so," said K.

"I don't buy that," said Begay. "In my experience people especially like to pick fights with pussies. It's less hassle. And you got yourself a better chance to win."

Begay went back to scrutinizing the screen. "I kind of lost my mojo here—How come you always do that to me? I'm minding my business and know where I'm going and then you throw some stuff at me. . . . And now I'm having to think about smiling being about fear. We Diné smile a lot. Does that mean we are afraid? Don't bother answering. Better tell me: What does Tiffany dig?"

"How should I know?" protested K. "I don't know her."

"I just told you: Tiffany needs to comment on something she likes. That's the way you catch friends—with compliments."

"Catch friends," mused K. "How about this one?" He pointed at a photo where the Odious Intern, glistening with sweat, was mopping his brow with the hem of his singlet, thereby exposing a well-oiled set of abs.

Begay raised his brows. "You sure you're straight?"

K shrugged. "I can promise you that whatever I am, or am gonna be, I won't be going for his type. But I got an intuition that Tiffany really digs him."

"He sure got a lot of likes here," Begay agreed. "Tiffany likes this. Maybe Tiffany should make a comment? Yep—Tiffany will make a comment: '*OOOOOhhhh, abs to die for and your teeth are soooooo white.*' Hey! Franz! Whaddaya think?"

"Sounds really annoying," said K. "As if she's appraising a horse or something. Just say something simple. Something that suits a short attention span. How about: 'Dreamboat!' And then you put some hearts after it, or whatever."

"I think you know more than you say," said Begay, "or you understand more than you think."

Somehow watching somebody being busy with a screen was more boring than just watching someone doing nothing, or watching someone reading, or watching someone watching paint dry. To make things worse, K's beer supply was running dry.

"Oho!" Begay wagged his finger. "Right away we got ourselves some boundary issues. Look at that! This here's all comments on your jock's fab abs. Of course it's only chicks—laydeez-—that comment, coz' the jock probably isn't that much into gay compliments, dig?"

"I would have thought that oily ab thing is at the very least crypto homosexual. And we know what Freud said about guns."

Begay groaned. "Anyways, here we got a whole bunch of your cheerleaders commenting on his abs. You can even kind of tell their personalities from how they comment."

K squinted at the comments. "Yikes! They don't pull their punches do they?"

"That's coz they're after pulling something else," said Begay distractedly.

"Pretty confident for such young people."

"Yeah?" snorted Begay. "What did you do? Draw up in a horse carriage with a bunch of roses?"

"We drank and smoked until inhibitions vanished or we passed out."

"Sounds great," said Begay.

"It was okay," said K. "What about you?"

"We were busy trying to find someone that wasn't related to us. Believe me, that took a whole lot of work and travel. Turns out all the cutest girls were clan-related. Nowadays there's hardly anybody who is bothered about fooling around with their relatives. That's why we are in such a mess."

K handed Begay's phone back with a shudder. "You don't call this a mess?"

"Not my business. Besides I don't mind what happens to Anglos. They got enough sins to pay for. Anyways—this was just a little recce. Leastways we found out that your jock knows your cheerleaders, so he shouldn't be dealing with their social media in an official capacity."

"Great," said K. "One more headache."

"Let's just see what we can do here," said Begay.

"I forgot why we started to look at this guy's stuff anyway. Why did we?" asked K.

Begay shrugged. "Because we can. Because you're worried his Uncle wotsisname is gonna push him to working on stuff he shouldn't be because of personal relationships. So that's one thing we know. Whenever you got a mind to, you can spring it on him and see if he still keeps smiling."

"I don't think so," said K, "because we aren't supposed to be looking at this either."

"True," said Begay unimpressed. "So I'll just keep working this connection and see how we go. So here's your gal, Seenthyia, poor kid, must've taken her to fourth grade to learn write her name, awww, she's kind of sweet. Kind of shy, is she?"

K tried to remember. "Yeah, I suppose so. She really did seem like the weakest link and she was the one who was most sorry for how Luisa was treated. Well—she seemed the most sorry."

"Well, she digs the jock. But she's kind of modest about it. Tiffany's just going to like and comment on Seenthyia's profile pic. What should I say?"

"How should I know? She's standing behind all those other kids, I can barely make her out. Just say she's looking great. I don't think you need to qualify."

"Look at the expert," said Begay. "Okay. Done. Now we just sit back and wait and hope that folks want to be friends with Tiffany. Just one friend will get Tiffany in there."

"What's Tiffany like?" asked K. That's where things had gotten to: asking questions on the psyche of fictitious tropes that only existed in cyber-space.

What would his greater namesake, Franz Kafka the writer, have made of virtual reality had he lived in these wretched times? Would Kafka have delivered the ultimate commentary on a reality cannibalized by cyber-fantasma? Would Kafka have come up with an audacious simile for the Zeitgeist, head stuck up its own ass?

More probably, a contemporary Franz Kafka would have vented his frustrations about his soulless insurance assessor's job, general tedium and relentless ennui via posting on forums 24/7.

Auf Wiedersehen: *Metamorphosis*. Servus: *The Trial*. Adieu: *The Castle*.

Hello: Pinned photo of *"Insurance Estimate for Tenement Building Obere Grinzinger Strasse"* defaced by fried egg stain: 847 likes.

"Tiffany: She got something for everyone," eulogized Begay, summoning K's attention away from speculations on Franz Kafka's alternative creative outlet. "She's sweet, but not too sweet; nice but not too nice; she rates others, but she rates herself too, coz it don't count for nothing if you're rated by some sorry body that doesn't rate themselves. She's cute enough that the boys fancy her, but not hot—understand? Coz if she's hot, she'll have all the other hot girls that are almost always bitches—why's that, do you suppose?—after her and they'll hound her and give her hell. She's

216

not too mellow, coz' that's boring, so she's kind of a middle of the road type of gal."

"Pass the sick bucket," said K. "I sincerely hope you are not right and that isn't how it works."

"This is one way you can work it," said Begay. "You can also go about it another way. You can make her the honey pot—or make her super badass so that others want to hang out with her. But if you got notoriety, that don't take you far. Then you got to construct loads of profiles. It's better to just stick to one that doesn't get in anybody's face too much."

The sitting around waiting was starting to get on K's nerves. And Wittgenstein was still schmoozing Begay.

"I think I'm starting to understand something about how they must feel, these kids, waiting for their friend requests to be accepted. It's like drip torture."

Begay nodded. "For us, we'd just go home after school was over and you didn't have to think about all those folks that bothered you until the next day. And you could hang out with your friends and not mind what you said, how you looked, if you behaved like a moron. People forgot, or they didn't notice. You always got another chance."

"I wish I'd known then how good we had it," said K. "As far as I remember it was bad enough then."

"Maybe it's always the same degree of bad, just a different kind of bad," said Begay.

"*Plus ça change, plus c'est la même chose,*" said K.

"Never mind, weirdo," said Begay "I don't need to understand."

"It just means even when things change they remain they same—the more they change, the more they stay the same."

"I don't know if I buy that," said Begay.

"But that's what you just said!" yelped K.

"Bingo!" said Begay. "Tiffany's just landed Seenthyia."

• • • •

While Begay ferreted around in the dysfunctional virtual world of the young-blood hope of this country, K switched from beer to wine.

"Did you know that the Arabs invented the distillation process?" asked K.

"It wasn't the Indians, that's for sure," said Begay, unimpressed.

"They introduced zero too," K said.

"Whoop-dee-do," Begay said.

"How's Tiffany doing?" asked K. "I'm getting bored."

It was not a state he was accustomed to. Usually the ebbs and flows in his headspace kept him busy, but the presence of another body in his territory—a body on a mission at that—was disruptive to his reverie.

Begay groaned. "Tiffany's liking loads of stuff. She's a regular cheering machine, that gal."

Good to know Begay hadn't been completely desensitized to this asinine madness.

"Is our Tiff making any tracks with the cheerleaders?"

"Just Seenthyia—poor kid. She shared some stuff from the hard cheerleaders' core that I'm going through."

"Anything relevant?" asked K.

Begay snorted. "Like I told you, the only tracks I can see is that there's no tracks to see. There's nothing here. That's the only thing that could be something."

"You're losing me," said K.

"Like I told you. You want me to tell you again?"

"Yes, please." said K.

Begay rolled his eyes. "The main clue I got for you is that there's no clue. When you're going through this stuff it usually don't take you that long to find something that's mean or nasty. Some trolling; some bitching; some bullying. SOMETHING, you know? There ain't nothing here. It's all likes and thumbs up and hearts and smiley emojis. . . ."

"Trolling?" asked K. A thought swam to the fore of his beer addled brain and dived away before he could catch up with it."Trolling. . . ," he pondered and gave up. "Maybe these kids are just nice?" he suggested.

"Was that the impression you got?" asked Begay.

"No," said K. "My impression was that there were three bullies to four followers. What about the Eastons? Anything on them?"

"Nothing," said Begay. "Just that their daddy's a hunter. Here he is with a big old elk, right in front of his cabin. Liked and shared by Seenthyia. Did you know Easton's a hunter?"

"I knew he's an asshole," slurred K.

"Easy on your Arab distillation, my friend," said Begay. "How long will it take you to sober up, you reckon?"

"What kind of a question is that?" asked K.

"You just talking about that fracking guy put me in mind of something I saw in your newspaper: There's another one of those uranium impact hearings in Oh So! Valley. All that talk about galvanizing people made me think maybe we should go?"

"Is that the hearing about uranium and cancer?"

"Lung cancer. Bone cancer. Leukemia. Kidney cancer. Ovarian cancer," recited Begay. "All scoring way high in our people. It's not just the ones who worked in the mines. It's the down-winders. It's folks that live near the old mines. It's everyone who drinks the water there. The water is still contaminated after all these years that they closed the mines. And it's going to be contaminated for a thousand years."

"At least they are having a hearing." The darkness in Robbie's voice worried K.

"You want a list of all my relatives that got cancer and died?" asked Begay, "Nothing's going to come of it. I have been to a bunch of those hearings. The government's just holding out until everybody of the old folks they sent to the mines without safety precautions has died of cancer. Case closed. Go get yourself another beer. I'm thinking it's a waste of time going."

"No wonder they're getting away with all their shit." Maybe it was the Arab distillation. Maybe it was the righteous cause. K felt furious. And galvanized. "We are going."

Begay shrugged.

"Don't shrug at me! This is not a matter we can be complacent about. Maybe it's too late for your relatives, but there's Lucky Easton and his fucking XOX that are creating new plaintiffs right at this moment. You should see what they are doing to Quorum. And we're all sitting by, doing nothing. Are we going to wait 'til the cancer rates over there rocket?"

"You gotta wait a few years until enough people are getting cancer," said Begay. "And then it's way too late anyways."

K got up and held a pint glass under the water tap. "At least we'll have tried."

CHAPTER TWENTY-FIVE

The road to Redwater climbed gradually toward a crest before descending to Redwater plain.

The setting sun had painted the far horizon a vivid orange. In the cooling evening air Needle Rock looked so close that every fissure and jagged edge, and its skirt of eroded rubble, stood out as if etched.

As so often, the view of Needle Rock lifted K's mood. Elation being a rare occurrence these days, K turned to Begay to share. Robbie Begay's face, closed and remote, dampened his desire to share his Needle Rock-generated joy. They continued the drive to Redwater in unrelieved silence.

K made a right at the traffic lights, passing the cluster of gas stations, drive-throughs and supermarkets that had sprung up in recent years and had turned Redwater from a backwater Rez hamlet, proud of its one KFC franchise, to a corporate bastion like any other, a transformation that no one but K seemed to regret.

Past Redwater the plain opened, signs of habitation became sparse with solitary trailers dotted here and there, tiny against the overwhelming, surrounding vastness.

"Why is it called 'Oh So! Valley'?" asked K.

Every time he crossed Oh So! Valley K wondered if it had been named by a passing Japanese traveler.

"'Hózhó'," said Begay brusquely.

At the crossroads K drove southwest on a road that skirted a range of volcanic rock sitting on sandstone that had once been sand dunes bordering the sea.

"Those massive changes that created this landscape help putting things into perspective, don't you agree?" said K.

"No," said Begay.

"You don't agree?" asked K. Served him right, asking Begay rhetorical questions. Rhetorical questions never worked on Robbie Begay.

"Fair enough," said K.

"You don't want to hear why I disagree?"

"No, I don't," said K.

The atmosphere hung heavy between them. It had been there all the way from Milagro, and maybe even before that.

"Hey," said K, "What's going on, Robbie?"

Begay shook his head as if trying to shoo off a fly.

"Did I do something?" K asked. It was unlike Robbie Begay to sulk and fester. Usually when Robbie didn't like something he let you know, there and then.

Begay shook his head again.

"The hearing is at the Community Center, right?"

"Where it always is," said Begay.

•   •   •   •

The Oh So! Valley Community Center was a long squat building, painted an earthy brown, with a sheet metal roof. K had trouble finding a parking space amongst all the pickups of various vintages.

Inside the community hall participants were sitting at tables in groups of eight, which gave the gathering an air of a senior citizens' social, except there was no food and most of the attendees looked as if they had long lost their appetites. There were a lot of wheelchairs, crutches and oxygen tanks about.

Begay took a moment to survey the room before setting off, weaving through the tables. K following at a distance, watched

Begay making the rounds, smiling, greeting and shaking hands with the frail congregation.

Begay beckoned K to join him. He radiated good cheer, launched into a detailed description of everyone's particular relations to him, embellishing his spiel with a couple of mildly risqué anecdotes that got one or two elderlies wheezing appreciatively.

Begay chatted, teased, listened, consoled, fizzed and sparkled with affability and conviviality. His gregariousness got the old and ailing folk to perk up somewhat. They nodded, smiled and issued phlegmy affirmations while filling out questionnaires that the federal uranium commission's agents had distributed.

Begay's bonhomie made for a strange contrast to this assembly of the moribund that made K feel like an intruder in God's waiting room.

"Must be ten times I filled out one of these," a wheelchair-bound woman hooked up to an oxygen tank said good naturedly, completing her form while her obstructed airways rattled with every breath.

"Ten times?" asked K.

"They have an inquiry every couple of years," wheezed the woman. "And then they go away."

"What about the results of the enquiries?"

"Sometimes we don't hear. Sometimes they tell us there is no problem."

"They are waiting for us all to die," said a man who did indeed look as if he had not long left on this earth. "Then this problem will be finished."

•   •   •   •

As soon as K turned the key in the ignition Robbie Begay lost his animation. They drove through the dusk-shrouded Oh So! Valley, the valley that now struck K as fraught with toxic menace rather than as the remote idyll that he had admired before.

K knew better than to start a conversation. Not a word was spoken during their eighty-mile drive.

When they arrived at K's home night had fallen and the orchard lay in darkness. Silhouettes of deer moved ghostlike among the trees.

"How about I get us some beers and we sit and watch the deer?" K asked.

When he returned with the cooler containing two six-packs Begay was still staring sightlessly into the darkness beyond the windscreen.

K opened two bottles and handed one to Begay.

Begay took a deep draught and set the bottle on the dashboard.

"Diné are not supposed to drink," he said.

K hadn't noticed that this had ever been a problem for Robbie before.

He dug out the thing that he knew about Diné and drink. "I don't think Diné knew alcohol."

"So?!" said Begay.

"So they wouldn't have had a prohibition against it," said K. "You can't forbid something that you don't know exists."

Begay shook his head. "We are not supposed to take anything or do anything that throws us out of balance."

Why start with beer? thought K. How about starting with those gas-guzzling trucks, or the diabolical internet, or soda pop and factory-farmed meat?

"There's a whole lot of things in modern life that throw us out of balance," K said judiciously. Maybe he was, with advancing age, acquiring the art of diplomacy after all.

"I'm not going to get into your nit-picking with you," said Begay.

K was momentarily stunned by the harshness of this remark.

Begay picked up his bottle and clanked it softly against the side of the dashboard. K tried his best not to let the relentless metronomic clanking get to him. He wound down the window.

The pitch-dark orchard brimmed with sounds: rustling undergrowth, the soft footfall of deer, the rhythm of chewing, the sleep-sodden grunts, croaks and tweets of the shy and secretive creatures that cohabited these grounds unseen and were for now its masters.

Begay clinked his bottle against K's and finished the beer in one long draught.

K opened the cooler and retrieved two more bottles. They drank in silence.

"Łitso," said Begay. "The yellow dirt. They say that in the beginning the Diné were asked to choose between the yellow corn pollen and the yellow dirt. They chose the corn pollen and promised to leave the yellow dirt underground. But they didn't stick to that promise. Maybe everything that is happening now, is happening because we broke that promise."

In the pond the bullfrogs were conferencing. They were loud and not particularly musical.

"We should have kept our promise and left łitso underground," Begay repeated. "Why didn't we keep our promise and go with the corn pollen?"

"Who sent your people to the uranium mines without safety precautions?" said K.

Begay shrugged.

"How come the bílagáana didn't send their own people into the mines?" K asked angrily. "Because they knew damn well how dangerous it was, that's why. They wouldn't have used Anglo miners as long as they could get cheap and dispensable Indian labor to do the dirty work for them."

"We didn't need to go and do their work," insisted Begay.

"They have a way of promising the earth when they're after something. The Diné aren't the only people falling for that. Haven't you seen tonight how they keep their promises?"

Begay clanked his bottle some more. "I got to thinking about this one bílagáana teacher we had, this old hippy that we liked to make fun of, because he was always telling us how wise the traditional beliefs are. He said they are not beliefs, they are empirical knowledge, developed out of centuries of observing all that's going on around them, really learning about it. He wanted us to be proud of being Indians.

"One time he told us this story about that old Hopi who was being bugged by this bílagáana who was probably after doing some mining on Hopi. The bílagáana asked that Hopi what happens if a person digs into the earth with a steel shovel? The Hopis are real strict about their environment.

"The old Hopi dude thought about it and said: "*We don't know what would happen if a person did that. But it would give us a darn good idea what kind of a person he was.*" Why was there was no Diné that said not to do it, when they started mining for uranium? We got strict rules too."

"Neat story about the Hopi," said K.

"Why didn't we stick to our ways like the Hopi did?" Begay insisted.

"Because the Hopi are a small tribe and they've been settled on those mesas for near a millennium. It's easier to come to an agreement if you're small and settled. Besides you had to put up with a lot: The Long Walk. The Livestock Reduction. Remember? You used to tell me about it."

"Did I tell you about Mutton Man too?" asked Begay. "Mutton Man ate some mutton that was contaminated with łitso and it made him develop special powers."

K laughed, a little more heartily perhaps than radioactive Mutton Man warranted. Begay joined in and they cracked open another couple of bottles.

CHAPTER TWENTY-SIX

"How come you're not at work?" Begay asked, looking bleary-eyed and sleep-sodden.

"I'm not on shift today. Maybe Becky forgot that I'm supposed to be back full time. I'm not going to complain. They got another school raid planned for today." K furtively turned over the page of the Milagro Gazette sporting an article on the federal government's announced intention to recommence uranium mining in the region.

"I had some dreams," Begay said.

"What kind of dreams?" K asked.

"Galvanizing ones," Begay said sardonically. "Fancy a road trip? Coz my dreams told me we should have ourselves a drive out there, where your fracking buddy's costing the earth."

•   •   •   •

"I forgot what a great place this is," said Begay.

They were traversing Desolation Valley. "Only a bílagáana could call this place desolate. What were they expecting to find?"

"Gold," said K.

They'd taken a detour looking for wild horses, but none were to be seen.

"Damn, I forgot my horse stick," said Begay. He went into a somewhat longwinded reminiscence about an uncle who might or might not have adopted or set free one or several horses whose pedigree might or might not have gone all the way back to the Spanish conquistadors.

K found it heartening that at least something Hispanic had survived in this heartland of God's Own Anglos, even though the conquistadors had not exactly been pussycats either. Anyways, there were no horses, Iberian or otherwise, to be seen, which was a pity because Begay would badly need something to buoy his mood—in view of what was yet to come.

•　•　•　•

They stood rooted to the spot and stared. Even though K had seen it before—twice—even though he had thought that he was prepared, he still felt the wreckage like a punch to the solar plexus.

Goosewash Wilderness—what had once been Goosewash Wilderness—looked even worse today than it had what now seemed weeks ago, but which was in fact only a few days ago, when it had reduced the mighty Amazon to a snot-nosed kid wailing in anguish. Maybe it was because the uprooted trees and bushes had withered and dried so that everything was now brown in color and skeletal in structure.

All that remained of the resilient and tenacious flora that had survived and thrived here for so long and so valiantly, despite the summers' scorching heat and the winters' bitter cold, were tangled, dead and desiccated roots stretching skyward, like the hands of the massacred on the set of a dystopian movie.

Above them XOX's Great Wall-size promotional billboard winked in the sunshine.

•　•　•　•

"That the tree?" Begay said roughly.

The oak was the only tree, indeed the only growth that still stood rooted, spreading its branches over destruction and decay, looking not unlike one of those more effective war memorials that brought home just to what depths man could sink.

"I don't get why they spared the tree," said K. "It's like they left a reminder of what they destroyed."

Begay shook his head. "Spared the tree? They couldn't get it down with their diggers, that's all."

"They are going to come back for it?" This possibility hadn't occurred to K.

"Sure," said Begay coldly. He walked over to K's truck and rummaged in the loading bed. He returned with a roll of police tape.

"Where did you get that?" K asked.

"Never go anywhere without it," said Begay and began cordoning off the perimeter of the tree.

"Wow," said K. "But is it legal?"

"Is this?" snarled Begay, sweeping an arm over the wasteland that once had been wilderness.

•　　•　　•　　•

"What was she like, when she was—"

"—Awake?" K interrupted.

"When she was awake," said Begay. He was balancing on a tree stump, scanning the hillside.

"Desperate," said K. "Devastated. She just couldn't understand that somebody could do a thing like this. Disrespect nature like that. Revel in destruction."

"That's what she said?"

"What?"

"'Revel in destruction'?"

"I think that's what she meant."

"But did she say it?"

"Not in so many words."

"You want to keep to what she said. Lucky I know the kind of weird way you talk, else you would've put me off the tracks."

"Off the tracks?"

"Like I said. Everything is tracks," said Begay. "Describe her to me again?"

"Tall," said K. "Really tall. Maybe a bare inch shorter than I am. I called her the Amazon—not to her face. It was just a name I gave her. A female warrior, but awkward with it."

"Yeah?" said Begay interestedly. "Awkward?"

"You know these tall kids that you feel all they really want to do is hide? It's bad enough to be self-conscious when you are a kid, but if you are a tall kid. . . . They always remind me of tortoises, the way they draw their heads in as if they wished there was a shell to go back into."

"Don't we all," said Begay. "So you got the impression she wanted to hide?"

K considered. "Yes, I guess so. That's the impression I got. An Amazon who was an awkward kid—not too long ago."

The memory of supporting her weight under the tree, her groaning, the rattling breath, the all-encompassing end-of-the-world panic he had felt then, started to rise.

"Hey," Begay said gently. "Back to reality, shik'is."

K resurfaced. "Leave off reading me, Mr. Allistracks, okay?"

"Okay," said Begay peaceably. "Let's go and have a look at that tree."

He headed off, striding over the torn-up soil and the rootwork of shrubs and the trunks of trees, as if they hadn't just stood eying the devastation united in grief and rage.

"Don't you need to look for tracks?" K called after him.

"Nope," said Begay. He stepped over the cordon and circled the oak tree slowly, scanning every inch of soil and bark, every branch.

"That looks like track reading to me," said K.

"Sure," said Begay.

"That's what I love about experts—they are not accountable to anyone," said K.

"Yep," said Begay amicably. "This is where she hung herself from? And this is where you climbed to get her down?"

K decided not to ask how this was evident.

Begay circled the tree again, stopped and looked over the wasteland down into the valley, then turned and walked up the incline toward the road. K trailed after him.

From the road there was a good view of the oak tree, the wasteland and Quorum Valley.

"See?" said Begay.

"No," said K. It was just as well to preempt the game of "twenty questions" that Begay was sometimes fond of playing.

"Right!" said Begay approvingly. "The only thing that you don't see is the part of the tree she hung herself from. Though you can see that pretty easy from the other side. It's kind of an open vista all round. It's about as open as you can get."

K surveyed the landscape. It truly was a vantage point, affording an uninterrupted panorama of Quorum Valley shimmering in misty sunshine.

Begay stood quite still, moving nothing except his eyes. K was reminded of the Indian Scouts in Westerns he had occasionally watched as a kid.

Begay stepped over the cordon and set off toward the truck.

"That's it?" asked K.

Begay opened the passenger door and hoisted himself into the truck.

"Where to?" asked K.

"Back to where we came from," said Begay.

"Anything you'd like to share, perchance?" asked K.

"Impatience is a bílagáana disease," Begay retorted sagely.

"And long-distance walking is a Diné strength," K responded, not quite as sagely.

"I ain't walking nowhere," Begay said complacently. "You are going to drive us around some in this beautiful valley."

•   •   •   •

Quorum Valley's two main roads, one circular, the other central, should have made for perfectly straightforward negotiation without any risk of getting lost, yet K somehow frequently contrived to do just that. Which might have been one reason he liked—had liked— Quorum Valley so much: it looked simple and yet was fiendishly deceptive.

Begay pointed westward. "Drive slow," he commanded.

Quorum Valley getting about twelve cars' worth of through traffic on a busy day, driving slowly was easy enough to do.

K obediently navigated at a speed suitable for ferrying a frail granny about, the while enjoying Quorum bathed in this peculiar radiance that maybe was due to the altitude, or to the surrounding ochre sandstone cliffs reflecting the sunlight, or to toxin-saturated particles released into the air by XOX.

"Left!" instructed Begay.

They chugged along an ungraded road that dipped and fell in gentle gradients and passed quaint homesteads nestling in the shadows of grand old trees. And so they meandered up and down the Quorum vale, taking lefts, doubling back by taking the next right, without K knowing what they were looking for, why and where.

Majestic weeping willows cast sun-dappled shadows on the gravel road. K was beginning to enjoy his chauffeur role.

Maybe the world was full of alternative career options suiting a clapped-out cop after all. There were worse things than moseying around the alleys and byways of what taken at face value was a paradisal bucolic idyll, if one turned a blind eye to the shadows cast by XOX's billboard spelling out future doom in lurid colors.

"Stop!" Begay said sharply.

The Datsun's brakes squealed like a nest of mice being trodden on.

"Better get those seen to soon," said Begay and hopped out of the truck.

K watched him in the rearview mirror walking along the irrigation ditch in which shallow waters gurgled. Begay jumped over the ditch and disappeared into the shadows of a weeping willow whose branches cascaded all the way down to the water.

In the absence of other distractions K contemplated whether his lack of agency was a curse or a blessing. Then he wondered if Begay was omitting to share his strategy and purpose because he thought K was too dumb to get it, or because he thought K wasn't dumb enough not to have gotten it, or because Begay was doing his own thing whatever that was, or because Begay was so wrapped up in sleuthing that he had forgotten K, or because Begay needed to go for a pee. This brought him to ponder on Americans applying the phrase "using the bathroom" even when speaking of their pets. Odd that a nation so comfortable with consumption and greed should be so coy about bodily functions. Which took him to another pet project: his thesaurus of euphemisms and the dirt they covered up. He was far into a contemplation of the implications of being told to "have a blessed day" in this context, when the truck door wrenched open and Begay hoisted himself into the passenger seat.

"Where does Sir wish to be driven to now?" K asked in his best posh retainer voice.

From Sir there came nothing. Eventually the silence became conspicuous.

K turned to look at Begay. "Hey!" he said. "Where—"

Begay was holding between thumb and index finger the straps of a bag woven from sisal or jute, with horizontal stripes in muted natural colors—ochre, brown, beige and dark red. The bag's rounded base was caked in dried mud that was peeling off in places, leaving flakes of mud on the truck's floor and passenger seat.

"What do you think this is?"

"A bag?" said K.

"Let's just open it, huh?" said Begay. He angled for the copy of the Milagro Gazette on the dashboard, spread it over his knees and started fiddling with the bag's zipper. "Darn, I can hardly get it to open. You want to have a go?"

The bag's straps were leather and felt brittle. "Vintage bag?" asked K. He straightened the rim of the bag with one hand while pulling the zipper with the other. The zip was missing teeth, which didn't make things any easier. "Here." He handed the bag back to Begay.

Begay sank his hand into the bag like a magician expecting to produce a rabbit. He drew out an embroidered handkerchief. "Who uses those?"

Then came a small fabric pouch.

"What's this? There's something solid in there."

The pouch housed a set of foldable cutlery: knife, fork and spoon of the kind that people used to take along on picnics and travels before plastic cutlery became ubiquitous. "Who uses that?" said Begay.

He rummaged some more and produced a bunch of keys without a key fob.

"I reckon those are house keys."

Begay pulled out of the bag a striped calico scarf in earthy browns and ferny greens. An opened roll of Swiss herbal cough drops. A tube of beeswax lip salve. A phial of homeopathic remedy. A coin purse with quarters and dimes.

"Anything else?"

Begay dug through the bag and drew out a crumpled piece of paper. He smoothed it out. It was an envelope.

There was a handwritten address on it.

"Laurie Sarslund," Begay read.

Sarslund had the sound of open waters and summer nights when the sun never set. And Laurie was a happy name, simple, unpretentious, wholesome.

"Lives in Gopher," said Begay.

"Is that everything? No phone? No ID? No purse?"

Begay turned the bag upside down. A few crumbs of what looked like granola dropped out, and two desiccated flower heads.

Begay was fiddling with his wretched phone again.

"I can't believe that you can't leave your phone alone, even now."

"Great reception," Begay said.

He squinted at the screen, sighed and passed the phone over to K.

"You're checking your social media? Here?" asked K.

"Not mine," said Begay. He reached over and drew his fingers across the screen.

"Have a look now."

Begay had expanded the image and K could make out the familiar, all-invading logo of the dratted social media site.

"Laurie Sarslund," said Begay. "That's her page,"

"You found her page just like this?" K said. "Wow! So we could message her to return her bag?"

"Look at the profile photo," Begay suggested.

Realization began to dawn.

"Laurie Sarslund is our Amazon?" K asked.

He had seen her tear- and snot- and grime-covered. He had seen her devastated. He had seen her gasping for air, after getting her off that oak tree. He had seen her motionless and far away in the hospital bed. Every time he had seen her, it had been in crisis and this last crisis was likely to last.

The image was of a young woman whose expression was simultaneously shy and determined; who looked self-conscious at having her photograph taken, in the way people once had, long ago. There was a tiny curve to her lips, as if she'd tried but had not quite managed to smile for the camera. The photo had been taken somewhere that looked like a verdant and flowering alpine meadow—perhaps it had even been taken here, in Quorum Wilderness, before everything went to hell.

"Laurie Sarslund," said K. "How young she wa—is,"

"How old is she?" asked Begay.

"Twenty-seven."

"That's not that young," said Begay. "I know some folks that are grandparents by that age—" He stopped abruptly.

K thought he ought to be grateful to have a friend-cum-foe who knew him well enough to read his thoughts, namely: "This girl is probably never going to be a grandmother now."

He turned the phone in his hand, scanning over her interests, her concerns, her communications. What a serious girl she had been. K found he lacked the fortitude or sangfroid to delve further into Laurie Sarslund's social persona and handed the phone back.

"What now?"

"Let's just drive back and see what's on the way," said Begay.

They traversed Desolation Valley and Great Spearstone Valley in silence.

On the road climbing out of Great Spearstone Valley to Petalia Plain K began to whistle "The bear went over the mountain, to see what he could see." Whereupon he realized, belatedly, what he could not see. "How did you find Laurie Sarslund's bag? Was it coincidence?"

"What's coincidence?" growled Begay.

"Chance," said K. "Did you find the bag by chance?"

"So we just take a leisure drive around Quorum Valley, coz that's a nice way to pass the time, and lookee here: we got ourselves the bag of a person we couldn't ID?"

"So it wasn't coincidence," said K. "How did you know where to find it?"

"Have you forgotten I'm the best darn track reader Redwater's got? That's why they put me on sick leave instead of booting my ass right off the force, even though I'm on to the chief's crystal-sideline."

"But this isn't tracks." K protested.

"How come you don't listen? Didn't I tell you a hundred times *everything* is tracks?"

"But usually there's something tangible . . . like dirt, or . . . a damaged tire, or a scent—even your stupid virtual crap is tangible. You can fish and lure people in like Tiffany does, and then you come up with tracks. That I can just about understand. But there was nothing here. . . ."

"Nothing?! There's tracks," Begay raised his thumb. "There's intuition," he raised his index finger "And there's a hypothesis," he waggled three fingers at K. "Like I told you. And," Begay began to count on his fingers, "One: Your Amazon Laurie; Two: A big old oak tree all alone; Three: No car, no purse, no ID; Four: The way out of Quorum is east. Let's drive, shik'is."

They drove on and K watched the silver-grey expanse of Great Spearstone Valley vanish in the rearview mirror.

"Did you dream it?" K asked eventually. "Did a dream tell you where to find her bag?"

"My galvanizing dream?" Begay asked sarcastically. "Why do you bílagáana always need to know how we get to know stuff? Why isn't it enough that knowledge comes to us, when we need it?"

"Was it a dream?" insisted K.

"Why does it matter?"

"Because," said K, "it would mean that there really is a world of dreams that speaks to us—like the old Lacandon lady believes."

"You would like that, huh?" said Begay.

"Yes, I would," said K. "I would like it very much."

CHAPTER TWENTY-SEVEN

Petalia Plain looked more scorched than usual at this time of year. K favored arid deserts maybe because they reflected the state of his soul, but this dryness was somehow different. It was desert drier than it was supposed to be. Even the tenacious weeds and shrubs that normally prospered in their understated way looked as if they were about ready to give up. Even the heat rising from the pavement had a lifeless quality to it.

"I'm starting to feel parched," said K. He tried to remember if there was a café, or a grocery store or a gas station in Latep. "The library should have some drinking fountains." he pulled into the vast parking lot. "Plenty of parking space, I'll give them that."

"They took away all that land from us Indians to make it into parking lots," said Begay.

As K had guessed, Latep library had drinking fountains, two of them, so they were spared the tedious and perfunctory who-goes-first dance of manners. When they had slaked their thirst, Begay pushed open the glass door to the library and strolled in without waiting for K. The door fell shut in K's face.

K stood, his nose an inch from the glass, seething. He contemplated driving off without Begay—let him try out his ancestral skill set. His fuse seemed to get shorter these days.

He decided to take a minute to find his way to a more equanimous state of mind. Luckily someone had contrived to move the notice board—kittens in basket poster and all—into the lobby, so there was something to read. Maybe the notice board got more traffic than the library, and the librarian did not wish to have her knitting disrupted by the public perusing it. K knew knitting involved a lot of counting.

They seemed to have a good many bake sales in aid of one thing or another in Latep. And ice cream socials, whatever they were. There were For Sale notices for riding mowers, horse-trailers and quad-bikes. And heeler puppies; and a facial sauna, whatever that was. They really did use their notice board, these Latep people. Nobody seemed to bother to take old notices off before tacking new ones on and so the board offered a kind of chronicled archaeology of Latep's wants and needs.

K wondered if Mrs. Browning had ever found a day carer to help her look after her husband who had had a stroke. Or if the miscreants who had dug out the Contender Peach tree in the front yard of 8930 3rd had ever returned it. Or had they furtively planted it in a hidden corner of their own backyard? Given it away as a gift? To steal a peach tree was an oddly quaint misdemeanor. A misdemeanor fitting for Latep. By now his bad mood had evaporated and he was really getting into the notice board.

He was going to peel his way back through layers of notices to whenever they'd put up that board, two or three decades ago, damn it.

He lifted a couple of index cards off a foolscap page that seemed to be blank. To leave blank pages stuck on such a crowded notice board seemed injudicious. K nominated himself temporary Latep Notice board-Guardian-Organizer, pulled the pushpins out and took the index cards off the board.

The index cards had covered two foolscap pages, both of them with the kind of bold and colorful header that spoke of down-home grassroots initiatives.

Here, covered by handwritten index cards offering broken-down cardboard boxes for free, and a used wooden birdfeeder, $3, were the XOX- and the Quorum Downwinders' petitions—low-priority matters for Latep, natch.

Since K's last visit to the library the petitions seemed to have gained one signatory each, and as before, both petitions had the same number of signatures and, presumably, the same signatories.

Number One on both was Laurie Sarslund. Number Two: Eren Solanas. Number Three: Paprika Melrose and Number Four: Jim Westwood.

How come K hadn't noticed Laurie Sarslund's name on his first visit?

Because the name hadn't meant anything to him. Still, he should have recognized it when Begay identified her.

His archaeological notice board custodianship forgotten, K pushed his way through the glass door into the library. It was a small enough library, but Begay was nowhere to be seen.

Who he did see was Eren Solanas in a burnt sienna T-shirt, fitted denim skirt and bare tan legs in Cowboy boots. He wondered if he had some kind of bare skin and leather fetish that he hadn't been aware of.

Solanas turned round. "Hi there," she said with a slow, lazy smile.

K found it hard to smile when battling lust, so who knew what Eren Solanas made of his grim visage.

He laid the petitions on the desk, smoothing the creased paper.

"Do you know this person?" he asked and pointed to the first name.

Solanas narrowed her eyes and read the name. "Laurie Sarslund?"

She leant back her head, showing a smooth, strong neck, frowned, looking at the ceiling, trying to summon a memory. Finally she shook her head. "No."

"She may have come in to put up the petition. Did you talk to her then?" Solanas creased her brow. "I don't think so. I don't recall. I'm just a locum and part time. I can ask the main librarian, if you like?"

"You signed the petition though," said K.

"Sure," said Solanas. "It's rare to find an environmental petition in this library. Of course I'm going to sign it."

"This person was quite engaged in environmental matters. Are you sure you don't know her? A very tall young woman?"

"No," said Solanas.

From somewhere came the muffled ring of a cell phone.

"Excuse me," Solanas said. She went to the coat stand, reached into a rustic leather bag and produced the ringing phone. "Hello," she said. "Hello? Hello!" She shrugged and stuffed the phone back into her bag. "We shouldn't really use cell phones in the library anyways," she said with a mock-contrite grin.

"I suppose not," said K woodenly.

Begay appeared out of nowhere like an ominous genie.

"Ma'am," he said, "can you copy out this title for me? And that number too so I can order it in the bookstore in Gallup?"

"The ISBN?" asked Solanas.

"That number," said Begay and put a finger on the ISBN. "I really like those books where the good guy wins. Does the good guy win?"

"Louis l'Amour?" said Solanas. "I don't really know."

"I really like the cover too," said Begay. "That's why I want to order it. When I'm done reading it I can cut out the cover and put it up in my trailer."

Begay's accent was Jhon-South-of-Boondocks-Meets-Dances-With-Wolves.

Solanas passed over the piece of paper with details on Louis l'Amour's *Last of the Breed* that she'd copied out.

Begay thanked her effusively, boomed "hagone," and exited stage left.

K was unsure what to do.

"You do get some traffic here then," he said awkwardly.

"This one was kind of an exception," she said. "Latep folk are not so diverse."

K nodded. "How's the environmental work going? Any takers?"

"Around here? You must be joking. It's a couple of nano seconds before the apocalypse and these folks just drift along like in a daydream, while XOX is fracking right under their feet, polluting the groundwater, causing seismic damage, poisoning wells. These people won't wake up unless something drastic happens."

"Like what?" asked K.

Solanas shrugged. "Anything," she said lightly.

"Better be going," said K.

"Come again—before I leave," Solanas said.

"When are you leaving?" K asked.

"In a couple of weeks," said Solanas.

"I'll try," said K and fled.

In his mind a line from The Doors played: "Wrap your legs around my neck, Babe."

You needed Jim Morrison's husky voice to make that one work.

CHAPTER TWENTY-EIGHT

"Now look who's all hot and bothered," said Begay maliciously.

K decided it would be safer not to fall for that one.

"Have you ordered your Louis L'Amour or are you going to wait until you get to Gallup?"

"The cover's got an Indian and a helicopter on it," said Begay complacently. "How cool is that?"

"Very. Can't wait to see it up there on your trailer wall."

"Shik'is," said Begay. "I want to show you something, okay?"

"Sure," said K.

Begay set the piece of paper that Eren Solanas had written out for him on his knee and rooted through his pocket. He drew out the envelope that had been in Laurie Sarslund's bag and put it down next to the other piece of paper. He ran his finger under the number written on Laurie Sarslund's envelope and under the ISBN.

"In case you're fixing to ask me what it is you are supposed to be seeing: this is the same writing. I studied it some and the person's that written both these numbers is your hot librarian in there."

"So?" asked K. "That's not necessarily a problem is it? I mean, she could have forgotten that they met. . . ."

"Ah, shik'is," said Begay sorrowfully. "This number?" He pointed to Laurie's envelope. "This number is your librarian's cell phone number."

"The silent phone call? It was you who called her?"

Begay nodded.

"Why?"

"That's the part that you call intuition," said Begay.

"You had an intuition that. . . ?"

"Drive shik'is. We don't want to be caught here by your librarian."

•　　•　　•　　•

Having decanted Begay at home by way of Drive-Thru Burgazz—"I deserve me some real food"—K made to the station where he found Córdoba on the phone, on the tail end of tying up some loose ends of a domestic situation.

"Sure, it is your choice whether you want to take up the place at the refuge," Córdoba said smoothly. "Like the other four times this month, when you chose not to."

K wandered over to the window from where he contemplated the cracks in the paving of the parking lot. When you screwed up your eyes they looked like an aerial view of rivers snaking through desert.

"The refuge is aware of your situation—if you do change your mind," said Córdoba. "And do call me—anytime you need to, okay?"

"Hey," said Córdoba next to him. She was such a light mover he had not heard her crossing the room. Shoulder to shoulder they stood and looked out at the paving.

"Don't you think the cracks look like rivers in a desert?" asked K.

"Rivers?" said Córdoba. "No."

"You don't think they look like rivers?"

Córdoba shook her head.

"What do you think they look like?"

Córdoba considered. "Claw marks?"

"Claw marks?" Rorschach eat your heart out.

"You came to ask me about cracks in the pavement?" Córdoba sounded as if she thought this a distinct possibility.

K dangled Laurie Sarslund's bag toward her.

"The young woman in hospital—we got her identity."

"Her identity?" asked Córdoba, her breath catching.

"Laurie Sarslund," said K. "Her bag was there in Quorum Valley, not so far from where . . . she was found."

"Who found her bag?" asked Córdoba. "Someone handed it in?"

K shrugged.

Córdoba looked at him in a way that it made it hard not to fess up. She looked at him as if she knew that he was struggling not to fess up to whatever he did not want to fess up to. She nodded.

"So her name is what?"

K fished out the envelope. Córdoba took it and walked over to the computer. It didn't take Córdoba any longer than it had taken Robbie Begay to come up with Laurie Sarslund's social media account.

"Would you like me to take this?" asked Córdoba. "Speak to her family?"

"Would you mind?" K said.

"I do it all the time," said Córdoba. "I got practice."

"It's better done by someone with practice," K said. "And skill," he added.

"I got more distance," said Córdoba. "I didn't find her."

K thought of their night vigil at the hospital; of Córdoba, bedside, arranging flowers in a vase.

"Everything you found is in this bag?"

K nodded.

"How about you get yourself a coffee and come back in about an hour?"

●　　●　　●　　●

"Her parents are on their way," reported Córdoba. "They should arrive sometime in the night."

"Are they having to travel far?"

"Five—six hours drive. Not so far."

"Are they coming to Milagro?"

"Sure," said Córdoba.

"But I thought they transferred her—Laurie—out of San Matteo General?"

"Oh no," said Córdoba. "She's back here. When they don't know about a patient's situation they go for the cheapest option."

"That would be a patient's financial situation?" asked K.

From time to time he toyed with the thought of moving back to good old Blighty, to the ever-rainy Welsh coast of his childhood, its hillsides teeming with bleating rain-sodden sheep, every hamlet in possession of a Methodist chapel and two public houses at the very least. And the National Health Service. The glorious NHS, where treatment was free at the point of delivery and where they would not, never would, shunt patients around on account of their financial situation. Here they called the NHS model of free healthcare "Socialized Medicine," and politicians got themselves elected for being against it.

Córdoba was studying his face.

"That would never happen in England," K said. For convenience's sake and to avoid confusing people he had taken to calling the British Isles "England." "We've got the NHS. The best health service in the world."

"I never heard you sound that positive about anything."

"Well, it is true," said K. His enthusiasm was in part due to the fear that the NHS-as-was days were numbered and that it was stealthily selling out, following the neo-liberal ideology of its big profiteering brother over the pond with all its floating islands of plastic debris the size of France.

"Anyways," said Córdoba. "Uhm—" She chewed her lip. "Do you want to be there too?"

"Sure," K said. "I'd like to come along."

"It might be kind of easier. . . ." said Córdoba. It was evident she did not ask for support very often. K briefly wondered what kind of child Córdoba had been. He couldn't imagine a toddler Juanita tottering unsteadily toward the steep learning curve that awaited all little people. It was more like she'd hatched fully formed, poised and competent.

"How did they react?"

"Shocked. But relieved too. They hadn't heard from her in a while. They are a close family. First they thought maybe she'd gone on a camping trip or something. They were just starting to get real worried because there'd been no word from her and her cell's switched off. Where is her cell?"

"It wasn't in the bag. What is in her bag is all we have."

"No cell. No ID. No driver's license. Weird," said Córdoba. "Do you know what's weird too? There was this phone number on the envelope with Laurie's name. So I called that number."

"Uh," said K, studiously keeping his face blank.

Córdoba scrutinized him. "You didn't try to call it?"

"No," K said. Which was true. He had not tried to call that number.

"Anyway," said Córdoba. "The person I spoke to wasn't cooperative at all. Hardly wouldn't say anything, except that she didn't know anyone called Laurie and she didn't know how her number got onto that envelope. Of course we don't know who wrote that number down. It could be Laurie or that person or someone else altogether."

"I guess," K said. "Why is that weird?"

"What?" said Córdoba.

"Why did you say that was weird—the way you told it this is just about someone saying they don't know Laurie Sarslund."

"You get a feeling," said Córdoba. "My feeling was that this person wasn't telling the truth. In fact I got a feeling she was proactively trying to cover up the truth."

"A suspect?" asked K.

Córdoba shrugged. "It was a suicide attempt, no? That's the responsibility of the suicidal person."

"What about aiding and abetting?"

"Like I said. Suicide isn't a crime."

There was verbal and nonverbal communication. Just now there was an apparent conflict between Córdoba's verbal nonchalance and the penetrating look she was giving K, as if she damn well knew that there was something here that wasn't kosher and guessed too that K knew more than he was admitting.

K didn't even know why he was holding back. Surely a bit of off-time sleuthing with a qualified buddy wasn't a crime—at least not a crime that Córdoba would worry about. Just a slight blurring of boundaries—but let's face it, without Begay they would never have found Laurie Sarslund's bag and without the bag the girl might have remained the nameless Amazon until—

K shuddered.

"You okay?" asked Córdoba.

"Sure," said K.

CHAPTER TWENTY-NINE

Once more K's imaginings proved wrong. Far from being Viking colossuses bestriding the land, the Sarslunds were of average size.

Mrs. Sarslund exuded the type of home-knitted wholesome integrity that was wont to breed offspring of conscientious responsibility of the higher order, or feckless hedonism and moral depravity, depending on how the dice fell.

She wore her blond-grey hair in a bun from which sundry strands had escaped that she kept brushing out of her face. The description "apple cheeked" was no cliché. Mother Sarslund's cheeks were cherubically rounded and of a pinkish hue that spoke of outdoor pursuits, a healthy diet and a clear conscience.

Mr. Sarslund's stoop and horn-rimmed glasses spoke of a bookish introvert. He looked like a cross between Atticus Finch and Samuel Beckett and so approximated K's ideal father figure. He fell for the man immediately.

The Sarslunds looked stricken, though it was evident that both were mindful not to burden the cops before them with their woes and sorrows.

"Thank you so much for contacting us," Mrs. Sarslund said. She was one of those rare people who managed to feel and convey gratitude even in the depth of a personal crisis. Atticus nodded. K saw that they were holding hands, holding on to each other. He wondered what Córdoba had told them. He was pretty sure that Córdoba, always professional and never one to shirk responsibility, would have done her best to prepare Laurie's parents for what was awaiting them.

They had waited for the Sarslunds at the station and then accompanied them to the hospital.

Córdoba had covered all the groundwork. This time they did not have to bear down on an underpaid healthcare assistant carrying the nightshift on her own, or chase up a charge nurse holed up in some back office playing computer games. There were a nurse manager and a staff nurse waiting for them in the hospital's reception area, which was eerily quiet at this time of night and cast in a bluish hue by dimmed lighting.

The nurses were friendly albeit matter of fact, and, to K's relief, went easy on stock phrases meant to convey optimism and reassurance.

They led the way across the reception area along a corridor hung with framed Georgia O'Keefe prints, an either thoughtless or brave choice depending how you looked at it, given that O'Keefe's blooms and petals invariably bore striking resemblance to the human reproductive anatomy.

They got into an elevator that took them to the basement. K had not known the hospital even had a basement. They walked along an unadorned corridor that could have used a fresh coat of paint; past a canteen where a woman in bright pink scrubs was cleaning vitrines and whistling tunelessly; took a right onto another corridor; then a left—K was losing all sense of direction and wouldn't have been surprised if they were being led to a secret steel-paneled nuclear bunker containing a scheming, criminal overlord stroking a white cat, muahaha.

They turned into another corridor, this one painted in what K thought of as Institutional Green, one of those colors that didn't even look like a good idea on posters in the showroom, a color that was possibly especially designed to signalize low status, low priority and lost hope.

K glanced at the Sarslunds, who walked along, hand in hand,

hopefully oblivious to the decline of standard in their surroundings.

The nurses walked ahead briskly, apparently similarly insensitive to the ambience.

The charge nurse opened a door at the end of the soylent green corridor and stepped aside to make room for the visitors.

There was no hesitation, no slacking of pace for the Sarslunds. They stepped into the room as one and walked straight up to the bed that stood under a barred window. This was the basement after all.

The room itself was not quite as bad as it might have been. It looked as if someone, if not the corporation under whose auspices San Matteo General raked in its profits, had made an effort.

There were a couple of visitors' chairs each with a needlepoint cushion, a vase of silk flowers on the high windowsill and a poster of geese flying in formation across a cloud-patterned sky. If not original, this poster seemed at least a wiser choice for a sick room. You could practically read anything into a flight of geese; hope, hello, good-bye and everything in between.

K became aware of Córdoba looking at him looking at the geese. She wore a worried little frown that made it pretty clear that she for one did not think he was quite out of the woods, and felt he had yet to prove whether he was asset or liability.

K resisted the temptation to try to stare Córdoba down. She was his most reliable colleague after all, nearly a friend—were it not for her ever-professional self-containedness.

Then it occurred to him that he had looked at everything in the room: needlepoint cushions, silk flowers and poster—except for the person in the bed. That validated Córdoba's frown and confirmed him as a liability.

The view to the bed was obstructed by the parents Sarslund who stood, Atticus at head and Mrs. Sarslund at mid-bed level, holding onto Laurie's hands and stroking her hair; Laurie, who lay quiet, unmoved and unmovable, though who knew— who knew.

She certainly looked a good deal better than she had when K had hoisted her body off the old oak tree.

He could almost look at her now and not see the blue-faced Amazon, blackened tongue protruding, eye sockets sunken, vivid red welt snaking round her neck turning into black-blue bruise.

He felt a hand on his arm, Córdoba's hand guiding him out of his reverie.

He carried one needlepoint cushioned chair over to the bed, then the other. The staff nurse pointed out the call button and described the location of the kitchenette, which the Sarslunds were welcome to use. The nurse offered tea, coffee or water, which the Sarslunds declined with thanks.

Córdoba made a minute "let's go" motion with her head and K nodded. Córdoba told the Sarslunds they would be back in the morning.

The Sarslunds, sitting somberly and tenderly close to their far-away child, nodded.

K doubted they were taking anything in, so caught up were they with holding onto their daughter.

CHAPTER THIRTY

"I thought you hooked up maybe," said Begay. "Rough night, eh? I'll brew us some joe."

K sat at the kitchen table and rested his head on his arms. He woke up when Begay set mugs and the percolator on the table.

"Maybe you should get some sleep?" Begay asked.

"I got to go back," said K and reached for the steaming mug.

"Back?" asked Begay.

He listened in silence to K's slurred account of last night's happenings. If he resented that Córdoba had matched his own web-sleuthing skills, he didn't let on.

"So the parents are here?" he asked. "That's good. It is good that she has folks that are close to her."

"They are good people," mumbled K.

"What was that thing about Córdoba calling your gal?" Begay asked.

"My gal?"

"Your hot lying librarian," said Begay.

"She did lie," K confirmed. "I don't get why she keeps lying. She lied to me and she lied to Córdoba. What's the big deal about knowing Laurie Sarslund? I mean, there must be hundreds of people who know Laurie. And Solanas and Laurie Sarslund move in the same circles. They are both environmentalists. Why the lies?"

"I'll give you credit for being tired," said Begay.

"Huh?" said K. Maybe he needed to lie down after all.

"You really don't get why Solanas is lying about knowing that girl?"

"No," said K. "It's unnecessary. It's not as if she's implicated in anything illegal. Suicide's not illegal after all."

"Maybe you do get it after all," Begay said.

"What is 'it?'" K asked. He was starting to feel pissed. Feeling pissed woke him up some. "I'm not in the mood for this guessing crap. What are you trying to say? Just say whatever you got to say and be fucking done with it, okay?"

"Solanas put up your Amazon to hang herself on that oak tree," Begay said. "Can't get better PR than that."

"She what—?" stammered K. "She did what?"

"I'm pretty sure that this is how it went," said Begay. "And if this is how it went there's nothing that we can do about it."

"Inciting suicide?" asked K. "Is that not like murder?"

"Failure to provide help? It's not a crime. All she did is strengthen this girl's resolve to do something radical and give her a ride to the oak tree." said Begay. "And she probably was the one that put the idea into that girl's head."

"That's awful," said K. "Why would she do such a thing?"

Surely, when Solanas said that something drastic had to happen before the people of Quorum woke up to XOX's environmental destruction she couldn't have meant sacrificing a life?

"She's one of those fighters. She really believes in the cause. And she probably thought that she's more use to the movement than that poor Amazon girl of yours. Your librarian's the mastermind."

"I still don't get it," said K stubbornly. It was quite possible that his brain did not want to get it. "Why?"

"She hoped there'd be a scandal. She was counting on the girl being found dead, hanging there and it would have been a way to get some bad publicity for what XOX is doing."

"She drives Laurie to the tree? And then she takes off with her bag and dumps it in a ditch? Why?"

"She didn't want that girl to be identified." Begay said patiently.

"But why?"

"If there's a person that suicided that is not identified, that case gets a lot more airtime. When you got a name, that person gets barely a mention. But if it is a Jane Doe they got to put in some work, see? That makes it interesting. The more interest, the more PR, the more people are going to mobilize for the cause, get it?" Begay explained.

Whenever K thought he'd hit rock bottom or had peaked, whichever way you wanted to look at it, cynicism-wise, along came another summit to climb or pit to fall into.

He thought that he'd left the soothing binaries of his child-hood—if they'd ever existed—long behind and now it turned out he couldn't deal with heroine turned villainess. Environmental activists were supposed to be the good guys here, what with Mother Earth and all that.

Solanas had sacrificed Laurie Sarslund to the cause—strange fruit hanging from an old oak tree.

"It all don't make sense without a suicide note," Begay said. "There must have been a suicide note. I bet your librarian helped that girl write a real punchy letter that would get them some coverage and make trouble for XOX. But where is it? Maybe it blew away? Or got lost?"

"I can't believe she's that callous," said K.

"Not callous," said Begay, "fanatic. She's a fanatic. There's loads of them about nowadays, with all kinds of things to be fanatic about. You're just shocked because she's supposed to be on the good side."

And then it occurred to K that the first time he had met Eren Solanas at Latep library, when she'd come in wearing dirt-crusted hiking shoes, she had just come from dropping off Laurie Sarslund at the Gamble Oak, the designated spot for Laurie's statement suicide.

Eren Solanas had sorted books and calmly chatted to him—all the while knowing that Laurie Sarslund was out there by the oak tree, alone, dying for the cause.

CHAPTER THIRTY-ONE

Solanas reminded K of one of those wild cats, with tails twitching, that are about to let fly, all claws and teeth and blood-curdling hiss.

When he had turned up at the library she had looked pleased. She had taken his visit as a personal call, maybe wasn't averse to "hooking up" with him, as Begay called it.

K, however, couldn't connect to his erstwhile lusty fantasies. What he saw was a ruthless manipulator literally prepared to up her cause via body count. The bare skin in leather now spoke to him of a predatory nature, the glittering hazel-green eyes put him in mind of a rapacious jungle creature out on the prowl.

"Don't you want to know what happened to Laurie Sarslund?" he asked.

"Who is Laurie Sarslund?" asked Eren Solanas.

"Isn't there something about Judas denouncing Jesus three times?" K said.

It sounded pretty corny to him, but then he was agnostic.

It had an effect on Solanas, whose nostrils flared and whose wide mouth compressed to a hard line.

K met the hatred in Solanas eyes with a level look.

"Where's the suicide note?" K asked.

Solanas' face was bone white now, her eyes narrow slits. She did not answer.

"There's nothing we can do to you. Legally there's nothing we can do," K said. A cold fury burnt within him. "I hope that every one of your days from now on is tainted with the memory of what you did."

Solanas' nostrils flared. The sinews on her neck bulged.

"Every single one of your days tainted," K repeated slowly and carefully. "Mail Laurie's ID and license and suicide letter to Milagro PD, c/o Kafka."

• • • •

The ferocity of Solanas' fanaticism ignited K's anxiety. Now that the Lacandons had taught him to believe in dreams, what was there to stop him believing in the powers of wish and thought—be they healing or destructive?

Should Laurie come to grief her fate could still be usefully exploited for the cause, he supposed. He did not really think that Solanas had it in her to be a fully fledged assassin, but he felt disquieted anyway, so he made a detour via first the grocery store and then the hospital.

He found the Sarslunds as he'd left them in the night: seated on the needlepoint-cushioned chairs beside their daughter's bed, stroking her head, holding her hands and reading aloud.

"What do you mean less than nothing? I don't think there is any such thing as less than nothing. Nothing is absolutely the limit of nothingness. It's the lowest you can go. It's the end of the line."[1]

K tiptoed nearer.

"How can something be less than nothing? If there were something that was less than nothing, then nothing would not be nothing, it would be something — even though it's just a very little bit of something. But if nothing is nothing, then nothing has nothing that is less than it is."[2]

Mrs. Sarslund looked up and smiled and Atticus laid down the book.

"Charlotte's Web?" whispered K.

Atticus nodded.

"It's Laurie's favorite."

"It's a wonderful book," agreed K. Though he didn't know if a story that contained so much death and rope dangling was really appropriate for someone who had tried to hang herself.

Laurie—Laurie really did look better. Maybe he was imagining it, but it seemed that there was now some color in her sallow sunken cheeks and the circles around her eyes were beginning to fade and there was a ghost of a smile—was there?—on her face.

"She looks much better," said K.

"She does, doesn't she?" said Mrs. Sarslund, and beamed at him. "She knows we are here."

Atticus was looking down at his daughter and holding her hand.

K handed over the mixed fruit platter he had picked up from the store —you couldn't go wrong with fruit.

"Oh," said Mrs. Sarslund. "How kind!" Disconcerted, K saw that her eyes had filmed with tears.

They had not cried when they first saw their comatose daughter lying in the paupers' section of a hospital, but they cried when given the trivial gift of a platter of fruit by a passing policeman.

People. Go figure.

1. White, E.B; Charlotte's Web; Kindle Edition
2. Ibid

CHAPTER THIRTY-TWO

"Luisa's website," said Córdoba. She looked at K's blank face. "Luisa's website," she repeated. "The porn profile. It is fake."

"How do you know?"

"A hunch," Córdoba said vaguely. "I had a friend check it out for me. And when they said it was fake, I forwarded it to Delgado's IT people and they confirmed it. It is fake."

"So the porn profile is fake?" K said with studied nonchalance. Only then did the outrageous proposition hit him. "Fake? A fake porn profile? Who would do such a thing? Why?"

"Revenge porn's a whole new genre," Córdoba shrugged. "Using porn to get at somebody you are mad at," she explained.

K shook his head.

"It's getting to be a normal way of getting at each other," Córdoba said. "Teenagers like it especially."

A man could live for so long and think he knew about life and understood about people only to realize he did not know anything and understood even less.

K walked over to the dragon tree withering in its pot and pulled at its dry brown fronds. "But why do that?"

Córdoba sighed. Even her patience had its limits. "Like I said: to get at someone."

"It doesn't make sense though, does it?" said K. "If it was about getting at Luisa—Luisa didn't use social media. She wouldn't even have known that there's this stuff on her."

Just as it would take thirteen blue moons for K to know about any stuff on himself that might be out there whirring around on the toxic web, spawned by corrupted minds and noxious notions.

"She did not have to know," Córdoba said finally. "It would be enough if someone knew about her."

"If someone knew about her. . . ?" repeated K.

Córdoba cleared her throat. "It has been done . . . all kinds of stuff . . . People have been set up to be raped—"

"Set up to be raped?"

"It's not so rare anymore," Córdoba said. "I had a case just recently."

"A case where somebody was set up to be raped?"

Córdoba nodded. "It was a pretty brutal rape, there was some branding involved too—and they found that it was set up by putting up a fake profile on a hookup site."

"Who does that kind of thing?" asked K. He did not dare ask what branding was.

"Mostly it's ex-boyfriends or husbands. In that case we think it was the wife that set up her husband's girlfriend. She set up a profile for her on a BDSM site. The husband had come clean and she knew just about everything about this woman, including where she kept her spare keys, which came in pretty handy."

"So the wife and the rapist are both convicted?" asked K.

"I'm not holding my breath. The wife is the wronged party; the rapist believed he was obliging the victim by acting out a fantasy."

"What is—uh—branding?" asked K.

"Putting your mark on someone, like you brand a cow," said Córdoba.

"They thought she wanted to be branded?"

"The girlfriend had some history on BDSM sites. Bondage, Domination, Sadism, Masochism," she explained.

"Submission," said K, "S is for Submission,"

"Uh," said Córdoba.

"We live in an age of language sanitization," said K, "everything else is getting dirtier. Our language is getting cleaner,"

Then he remembered how these days politicians spoke about migrants, the unemployed, the poor; and he reconsidered. He didn't think there was a need to share this change of mind with Córdoba, who didn't seem that bothered. In contrast to K's habitus, Córdoba was a doer, not a theorizer.

"Well. . . ," said Córdoba, and shrugged.

Like arsenic invading the bloodstream, the true extent of the diabolic scheme of revenge porn was beginning to hit K.

"So there is a chance that Luisa may have been taken by someone who accessed the hookup site? Somebody could have found her and harmed her?"

"It is possible," said Córdoba. "Loads of kids do it. You saw how they were—those girls. It's a real easy way to get at somebody you don't like."

"How did you know that?" asked K.

"I didn't know anything," said Córdoba. "I was going with the stuff we knew."

·   ·   ·   ·

When K entered the break-room, debriefing of the teacher-training posse was in full flow.

If Miss Caulfield of Merced Elementary was acing it in the educators' arms-race, Mr. Pierce, San Matteo High Superintendent, achieved a very close second. Pierce had committed himself to arming all staff, especially canteen staff, by the end of the next school year.

"Isn't Pierce running for County Commissioner?" asked K.

"Sure is," said Smithson.

"Is he going to have enough time? All that tooling-up of his school must be keeping him pretty busy."

"Better go 'n listen to your crank calls," Young suggested.

"There've been some more?" asked K.

"You're getting calls on that girl?" Dilger had sidled up.

"Some," K said flatly, leafing through the pile of messed up forms that littered the sticky counter. If only taxpayers knew how much of their hard-earned dollar went into wasted forms that cops had been too dumb to fill out correctly. What was here was enough to fuel a hearty bonfire for a couple of hours or so.

"If you need a body to go through those calls for you—I got just the guy," said Dilger and snapped his fingers.

Out of the recesses of the break-room materialized their very own NRA-sympathizing jock of the oily abs, aka the Odious Intern, about whom K knew much more than he could let on. The Odious Intern in the flesh was a corn-fed youth who was spending his time at Milagro PD brown-nosing whomever he thought counted.

"I'd be happy to undertake that task, Sir," said the Odious Intern obsequiously.

"I'm sure you would," said K. "Which school did you graduate from?"

"MMHS," said the jock. "It's great to be here, Sir," he gushed. "I'm learning so much. I'm aiming for a football scholarship. . . ."

"I'm worried about the potential conflict of interest." K interrupted the young future's roll call of dreams.

"Sir?"

"I wouldn't want you to compromise yourself," K said gravely.

"No problem," said Dilger heartily, an avuncular hand resting on the jock's shoulder. Nepotism was what had brought the Odious Intern to the squad, and nepotism was what would guide him straight into the murky waters of conflicts of interest and compromised ethics—not that any of these posed a problem for Dilger. "My nephew's a real wiz with all that social media stuff too, if you need anything doing."

"I bet he is," said K.

"I promise I'll do a good job, Sir," the OI assured him.

"It's always great to welcome young blood," said K. "I'm

sure we'll find a suitable outlet for your talents." Like Principal Weismaker-Coffee Taster, Head Dirty Cup Collector or Managing Spoilt Form Shredder.

K's personal God/Guiding Spirit/Guardian being mustard-keen as usual, retribution for ethical over-thinking was swift, and came in the form of a deluge of recorded messages on the Luisa Alvarez info line that K had now condemned himself to listen to.

•　　•　　•　　•

"Ooooh, yeah baby. Ooooh, she's hot. Yeah. She's a hot piece of ass alright. I got me a hot piece of ass alright. Bet you wouldn't mind having yourself a hot piece of ass like I got myself here right now. Ooooh, baby. C'm'on and find me. Ooooooh. . . ."

"We don't need you to waste our taxes on looking for a cheap little whore like that. Go out and do some real work for citizens that deserve it! My car got keyed and you still haven't caught the criminals who did it."

"Here's some information that will help you: My neighbor has her. He's not opened his curtains for four days. He has her in there. He always tries to talk to the kids. And his dog has a pink bandana. He's weird. Road 27.2. Brown trailer in the messy yard. Don't tell him it was me that told you."

"I know where she is. But I ain't telling you. . . ."

There were fourteen messages all in all, and most of them pervy.

A good proportion of callers seemed to be perusing Luisa's fake website whilst on the phone.

There were teasers, taunters and fantasists, conspiracy theorists, the lost, the lonely, the pathetic and the desperate and everything in between; old hands and seasoned hoaxers; repeat offenders;

jokers, novices and neophytes, not one of them, it had to be said, a particular credit to Milagro town and San Matteo County.

•   •   •   •

"We are just in the neighborhood, checking," K said. "Making sure everything is alright."

The living-room was stuffy with dark red velvet curtains drawn; sofa and arm-chair upholstered in a deep pile material; the carpet dark brown, all combining to a wintry atmosphere.

The woman was in her seventies perhaps, small and wizened and with an immobile face marked by long periods of silence and solitude.

As soon as she had opened the door, she had asked him in and insisted on making him a coffee, which had taken her ages. Then she had insisted that he take a second cup. Then she had brought out some cookies. Then she had introduced him to her cat. Then she had told him about her friends who had died. With each friend she had gone into considerable detail as to their personality, their circumstances, the sad manner of their death.

When he made to get up and go, she started to talk about the rising crime rate.

The cat had taken position in front of K, meowing, as if keen to participate in the conversation.

K gave her his card. "Anytime you need something, call. If your cat goes missing, or kids bother you or you need to check in with us, just call. That's what we are here for. And it makes us feel useful. Do call me, you'll be doing me a favor."

The old woman stood in the doorway and he saw her waving until she vanished in his rearview mirror.

He wondered if she had understood what he hadn't dared spell out: that she did not have to call an automated phoneline with false information, just to cope with her loneliness.

CHAPTER THIRTY-THREE

"So the kid's hookup profile is fake?" asked Begay. "Are they sure?"

"It's been verified by Delgado already," said K. "I can't believe we didn't think of checking it out earlier. What are we going to do? Delgado said there's no sure way to determine who set up the fake profile, not if they used a public computer. Want to know the worst? Córdoba contacted the site administrators to take the profile down and they said it will take two weeks, because they got to verify our request. Can you believe that?"

"Sure can," Begay had stopped listening and was fiddling with his phone.

"I'm starting to feel that your phone is our third housemate. How about you try making it wash the dishes? Bake a cake?"

"Hmm cake," said Begay distractedly.

"Hey! Talk to me!" K felt irritated, borderline outraged, that even at times like these, when an innocent girl was being put at risk right at this very moment, Begay was fiddling with his phone.

"Oy! Listen up! What are we going to do? Right at this moment all these perverts are copping a good look at Luisa's fake profile. And then they are going to call in with their nasty little fantasies."

It occurred to K that the perverts who did call in were probably less dangerous than the perverts who didn't. It was a seriously disturbing thought. "Robbie!"

"I'll be with you in a moment," said Begay, sounding like

some call-center-customer-service-associate putting a querulous customer on hold.

"Great time to be having fun with your phone," K was starting to feel seriously pissed.

"Sure am. Hope it's gonna be worth it—hold on. Almost done. Here! What do you think of this?" he handed K his phone.

"Why are you showing me this?"

Bloody Robbie Begay. It was unbelievable. All K needed to rock his day was to look at yet another pornographic pic. This one was a nude with a remarkably grim facial expression.

"She's got a very young body for her age." K was tempted to throw the phone at Robbie.

"You don't recognize that body?" Begay asked.

"I don't go on those sites." K was furious. "You've known me for a long time. How come you don't know me at all?"

Begay muttered under his breath.

"Did you just call me dumb-ass?" asked K.

"Sure did," said Begay. "The body you are looking at is the same body they used for the fake profile."

"It is?" Slowly the penny dropped.

It was the nubile body of a young woman crowned with the forbidding face of a matron of advancing middle age.

"You hacked it?"

Begay nodded modestly.

"Whose head did you put in there?" K asked, against his better judgment.

"My boss' wife," said Begay casually.

"What?!"

"He's living it up with hush money from the meth-pushers. And she's a real dragon."

"I don't know what to say," said K.

"Just say 'Great job' coz that's what it is. Besides—when they see this, the site administrators are going to know it's been hacked and they're going take it down right away."

"What if your boss finds it?"

"That's what I'm hoping. I'm really hoping he'll browse some hookup sites and he'll find his lady-wife on there."

"What if he decides to take action?"

"What's he going to do? Tell everybody he's going on hard-core hookup sites? Tell them his wife's on there? There's loads of people that are just going to love this. This is going to go viral in no time. You want to know what I'm sorry about? That I'm not going to be there to see his face when he finds this."

CHAPTER THIRTY-FOUR

In just two short weeks the Odious Intern had become one of the squad. Here was Uncle Dilger's pride and Milagro's shining future regaling the brouhaha brothers with the exploits, real or imagined, of a plenitude of awed and willing female admirers of his footballer's prowess.

Somebody loudly cleared his throat, possibly suffering from an irritation brought forth by a K-related allergy, and the Odious Intern seamlessly changed subject, announcing the glad tidings that he had secured an internship with XOX Energy Corporation; launching from thence into a singing of praise of XOX that was verily puke-inducing.

K listened to the OI's unconstrained, unbridled and unqualified enthusiasm that bore more than a passing semblance to Lucky Easton's website mission statement, while busying himself looking for the coffee jar and thinking up pithy phrases with which to scythe down the misguided fervor.

"This guy don't really rate XOX, dontcha, buddy?" Uncle Dilger pronounced with lethal joviality.

"That's putting it mildly," K, seizing the opportunity, said warmly. "It's more like I hate them worse than the plague; regard them as lower than the lowest scum of the earth; hope that the bubonic plague will raze all their houses; that giant rats will feast on their entrails nom nom nom; that they and their descendants will reap downwinders' benefits for evermore and that living on fault lines will move their spirits in perpetuity. Hallelujah."

He smiled wide-eyed and benignly into the Odious Intern's troubled face.

From somewhere there was another throat-clearing. Young broke the silence to expound on the hunting season and a new brand of pheromone spray that was sure to get the elks interested. He'd got the tip from Easton, Lucky Easton, who was a great guy, a real great guy and Lucky Easton had been extremely lucky with that spray, because he'd been sitting there in front of his cabin, just browsing on his phone, when this huge elk—rack must've scored 475—came by to look for this lil' elk lady and—bam!—Lucky shot him right then and there, from his folding chair. How cool was that? Lucky Easton was a great guy, a great hunter and he had a hunting cabin on Calvary Peak, near to Young's own cabin. Easton's cabin was real fancy and had a fancy name, 'Hermitage'—"

"Hermitage?" asked K incredulously. Easton didn't seem to be a hermitage kinda guy.

In a tone of "not that it's any of your business," Young explained that Easton's cabin used to belong to some old guy who lived there full time and wrote books, making it sound as if writing books was a pretty deviant occupation.

K, having outstayed both his welcome and his forbearance, made off to listen to some more crank calls which momentarily seemed almost tolerable, proving that all was relative and that there were upsides to things getting worse.

•　•　•　•

There were seventeen new messages and most of them featuring familiar voices from persons who had perhaps accommodated the making of crank calls in their daily schedule. Lunchtime? How about a French dip sandwich and a pervy phone call to Milagro's finest?

K listened with half an ear, while continuing to work on what had started as a doodle and was emerging to be a drawing of a fantastically ornamental griffin-type creature, with curled claws and scaly legs and intricate pluming. K resolved to bring in some color pencils next time. The gasps, hoarse whispers and malicious insinuations literally went in one ear and out the other, K having established a play-stop-erase routine that allowed him to get through the whole sorry mess in record time. A muffled voice came on—the message so short that K had erased it before he could check himself.

Which was a pity, more than a pity, because this had been a new voice, a disguised voice, and it had not sounded like a crank call. It had been too short, the voice too nervous, to be a crank call. And now it was gone. Erased forever. But K was pretty sure that he had the message right.

He raced out of the building, threw himself into the truck and kept his foot on the accelerator flying up the Aleppo Road, tore open the door, bounded up to the sofa where Begay was snoozing with Wittgenstein on his chest, bellowed "Wakey, wakey!" in Begay's ear, set his boots before him and commanded, "Chop chop, Mr. Private Investigator! Your services are required!"

CHAPTER THIRTY-FIVE

"I don't know that I feel entirely comfortable with this," said K.

Robbie Begay, he had to hand him that, hadn't taken long to be fully awake; had taken even shorter to understand the implications of what K was telling him; and had been way ahead of K in terms of devising a plan of action.

"You really like to worry, huh?" said Begay. "We both got legit IDs and we got legitimate cause."

"We got all that," admitted K. "But not in the right combination."

"It's just a lil' recce we're on anyways. Just some preliminary fact-checking, to make sure we're on the right track. No big deal."

"Hm." K remained unconvinced. In his opinion Begay was enjoying himself a tad too much.

"What are you afraid of? You don't rate your job anyways. Neither do I. So what's the worst that can happen? We get thrown out."

"Is this a version of suicide by cop?"

"Trust you to always come up with death," said Begay.

• • • • •

She had none of the effusive joviality, the manic bonhomie that was so often used to mask that all-pervasive American fear: the fear of the stranger.

She was as slim, as carefully groomed, as conventionally presentable as was to be expected of the wife of an important man, a wealthy man, harbinger of prosperity, employment and environmental destruction, and of the mother to a twin set of ice queens.

She looked as if she could freeze a man's balls off at twenty paces.

Surprisingly, she bought their mealy-mouthed pretext for the purpose of this visit.

The purpose of their visit was, according to Robbie Begay's edict, the entirely routine matter of following up on Lucky Easton's mandated DWI compliance.

"Please," said Mrs. Easton and gestured in the direction of what K believed was called a den, an annex space to accommodate children, less desirable visitors and perhaps the gardener on his coffee break, who had to make up to plants entirely unsuited to these climes what nature could not deliver.

To get to the quarantine zone of the den they had to traverse commodious expanses of dazzlingly varnished wood flooring, tiled walkways and a high-ceilinged, light-flooded hall where humongous Pueblo pottery stood about on adobe plinths.

Begay stopped next to a shining black pot with the dimensions of a cauldron erstwhile used by cannibals to get some use out of missionaries.

"Maria Martinez," said Mrs. Easton sharply.

"Maria Martinez?" asked Begay, undeterred, running a finger along the pot's rim.

Mrs. Easton looked as if she was getting ready to get out her taser.

Begay stroked the smooth black glazing. "Auntie Maria never lost her gift, even when she was just making pottery for tourists," he said dreamily.

"Auntie?" said Mrs. Easton.

Begay nodded in a way that conveyed that he had already said too much, and wouldn't say any more, what with ancient Pueblo pottery clan secrets and all.

Mrs. Easton's mien turned from glacial hostility to brittle reverence.

In the den she retrieved an embossed folder from a heavy oak shelf and began rooting through it.

"Did you go see my husband at his office?" asked Mrs. Easton.

To K's horror Begay nodded.

"Could he not help you?"

"He wasn't available, Ma'am," said Begay.

"He wasn't available?" asked Mrs. Easton. Watching her face was like watching water freeze over during an ice storm.

"There's nothing here on his DUI," said Mrs. Easton through clenched teeth, and snapped the folder shut.

"Is Mr. Easton at his hunting cabin?" asked Begay.

"Up at Calvary Peak?" said Mrs. Easton.

"Calvary Peak?" yelped K enthusiastically. "One of my friends has a cabin up on Calvary. Great hunting there."

"He won't be there. The cabin's closed." said Mrs. Easton.

"You keep your cabin closed during hunting season?" hunting-enthusiast K asked incredulously.

"There are some repairs scheduled, so we are not using it this season."

"Our friend's cabin is called 'Deliverance,'" said K. "Do you happen to know it?"

"Can't say that I do," said Mrs. Easton.

"Deliverance is an original name for a rural hunting cabin, don't you think?" asked K.

Mrs. Easton looked at him as if she was getting ready to call in the psychiatric crisis team, and did not answer.

"What's your cabin called?" asked Begay jovially.

"Hermitage." Mrs. Easton got up from the table and led the way to the door.

• • • •

"Maybe I can get a discount on one of her pots by your Auntie Maria?" said K in the car.

"Sure," said Begay. "She likes having her pots in as many bílagáana hogans as possible."

"Auntie Maria negotiates from beyond the grave?"

"You wouldn't believe the stuff she does," said Begay cheerfully.

"I look forward to my masterpiece," said K.

"Auntie's magic," said Begay. "She got me from lowlife Indian to artisan Native in no time at all."

"Do you have many aunties and uncles?" asked K.

"Me? I'm practically related to everybody: Zuni, Hopi, Santo Domingo, Acoma, Santa Clara."

CHAPTER THIRTY-SIX

The road to Calvary was not smooth.

The road to Calvary was an obscure turnoff at the north end of County Road Q, an ungraded washboard path that turned into a narrow, steep, stony and potholed affair.

K's Datsun truck careened over potholes the size of craters, revved up 25 degree inclines and bumped along a sheer drop. A couple of times he thought he could hear Begay wince.

Gradually the path broadened and smoothed out, and they entered a clearing which soon opened onto a vast alpine meadow.

"Pretty neat, huh?" said Begay.

The meadow was studded with yellow blooms, the latest, probably the last of the season. How like humans to disrupt these last mild weeks before the harsh season set in, and which animals needed to fatten up against the long winter months. How like humans to terrorize all these creatures with their murderous pursuits.

At the far end of the meadow, at the forest edge, sun light reflected off glass.

"Whereto, my guide?" asked K.

Begay studied the meadow, looked up at the sun and pointed in a westerly direction.

K obediently drove in the appointed direction. The rough track made him fear for his axle. They rounded the meadow. Begay pointed to a track leading into the forest. The track was another steep one. Tall conifers loomed, casting dark shadows. The track led to a small clearing on which stood a redwood cabin.

"Is that it?" whispered K. "The Hermitage?"

"Why are you whispering?" said Begay. "No need to whisper. We are legit, remember? Besides, there's nobody here that counts."

Begay jumped out of the truck and approached the cabin as if he possessed a lease for it. He circled it, whistling loudly.

"Do you have to be that conspicuous?" hissed K.

"Do you see that?" Begay boomed, and pointed. He walked up to the solid wooden front door, adorned with a brass knocker the shape of an elk's head.

"Tasteful," K said.

"Hello!" boomed Begay, lifting the elk's head and letting it drop with a clang. Begay listened. "Ain't nobody in," he said.

He set off and K followed him. Begay did another circle of the cabin. At the back of the cabin a path led from the woods to another door, narrow and unadorned by brass fittings and knockers.

Begay walked up to the door, peered at it, examined the lock and pushed at the door. It gave.

"It's open?" asked K.

Begay nodded and put a finger to his lips. It seemed a bit late to be worrying about making noise now, but what the heck.

They entered an impressively appointed living room with a high ceiling and a stone-clad fire place that took up the entire wall, with a bear rug in front of it. Colorful woven rugs were scattered about. An enormous sofa, draped in another bearskin, faced the fire place.

Carved oak doors fanned out from the living room: bedrooms and bathrooms probably.

Begay disregarded the oak doors. He seemed interested in only one door, a narrow white door that blended into the wall; a door that they might have overlooked, had it not stood ajar.

Begay approached the door, listened, slowly and carefully pushed it open, revealing a space of cavernous darkness.

K looked at the flight of stairs leading into obscurity. "I didn't know log cabins have basements," he said.

"Some do, some don't," whispered Begay.

They tiptoed down the stairs.

"What's that smell?" whispered K.

Begay led the way and did not answer. The light from the living room did not penetrate where they were going.

"I can't see anything," K whispered.

K heard Begay digging into his pockets. A click and a narrow beam of light appeared on the wall facing them. The torch's beam danced along the raw stone wall and came to rest on another door.

All K could hear was the sound of blood pounding in his temples, and Robbie trying to control his breathing.

Begay walked softly to the door and pushed it open.

He let the light beam travel across the room, over the floor, over the sleeping bag on the floor, the empty water canister, the bucket. . . .

"Ugh," said K.

Begay swiped the torch across the room once more and walked to the door. He shone the torch at the lock, nodded, walked on up the stairs, examined the basement door, nodded again and made toward the back door, checked out the lock and nodded some more. He crouched down, examined the path leading from the cabin's backdoor into the woods and set off on it without looking back.

How Begay knew where he was going, K did not know, but it surely looked as if he knew where he was going. Begay was picking up the pace, leading the way around a thicket, through a cluster of bushes, through some trees and up a steep incline. Then he stopped. They were standing on top of a steep promontory. Through the trees they had a good view across the vast alpine meadow.

They must have climbed farther than K had realized. Begay turned and made his way along a slippery path that sloped steeply down toward a hollow covered in undergrowth.

Begay stopped and stood, like an animal taking up scent, K

thought, and very slowly turned his head as if listening to something.

Across the usual forest noises, bird call, falling pine cones bouncing off soft forest floor, the crackling made by animals moving through undergrowth, K thought he could hear something too. And what he heard made his blood run cold.

"Do you hear whimpering?" he whispered.

Begay nodded.

They got down the slope half walking, half sliding. Up here it must have rained not so long ago, and the narrow track was slick with mud.

The sound was more audible here.

Begay picked his way through bushes, shrubs and undergrowth and stopped under a stunted oak tree.

K sprinted across the undergrowth and vaulted over dead wood, ripping loose from thorny branches that held onto his clothes and skin.

Together they looked down at the ragged whimpering bundle folded into itself in a fetal position.

"Luisa?" said K softly. "Luisa?"

The bundle whimpered.

"We are going to take you home, Luisa," K said. "Don't be scared. All is going to be alright now."

•　•　•　•

"How did you find her?" asked the paramedic.

"Just out on a hike," said K.

The girl's clothes were dirt-crusted and blood caked. Blood was seeping from multiple cuts and grazes. Her hair was matted, her lips cracked and her skin translucent.

There was no telling how severe Luisa's injuries were.

Begay and K hadn't dared risk carrying Luisa up the slope. They hadn't dared taking the risk of driving her down to Milagro in K's rickety truck.

Of course they couldn't get a phone signal on Calvary, so K had to drive all the way downhill. From the foot of the mountain he had called emergency services. Emergency services had sent out the mountain rescue paramedics. Mountain rescue had taken a pretty long time, because K had not been able to pinpoint their precise location.

"All's going to be fine now," the mountain rescuers said to the girl they were carrying on the stretcher, unconsciously echoing what K had told her before.

CHAPTER THIRTY-SEVEN

K was learning to be grateful for small mercies. After all it was better to find people whose cases one had been working on unconscious or comatose in the hospital, rather than having them croak.

There they were, both of K's charges, at Milagro General, just a few rooms apart.

Once the Sarslund's insurance coverage had been assessed, Laurie had been brought forth from the soylent green bowels of the hospital to the more august beige-walled and O'Keefe-adorned upper echelons.

K didn't think the Sarslunds noticed or minded one way or another.

At Luisa's bed the female members of the Alvarez family were holding vigil. Three generations of women; three ways of being; three ways of making a life in this country.

Luisa's cuts and grazes had been cleaned up and covered by plasters. Her hair had been brushed and braided and she was hooked up to a drip.

"She'll be fine," said the nurse who had caught K poking his head around the corner. The nurse's voice drew the Alvarez' attention to the door, precisely what K had wished to avoid.

K sheepishly handed over the sunflower that he had brought for Luisa, for no other reason than William Blake had penned a poem about a sunflower. K was conflicted about Blake's poem, which had a slightly morbid ring to it, but liked the sunflower without reservation. "Girasol"—the flower that turns with the sun.

The Alvarez family beamed at him as at a long-lost friend, and abuelita's gnarled hands fastened around his. She spoke in low soft Maya and Mrs. Alvarez translated.

The old woman was thanking him for bringing back her granddaughter; thanking him for helping them; thanking him for listening to her dreams.

K said, "It was your granddaughter Maribel who told me about your dreams first."

The old woman said something and patted her granddaughter's hand. Maribel's eyes filled with tears.

K wondered if her family could guess of how often Maribel had gone to the police station, how hard she had tried to make Milagro PD take her little sister's disappearance seriously, how she blamed herself.

K hung around, keeping in the background. He doubted that Luisa would be ready to communicate anytime soon. Still—it was better to be there, to be ready—just in case.

When Córdoba arrived K knew he could leave with a clear conscience. If anyone could get a statement from Luisa, it was Juanita Córdoba.

Córdoba was carrying a bunch of radiant dahlias.

"Lovely choice of flowers," murmured K.

"It's the national flower of Mexico," Córdoba said.

K hoped the Alvarez family wouldn't interpret Córdoba's bouquet as a 'Go back where you came from" message and his Blake-inspired sunflower as a "We're all gonna die" statement.

"Should we let the school know that Luisa's been found?" asked K.

"I already did," said Córdoba. "I talked to her teacher , Ms. Davies. She was real relieved."

"I bet she was," said K.

He tried not to show his disappointment that Córdoba had deprived him of one of the few pleasant encounters this case had to offer.

On his way out he looked in on Laurie.

The Sarslunds were still sitting where K had left them the night before. They were still reading Charlotte's Web to their daughter, or maybe they'd started over reading the book again and would keep on doing so until—? Until.

CHAPTER THIRTY-EIGHT

"Because I say so," said Weismaker sternly. The sheriff seemed to be getting sharper these days. Maybe it was all the budget cuts and the prospect of a "Hang 'em High" county commissioner. Still, K didn't see why Weismaker had to take it out on him.

"I was involved in the case from the beginning, Sir," he said. "I think it should be me. . . ."

"Precisely," interrupted the sheriff. "That's why it's not going to be you doing the questioning."

Who then, thought K.

Gutierrez—he had certainly carried his share of the case, but Gutierrez had conservative values, and he was critical of Maribel's lifestyle choices—if you could call them choices—so you could hardly call his slate clean either.

Córdoba was out of the running—even K had to accept that—because she had taken the lead role interviewing the cheerleaders, and however skilled her technique and however perfidious her ruses, it was likely that the suspects had learned their lesson the second time round and wouldn't spill in Córdoba's presence..

Who remained? Young, Dilger, Smithson, who'd all thought of Luisa as a teenage whore—who probably still did. Once those guys got a prejudice between their teeth, they didn't let go.

Myers? K could see Myers going through the motions, neutral up to a point. He couldn't see Myers getting very far though, because most of Myers' brainpower went on figuring out where to source spare parts for the junkyard assembly he called his "vintage vehicle collection."

"I'll do it," the sheriff said. "You can watch."

"Nothing will come of it anyways," said K sulkily. "As soon as you get near them, they'll lawyer up and that'll be the end of that."

"Hasn't anyone told you?" asked Weismaker. "We got them in already."

•   •   •   •

The Easton twins did not need a lawyer. Though questioned separately they were a fine-tuned alternative fact machine churning out bland denial after bland denial.

The Easton twins admitted to Luisa Alvarez being at the Hermitage.—Yes, Luisa had stayed at the hunting cabin. No, they hadn't taken her there against her will.

What about Luisa telling police that on the day of her abduction she had accepted a ride from the Eastons, believing they would take her home, but instead she'd been taken to the hunting cabin against her will?

—Luisa was probably afraid of her family's reaction. Luisa had simply needed some time away from her folks.

Was that why they had kept her locked in the basement with a bucket as a bathroom?

—Luisa felt nervous alone in the cabin. She felt safer in the basement.

And the bucket?

—Luisa had just been too frightened to walk through the dark house on her own.

Why had Luisa broken the cellar-door lock and the backdoor lock and tried to flee?

—No idea. Maybe she'd heard a noise and it had freaked her out. Luisa was a nervous type of person.

What about the fake porn profile that had been set up for Luisa?

—Fake porn profile? Nasty! They didn't know about anything like that. Chelsea at least had had the grace to blush.

Maybe, suggested Taylor, they should have a look at that boy—what was his name—Coo-aw-tee-mock? He'd been creeping around Luisa. He might have felt angry he wasn't getting anywhere with her. There was all kinds of stuff, virtual and real, he might have tried to do to her out of revenge. Mexicans had this macho attitude toward women. When they couldn't have what they wanted they got mean and nasty. That was well known. Better check his papers too—Oh, by the way—had they checked Luisa's family's papers? Nowadays you could never be sure who was legal and who wasn't. . . .

Watching the farce, K was losing the will to live.

Through all this time with Chelsea and then with Taylor Easton the sheriff never lost his composure, nor his somewhat distant neutrality. Here was a man who was doing his job; a professional who wasn't invested one way or the other, whose task was merely to find out what had happened. And if he didn't—to know that he had done his best to cover all bases.

From the first minute of questioning it had been clear to K that neither Chelsea nor Taylor Easton were going to crack. So K assumed that Weismaker too hadn't any illusions how these interviews would conclude.

You had to hand it to the sociopath twins: their explanations for Luisa's presence in the hunting cabin were, if not entirely convincing, then at least plausible. Pointing the finger at Cuauhtémoc as the possible creator of the porn profile was fiendishly clever and entirely ruthless.

K had no doubt that the majority of his cherished colleagues would happily believe that a Mexican family's love was so stifling that a sleeping bag and a bucket in a basement were a preferable alternative to it—that or running away to make it as a teen porn queen. And everyone knew about priapic Latin machos and their notorious disregard for women.

There were few things worse than sitting in the observation suite, behind the one-way mirror, powerless, observing questioning going nowhere.

As per usual Weismaker had been right. K was too invested in the case, too partisan. There was no way he would have been able to keep it together as the sheriff did right now, calmly seated opposite the demonically glacial and freakishly self-possessed Taylor Easton, clad in modishly distressed jeans, pink short-sleeved T-shirt under a rhinestone studded denim vest, idly fiddling with a strand of golden hair, occasionally crossing or uncrossing her legs, answering every question in a tone as if discussing the weather.

K saw clearly now why the world was in the state it was in: It was because it favored people who possessed the Easton twins' moral vacuity and social skill set. The Eastons would go far, that much was clear. Had an Ivy League establishment witnessed these interviews both Easton girls would have been offered unconditional admission, he was ready to bet.

He was beholding the full glory of the post-truth world, a whole new golden dawn for a generation who had been taught the art of unaccountability by the highest in the land.

K wondered when the sheriff would feel sufficiently bloodied by trying to pound blood out of stones to terminate the interviews.

Conducting an interview with suspects who were clearly not going to crack—no matter what—was maybe even worse than just observing it. At least K could just get up and go whenever he pleased.

Just as K had resolved to do just that, there was a knock on the door of the interrogation room and Becky entered. The sheriff courteously thanked Taylor Easton and declared the interview concluded. Becky would see her out.

The only time K had seen Taylor Easton marginally flustered was when the sheriff thanked her.

Becky's nostrils were pinched and white. Never a good sign.

K went through to ask Weismaker if he was wanted for anything else.

"Yes," said Weismaker. "There's just one interview to go and you might as well stay."

"It's like watching Sisyphus pushing his boulder uphill," K said ungraciously. To be fair, much of his life was like that anyways.

Besides, one probably had a better chance of happiness by letting go of one's lily-livered, liberal-claptrap, snow-flakey ideas on justice, integrity, ethics and all that jazz.

CHAPTER THIRTY-NINE

K sipped his cold coffee and watched the sheriff arranging chairs in the interrogation room. Apparently Weismaker expected two people.

K couldn't figure whom the Sheriff was going to interview. He had questioned and released his two prime suspects barely half an hour ago. It was bound to be someone and their lawyer, which wasn't good. Any lawyer worth their salt would not take long to ferret out that nothing about K's involvement in the case was kosher and that it was thin ice all around that he—and by extension the case—was standing on.

The version of finding Luisa that K and Begay had settled on did not bear much scrutiny: they had been on an innocent hike, tralala, just stretching their legs and getting clean mountain air into their lungs, balancing along a muddy slope off the trodden path as one does, when they heard a noise, followed it—and found Luisa. Voilá.

As to the basement situation and the bucket and all that, Begay had been led to Lucky Easton's hunting cabin basement by following Luisa's tracks in reverse. Begay had given a statement to that effect, dazzling them with detail and blinding them with track-reader jargon, and had managed to be a damn sight more convincing than K had ever succeeded in being. When K attempted to lie he had so many tells that it was like a giant neon sign lit above his head spelling 'Pants on Fire!' with a giant index finger pointing at him. Flick on; flick off.

Lacandon DREAMS

• • • •

As usual when he was sitting in the dimly lit observation room looking out into the *Interviewing Suite* as on to a stage, K's *wanderlustig* mind embarked on a reverie. How weird to be here, of all places, this country, this small town, this police station. This POLICE station. How come he'd become a cop? He of all people?

It had all started as a joke. The joke had been to find the job that he deemed furthest from his sensibilities. He didn't remember if he'd pursued this challenge in the spirit of self-improvement or self-destruction. But life had a habit of surprising you. Because against all odds there were things he liked about this job. There were many things that he didn't like, for sure.

But then there were moments—like the time spent with abuelita and Mrs. Alvarez pondering on Lacandon dreams—that he cherished.

Or beholding the Sarslunds reading *Charlotte's Web* to their daughter. Maybe such moments weren't strictly police business, but they were the unexpected gifts that police business sometimes brought with it.

Abuelita's dreams hadn't helped at all with finding Luisa, but they had opened a door, like Magnusson had said. The door that had been opened for K was the permission to take seriously his internal life, his unconscious, his dreams. The open door was to acknowledge all that nurtured him, all that disquieted him, all that was important to him and that he had kept to himself, as a legitimate, meaningful part of his life.

Knowing that there was a whole bunch of people—an entire tribe—in a rainforest thousands of miles away, the fabric of whose social life revolved around dreams, went some way toward K's own dream-world and dream-time; his secret, hidden life that hereabouts he didn't share, that he had always been slightly ashamed of.

Knowing that there was an old woman as far away from her

people as he was from his, with whom there had been a meeting of minds, a meeting of souls even—that helped.

The door opened and the Sheriff appeared. He held open the door and ushered in two women. The women were tall, slim, possessed of glossy tresses and attired in tailored jeans and fitted shirts.

Weismaker motioned toward the chairs and each woman took a seat, crossing left leg over right, sitting upright, straight-backed. Their pose indicated that they wished to spend as short a time as possible in the interrogation room, even though it was now called the Interviewing Suite.

The women looked alike and of a similar age. K couldn't remember if, excepting the Easton twins, there had been any other sisters involved in this woeful case. And then he recognized one of them. The young woman with the superior smile bordering on sneer was Ava Byrone, the third in the triumvirate of cheerleader leaders.

Slowly it dawned on K that the other woman was Ava Byrone's mother, not Ava's sister as he had first assumed. There was a whole new phenomenon of mothers and daughters preserved and got up to looking like siblings. Mothers looking the age of their daughters, were as disconcerting and plain wrong as daughters calling their mothers their "best friend."

K remembered a controversial lecture by a professor of sociology who had been too old to give a fuck. The old brontosaur had opined that far from being a biological imperative, incest avoidance was not an inbuilt human imperative—it was merely due to historically shorter fertility spans and later sexual maturation. By the time their children were of a reproductive age, parents commonly were fast approaching the big sleep. Fathers were simply too old, too tired, too decrepit to take sexual advantage of their daughters. Nowadays however, the old professor said, when mothers and daughters looked like sisters, who could blame fathers for being erotically confused? The lecture had provoked a stampede of walkouts, as far as K remembered. Nevertheless, he wouldn't have minded sharing the professor's incest-theory with the Byrones.

There was much more at risk than age-deniers dissolving generational gaps. Once generational gaps had been dissolved, it was but a short step to upending the natural order and from there just a hop and a skip to mayhem and chaos. You just had to look out at that creepy mother+daughter=besties mashup to see how these things went.

K's unquiet mind migrated to Miss Williams, the buxom geography teacher, who had one afternoon cornered him in the supply room and performed on him what was euphemistically called "a sex act." He'd never told anyone about the supply room incident. At fourteen, you didn't tend to look a gift horse in the mouth.

K emerged out of memory lane. The observation suite seemed to encourage reverie. A couple of times K had missed dramatic turns and spectacular disclosures because his mind had been elsewhere.

Right now however it didn't look as if a breakthrough was imminent. The interview had been going on for quite a while and Ava was glibly fielding and denying her way through Weismaker's questions.

"Do you know of any reason why Taylor and Chelsea might have disliked Luisa?" asked the sheriff.

Ava shrugged her shoulders.

"Is that a yes or a no?" asked Weismaker mildly.

Ava sneered. "No."

"No?" asked Weismaker again.

"No," said Ava.

"Not even because Taylor and Chelsea's father has an affair with Luisa's older sister?" Weismaker asked.

Ava did an elaborate shrugging and shaking-head thing.

"What are you saying?" Mrs. Byrone the elder had the husky voice of a film noir femme fatale.

"Mr. Easton is having an affair with Maribel Alvarez, Luisa's older sister," Weismaker said matter-of-factly.

How exactly had the sheriff come by this information? It surely wouldn't—couldn't— have been prudish Gutierrez grassing on a fellow Mexican-American? How?

"Lucky?" Mrs. Byrone had uncrossed her legs and was rearing in her chair like a cobra ready to strike. "Lucky Easton is having an affair with that girl? The Hispanic girl who works in his office?"

Weismaker nodded mildly. "A love affair. It has been going on for a while. It is serious. I believe there has been talk of Mr. Easton leaving his wife."

"He is going to leave his wife?" Mrs. Byrone rasped.

"I believe so," Weismaker said.

"He is going to leave his wife?!" Mrs. Byrone leant forward, eyes flashing. Enraged, she was a truly formidable sight. "For that little—? Let me tell you something—"

"Mom," Ava said warningly.

Mrs. Byrone clawed at the air with crimson nails. "I will tell you what happened—"

"MOM!!"

"The Easton girls wanted to scare Luisa. They could not stand her, the little Pollyanna, with her great grades and being the teacher's pet, with her family that are illegals I bet, taking advantage of the system—"

"Mom. . . please. . . ."

"Lucky and that little bitch . . . I knew he couldn't keep it in his trousers, but this. . . . He's got no standards. No standards AT ALL. . . ."

"Mommy!!"

"The Alvarez girl—they meant to scare her. Teach her a lesson. I hope those goddamn illegals were scared. I especially hope they scared the hell out of that little beaner whore."

"So the Easton girls took Luisa to the hunting cabin?" asked Weismaker.

"To scare her," said Mrs. Byrone.

"You knew this?" asked Weismaker.

"They tried to pull my daughter into it. My daughter tells me everything," said Mrs. Byrone.

"Mom!" whimpered Ava.

"He's destroyed his family. Lucky's lying has destroyed his daughters' lives. They'll be charged. They'll be detained. They'll never get into a good school now. Their future's all gone," Mrs. Byrone smiled triumphantly. "Make sure you tell him that. Make sure the goddamn son of a bitch understands what he has done."

CHAPTER FORTY

K turned the brown envelope in his hands. It was addressed to Officer Kafka c/o Milagro PD, no sender, and K had an inkling what it was. The only safe and quiet spot he could think of was Lorinda's supply room.

His favorite refuge, the Observation Suite, was occupied by Myers training Young how to record an interrogation.

K pulled the door to and switched on the lights. The supply room smelled strongly of bleach and the citrus-scented cleaning fluids that Lorinda preferred. The only place to sit on was the four-rung stepladder.

The envelope wasn't stamped. It would have been dropped through the station's letter-slot.

K contemplated donning a pair of Lorinda's disposable latex gloves, and decided against it. The envelope was glued shut. K tried to prise apart the edges, gave up and tore it open.

The envelope contained some folded handwritten sheets of paper, a social security card, a driver's license and two bankcards.

K put the cards back inside and unfolded the letter.

It was written on plain paper, in a large, rounded, almost childish hand by someone who was used to writing on lined paper, or in any case had trouble writing in a straight line. The closer the writing got to the end of the page the more it sloped downward. Graphologists would know a thing to make of that. Here and there a word and been whited out and overwritten.

K wondered how many suicide letters sported Wite-Out corrections.

Having read the letter to the end, K returned to its beginning.

Strictly speaking it wasn't so much a suicide letter as a manifesto; a political call for action; a rallying cry to environmentalists; a finger of blame pointing to the XOX corporation and its heinous acts of destruction.

What was missing was any trace of Laurie Sarslund as an individual; any suggestion of personal commitments and attachments beyond the environmental cause. No mention of family, friends, foes, lovers. No hint to a life other than that of an activist fighting for a greater cause.

It was a letter well-written; a letter that made its points concisely and effectively; a perfect letter for passing on to a newspaper—and definitely not a letter written by a suicidal idealist.

K went to the squad office and placed Eren Solana's manifesto somewhere in the middle of Laurie Sarslund's file. He doubted that anyone would be interested enough in the Sarslund file to find it, and if they were, there was a good chance that they wouldn't think to ask how the letter had gotten into the file.

Sloth and slovenliness had some advantages.

•   •   •   •

That night K dreamt of coming upon a white horse in a clearing. It stood as if waiting for him, and when he got closer he saw that it wasn't a horse, but a unicorn. He stretched out an arm and the creature reared on its hind legs, took a flying jump and was gone.

The disappointment of the vanishing unicorn awoke K.

In this more prosaic lucid state K realized the shortcomings of his anthropological approach to the interpretation of Lacandon dreams and his narrow assumption that people dreamt of what made sense to them and what fitted into their cultural frame of reference.

Because even dreaming of jaguars and spider monkeys would

have been more plausible and appropriate to K's context and circumstances than dreaming of a unicorn.

CHAPTER FORTY-ONE

The Sarslunds received Laurie's effects, driving license, social security and bank cards without querying their provenance. Once again K had squandered emotional energy and valuable headspace on a scenario that had remained imaginary.

In any case the Sarslunds were too elated, too excited to ask questions.

Laurie had smiled.

K did not dare look to the nurse who'd just entered the room for confirmation. It was a common thing for relatives of comatose loved ones to detect positive and definitive signs of consciousness.

It had been a definite smile, said Mrs. Sarslund, as if psychic.

Laurie's dad had been reading: *"Fern was up at daylight, trying to rid the world of injustice. As a result, she now has a pig,"*[1] and that had made Laurie smile.

That place in the book had always made them laugh as a family.

More precisely: *"As a result, she now has a pig,"* was what had made Laurie smile, and Mrs. Sarslund had grabbed hold of her husband's arm, forgetting the cup of coffee, and the coffee had spilt and stained the book—it was the book that Laurie had had since her eighth birthday, and they hadn't been sure if the story wasn't too heavy perhaps for an eight-year-old, but Laurie had loved it and understood what it was about—and maybe had chosen to become an activist because of it.

"Up at daylight, trying to rid the world of injustice" was very Laurie.

Rather than stained, the book was soaked top to bottom, cover to cover, in coffee. It must have been a big cup.

"What will you read to Laurie now?" K asked. He doubted that the book could be salvaged.

"We'll get another one for when Laurie wakes up," said Mrs. Sarslund.

"We know it by heart now anyway," said Atticus.

• • • •

"I shouldn't have thought that's your reading matter," said Agnes Prohaska. "It's a great book, but for another type of cloud head than you are."

Agnes Prohaska's heavy accent took some of the sting out of "cloud head" and made it sound almost affectionate.

K relayed the tale of Laurie and *Charlotte's Web*.

"You don't believe she smiled?" asked Prohaska.

"You have to try not to get up your hopes too much," said K.

"Not get your hopes up too much?" echoed Prohaska. "What is wrong with you?"

"You should approve," K protested. "Opium for the people and all that. Once you believe in miracles you might just as well call it a day and go for religion."

Prohaska laughed. "Touché," she said.

"I will miss you, you know," K said.

"You still have time to think about my proposal," said Prohaska. She shook loose a cigarette from a packet of Gitanes, put it between her lips and struck a match. A cloud of smoke rose like Beelzebub and the smell of sulphur and burning tobacco enveloped them.

"Come along then," she said.

K followed her along countless rows of shelves, here and there the title of an old favorite catching his eye; a cover beckoning; a couple of words promising a new discovery, a new world. They side-stepped boxes spilling over with books, chairs piled with books, stacks of books collapsing against shelves.

Prohaska led the way to a side room K hadn't known that was there, lined with glass-fronted book cases; she opened a case, stood on tip-toe and angled for a book.

"Here." She passed the book to K.

It was an unblemished copy of Charlotte's Web in hardcover, complete with dust jacket. "That must be one of the early editions?" K said, opening it.

He did a double take. "Is that what I think it is?"

"How should I know what you think it is?" growled Prohaska.

"A signed copy," said K.

"It is," said Prohaska.

"That's not in my budget, I'm afraid," said K.

"Did I give you the first edition?" Prohaska asked.

K squinted at the book: "Third. Still—it's bound to be really expensive. You have a signed first edition?"

"I think so," Prohaska said. "Mind: If you happen to agree to my proposal—I still haven't made up my mind what I want to do with my signed first editions."

"Bummer," said K. He was trying to calculate what he could afford to shell out on a signed third-edition copy of *Charlotte's Web*. He decided he didn't mind making his wallet squeal. As with any magical thinking, you had to hurt a little to make something work. Provided the truck didn't throw up any repairs in the next three months. . . .

Prohaska pressed the book into his hands. "Take it. Compliments of the house."

"But. . . ," K protested.

"And may a miracle happen," said Agnes Prohaska.

1. Ibid

CHAPTER FORTY-TWO

It was only when he had to brake sharply at a red light that K noticed he had been doing 55 in a 35-mile zone. He turned into Anasazi. At the pedestrian crossing the lights were flashing, which meant that school was out.

How he found himself on Milagro Middle and High School's parking lot, he couldn't say. It was the part of the parking lot dominated by Subarus, VWs and Toyota Prius—probably where staff parked their vehicles. K got out of his rickety Datsun pickup and leant against the cabin. He needed to clear his head.

"Officer Kafka."

Siwan Davies was wearing something light and summery, her skin the hue of a sun-kissed peach and—Oh Lord Have Mercy—she was blushing.

Siwan Davies' blushing was like Viagra to K, damn it.

"Is it about Luisa?" she asked anxiously.

"No," said K. "Luisa is doing fine. She is due to be discharged from the hospital in a couple of days. You can go and visit her if you like."

"I will," said Siwan Davies.

"I came because I need some advice—" K said.

"Advice?" asked Siwan Davies.

"How about I buy you a coffee and tell you?" said K.

"Sure," said Siwan Davies lightly. "Advice is part of our job description."

K took Siwan Davies to the independently owned Conifer Coffee House whose rickety furniture, coffee-stained doilies and yellowing net curtains he hoped would keep his mind from straying to untoward thoughts.

He bought them each a coffee, which was served in quaint blue-and-white-striped ceramic mugs. Siwan Davies declined the offer of a pastry and took her coffee black. K spooned some sugar into his cup. Stirring gave him something to do.

Siwan Davies' luminous eyes were fixed on his face. Her expression was somber and attentive. No blushing now.

"You think your life is pretty much set on its tracks and then something comes up." Too late he noticed how this might sound—a wordy and hackneyed prelude to a declaration of romantic interest of the kind you saw in old movies—which were the only kind of movies that K ever watched.

But Siwan Davies nodded earnestly. Here was a dame who could tell the difference between wooing and counsel.

"Do you know the bookstore?" K asked. In the near-half-century of her tenure, Agnes Prohaska had not found it necessary to give her shop a name. She had retained some of the austere pragmatism of her communist homeland. "Agnes Prohaska's bookstore?"

Siwan Davies' face brightened. "It's really something, that store. I wouldn't be surprised if people got lost in it and you'd find them years later—mummified." The thought was less fanciful than it was off-putting.

"Ugh," K said.

"I was joking," Siwan Davies said.

"You may have helped me make up my mind," K said, and he told her about Agnes Prohaska's proposition.

Siwan Davies' eyes shone with enthusiasm.

"You seem to really like the idea," said K, somewhat grudgingly, because he had banked on her talking him out of it.

"Don't you?" Siwan Davies asked. "If you weren't contemplating it, I don't think you would have asked for careers advice,

301

do you?" She paused. "I am not your careers counselor," she said, "and so I'll take the freedom to tell you what I think: I love the idea. I think it is an opportunity for you. I think it will do you good and it will get you out of your rut—"

"You seem to know a lot about me," said K.

"It's pretty obvious," said Siwan Davies heatedly. "Besides—there's not that much risk. That's what you just told me Agnes Prohaska said. You could just try it for a while and see how it goes, and at the end you may have opened a new door, or at the very least you'll have learnt something about yourself. Maybe that new thing will be that you shouldn't run a bookstore—but give it a chance, do."

"With everything that doesn't work out a bit of hope dies," K said.

Siwan Davies' eyes were of the deepest blue and she looked at him with an expression he could not read.

"Does that mean you should not try it?" she asked finally.

"It would be a reason not to try it," K said.

"So one should just wallow and conduct one's life with disappointment avoidance as its imperative?" asked Siwan Davies.

It sounded dreadful.

"A bookstore run by Franz Kafka," said Siwan Davies dreamily. "I'd definitely go there. He's one of my all-time literary heroes. Isn't he yours?"

"I don't mind him," said K.

"You don't mind him?" Siwan Davies laughed and shook her head, making her red curls dance. "That's big of you. To me Kafka gets how things are. That metamorphosis thing. It is like he foresaw what would happen to the earth. Like he predicted the state we are in now."

"You read "The Metamorphosis" as a work on ecology?" asked K.

"Sure," Siwan Davies said. "Don't you?"

"It hadn't really occurred to me," said K.

Siwan Davies looked at him thoughtfully.

"What?" K asked eventually.

"You've got this wonderful name. And it kind of suits you too. And it doesn't seem to make you happy at all."

"We are back on our previous point," said K.

"You are back on your previous point," corrected Siwan Davies. "If you ran the bookstore, you could have loads of discussions on whether "The Metamorphosis" is a work on ecology—what do you read it as, by the way?"

K thought. "There's many ways to read it. I mainly read it as a work on puberty—the havoc that sexual maturation wreaks on a body: Gregor Samsa wakes up and is transformed into something monstrous and repulsive. Both Gregor himself and his parents are similarly repulsed and alienated by this body that cannot be controlled, that won't function as it did before." He looked up at Siwan Davies and said defiantly, "Every adolescent boy will recognize that. Metamorphosis is more realistic than surreal, believe me. I told you before—I take Kafka for a realistic writer."

Siwan Davies shuddered. "You did tell me. I remember. It's plausible—but disturbing and less enchanting than other possible interpretations. . . ."

"Interpretations? Over-interpretations more like. Mostly they serve critics' egos more than they reflect the authors' intentions. I loathe over-interpretations."

Siwan Davies laughed. "Just imagine! You could have discussions like this all day long."

"With you?" asked K and watched Siwan Davies blush.

•   •   •   •

Maybe Mrs. Sarslund cried every time she was given something, First the platter of fruit had made her cry and now her tears fell onto the copy of Charlotte's Web that she held in her hands, fell onto the pages she turned, would fall on E.B. White's signature. . . .

Atticus took the book out of his wife's hands. "Up at daylight, ridding the world of injustice?" and looked at K in the way that, in theory, he wished to be looked at—probing, and tender, and perceptive. In practice, Atticus' searching and affectionate gaze made K squirm.

K muttered his good wishes, assured them that Milagro PD was at their disposal and scampered.

In the corridor he ran into the nurse doing her rounds.

"Did she really smile?" he asked, before remembering that the nurse probably wouldn't be allowed to answer, due to medical confidentiality.

"She did," said the nurse.

In the depths of his solar plexus K felt the little caged bird of hope beginning to flutter.

"Really?" asked K.

The nurse nodded. "I think she's going to be okay."

"A miracle then?" asked K, before he could control himself.

"TLC," the nurse said.

"What is that?" K asked.

"Tender Loving Care," the nurse said and walked on.

EPILOGUE

On this day of handover, the last day of her reign, the spirit of the Beat Generation ruled Agnes Prohaska's Bookstore. Flaunting health and safety rules, the store's every nook and cranny was penetrated by a fug of smoke and the pungent, nostalgia-inducing smell of smoldering Gitanes.

In the fog K could make out Weismaker bearing a bottle of rye. There was Magnusson clutching an offering of a bottle of Tequila and one of vodka, shouldering his way through the throng. There was Siwan Davies with a serving platter of pesto pinwheels.

"You're not gonna hide in a corner?" chided Begay. "You got to get out and mix and mingle. These are your future customers, remember?"

"You let him boss you around like that?" Gloria asked.

K noticed Gloria and Robbie were holding hands.

"Wittgenstein misses you," K said.

"Tell him I'm gonna visit real soon," Begay threatened.

"Anytime," said K sincerely. He looked out at the throng of people mingling, drinking, teasing and conversing, and did not know how he felt.

"It's an experiment," said Magnusson the omniscient. "Not a lift to the scaffold."

"I told him that already," growled the sheriff. "I'll be expecting you to carry your full caseload! There ain't going to be extra leave days for any of this from Milagro PD, Son."

"You could punch it in as Outreach work," suggested K.

The sheriff pressed a glass of rye into K's hand, patted his shoulder and moved on.

"Was that a yes or no?" K asked Magnusson.

"It will be what you make it," said Magnusson cryptically.

"Perhaps you'd like to be my resident oracle?" suggested K.

"Apropos oracle," said Magnusson. "What happened with your Lacandon's dreams? Did they give you any clues?"

So much had happened, so much had changed, that K struggled to recall.

"Clues? Not as such, I don't think."

In the end the clue leading them to Luisa had been an old-fashioned one, a muffled voice on an info-line with a message that K had accidentally erased. A message by someone who'd served the wrong masters and who had finally decided to do the right thing. Seenthyia Breenhauser had found her conscience at last. K could not blame Seenthyia for wanting to remain anonymous. Taylor and Chelsea Easton were formidable foes.

The twins' vendetta directed at the Alvarez family had been relentless, well strategized and ruthless; they had ruled their entourage with an iron fist. K did not know if Luisa had ever found out about the fake profile the twins created for her. They certainly had wanted her to, slipping the web link into her school books, trolling Maribel and spreading rumors. The twins and their co-conspirators had gotten their just deserts and were going down, brought low by Easton's spurned lover whose wrath had been so boundless she had even been prepared to sacrifice Ava, her own daughter, for the sake of revenge.

Lucky Easton alone, the nucleus of betrayal, spoilage and destruction; original cause of Laurie Sarslund's attempted altruistic suicide; had remained unscathed and standing, and was, according to rumors, getting ready to run for political office on the back of four dozen semi-automatic handguns, ammo and lock boxes awaiting delivery to San Matteo County district schools.

"Will justice prevail, Mr. Oracle?" K asked Magnusson.

"Pinwheels?" asked Siwan Davies.

"I just had an offer for being the resident oracle," Magnusson said. "Should I take it up?"

"Any predictions?" asked Siwan.

"It takes a village to raise a bookstore," said Magnusson, "and beautiful strangers will become friends."

Siwan Davies blushed. Magnusson must have had a few. The big Swede was not usually that forward.

"Meet Ms. Davies," said K. "If my hopes are dashed, the sun of reality melts my wings of fancy and I crash and burn, blame her."

"That was quite a jumble of metaphors," said Siwan Davies. "Do let me know if you need a resident word police."

"I'm saying yes now," said K and watched Siwan Davies move away with her platter of pinwheels.

"Where do I put these?" Juanita Córdoba, clad in jeans and denim shirt, was hauling two bulging paper bags. "Duros and buñuelos," she explained.

"Homemade?" asked Magnusson.

Córdoba nodded. "Not by me. There's a couple of gallon jugs of agua fresca out in my truck too. It is sent to you by a very happy family."

There was a lump in K's throat. "They shouldn't have. We did our duty."

"You saved the life of a whole family," said Córdoba.

Whether he had saved anyone's life was debatable, but at least this time he hadn't been complicit in anyone's death—if one disregarded XOX's relentless advance to the core of Quorum Valley, its verdant heart and its sweet waters.

The earth's crust was a brittle skin above a churning inferno, upon which the human species, cloaked in grand delusions, conducted its petty affairs.

But for now there was nowhere that he would rather be than here.

"Who is that gentleman with the case of red standing by the door?" asked Magnusson. "Another grateful customer?"

"It's Atticus," said K and began working his way through the merry crowd.

BIBLIOGRAPHY—FURTHER READING

Bruce, Robert D.; Lacandon Dream Symbolism Vol. I: Dream Symbolism and Interpretation; Ediciones Euroamericanas Klaus Thiele, 1975

Bruce, Robert D.; Lacandon Dream Symbolism Vol. II: Dictionary, Index and Classifications of Dream Symbols; Ediciones Euroamericanas Klaus Thiele, 1979

Brugge, Doug; Timothy Benally; Esther Yazzie-Lewis; eds. The Navajo People and Uranium Mining; University of New Mexico Press, 2006

Lee, Lloyd E. ed.; Diné Perspectives: Revitalizing and Reclaiming Navajo Thought; University of Arizona Press, 2014

Pasternak, Judy; Yellow Dirt, An American Story of a Poisoned Land and a People Betrayed; Free Press; New York; NY, 2010

White, E.B.; Charlotte's Web; 1952

ACKNOWLEDGMENTS

It takes a village to write a book, so my thanks go to those people whose hospitality, friendship, support, generous help and sharing of their knowledge and experience helped shape these books: Judy Wolfe, Jeanne Fitzgerald, Kathryn and Rod Eckart, Gwen and Chuck Johnson, Anita Pete, Fernando Nakai and the Nakai family, Nancy and Bruce Maness of South Forty and 'the village', Diné staff and clients at IHS and DBHS.

Tania Medhat for valuable input and diligent proof-reading, Ruth Medhat for instilling a love of language in her brood. My uncles Jamshid Medhat and Ted Polk, testimony to family bonds spanning continents and generations.

Sharon Keating, friend, poet, writer, and Missy G., harbinger of happiness. Dorothee Shinoda and Gabriele Lindner—what would life be without friends with whom one can look back as well as forward! Dr Robert Snell, author of *Portraits of the Insane*, inspiring thinker and writer.

The Wenner-Gren Foundation for a fieldwork grant, which enabled my PhD.

My editor Lisa Graziano, Ann Weinstock and Sara Pritchard.

The next generation: Corvin Medhat, Ben Elliot, Shintaro Shinoda, Orville Billie, Franziska Finkenauer (young hope of German wine making): The future is yours.

Montezuma Moms Demand Action whose advocacy for gun sense provided thought and fodder for this book.

The treasure trove that is BOOKS of Cortez- and by extension to independent bookstores everywhere.

In memory of Maggie Scroggins, much missed, whose star shone brightly.

And by K's urgent request a special mention of the glorious

National Health Service (NHS) and its dedicated staff—may all continue to thrive and flourish in and through these challenging times.

THE AUTHOR

Katayoun Medhat is a medical anthropologist and psychoanalytic psychotherapist. Her first novel, *The Quality of Mercy* (Milagro Mystery #1), was inspired by PhD fieldwork in the southwestern US and the Navajo Nation, and won the 2016 Leapfrog Fiction Contest. She lives in the south of England, where she is writing *Flyover Country* (Milagro Mystery #3).

CPSIA information can be obtained
at www.ICGtesting.com
Printed in the USA
LVHW040136130819
627406LV00004B/4